Ash London is a renowned music journalist and media personality who has hosted major TV and radio shows, including *Ash London LIVE*, *2DayFM Breakfast* and *The Loop*. A music obsessive, her favourite memories include flying to Paris to interview Taylor Swift, scoring multiple piggyback rides from Ed Sheeran and, of course, seeing Ricky Martin live in concert when she was eleven. She currently hosts the podcast *Hopeless Romantics*, which is her excuse to read romance novels all day and call it work. Ash lives between Melbourne and Auckland with her husband and young son.

You can find Ash on:
Instagram: @ ash_london
Tiktok: @ashlondon

Love

ON
THE
AIR

ASH
LONDON

ALLEN&UNWIN
SYDNEY·MELBOURNE·AUCKLAND·LONDON

First published in 2025

Allen & Unwin
Cammeraygal Country
83 Alexander Street
Crows Nest NSW 2065
Australia
Phone: (61 2) 8425 0100
Email: info@allenandunwin.com
Web: www.allenandunwin.com

Allen & Unwin acknowledges the Traditional Owners of the Country on which we live and work. We pay our respects to all Aboriginal and Torres Strait Islander Elders, past and present.

A catalogue record for this book is available from the National Library of Australia

NATIONAL LIBRARY OF AUSTRALIA

ISBN 978 1 76147 045 5

Set in 13/18 pt Adobe Garamond Pro by Midland Typesetters, Australia
Printed and bound in Australia by the Opus Group

10 9 8 7 6 5 4 3 2 1

To Adi, of course

1

Up until the age of twenty-nine and a half, if I wanted something, I usually got it.

Not because I was pushy or mean or overbearing—I had simply made a habit of giving in to every single one of my urges and desires without a second thought.

From pastries to Balenciaga boots, I said yes to myself without hesitation or regret.

Of course, underneath the designer clothes and delicious lunches and scarily extensive day spa schedule, there was a reason for this life of hedonism and, naturally, it stemmed from my childhood (blah blah blah). But despite my understanding of why certain unfortunate (read: traumatic) events in my early years made me this way, I never had the desire to change. After all, I was yet to find a single one of life's disappointments that could not quickly be eradicated with something new and shiny.

Until I found myself falling out of a taxi and sobbing in my Aunty May's front yard at midnight, heartbroken and homeless.

Not even the limited edition bright pink Chanel Dad Sandals I purchased later that week could pick up my spirits. In fact, at one point I found myself wondering if I'd overpaid for them. And that, ladies and gentlemen, was how I knew that shit was getting real.

While not everyone can simply quit their job, press eject on life and start over, I knew I could and probably would. Because when I wanted to do something, I usually did it.

And that is how I found myself here, on a desert island 5000 kilometres away from home, with a raging hangover and a killer tan.

Eyes still closed, I reached down and rummaged through the sea of clothes and towels on the floor. The room smelled like a mix of herbal mosquito repellent and coconut sunscreen. My fingers finally hit a familiar hard spot in the pocket of my favourite Isabel Marant shorts, which were now looking a little worse for wear. It was a shame DHL didn't do express courier services to tiny islands in the middle of the Philippines. If I were back home I could have had a new pair on the doorstep by the weekend.

Pulling my iPhone close to my face, I tapped the screen, propelling several bits of sand back into my eyes and mouth, causing me to cough, splutter and drop an F-bomb.

It had no battery left.

My God, who was I anymore?

Two months ago, a phone devoid of battery would have signified a life devoid of meaning. Now, I was carelessly letting it die and then falling asleep in a damp bikini.

Is that how you get UTIs? I wondered. I added it to the mental list of 'things to google later'.

Please, God, let me not get a UTI. Not here. Not now. Amen.

At this point in life, I was pretty sure that God didn't exist. And after the last five months had unfolded the way they had, if God did exist, then he/she/it must really hate me. In any case, if God wasn't willing to even *attempt* to help me out while my entire life was tanking monumentally, then God wasn't going to lift a finger to save my urinary tract. Fact.

I rolled over towards the familiar mop of brunette hair on the pillow next to me. The same hair I'd been waking up to on and off since, well, forever.

A wave of gratitude washed over me for this fearless, intrepid woman who had dragged me around the world on adventures for over a decade. The girl I'd met on the first day of Year 6 who'd instantly become the sister I never had.

The girl who hadn't given me an option seven weeks ago when I called her crying from my car with snot running down my face and a half-consumed McDonald's thickshake in my lap. The one who was waiting on the shore thirty-six hours later, arms open wide, with a sympathetic look on her face, and who simply said, 'Everything will be okay . . . but first, let's drink.'

I reached over Vanessa's corpse-like body to find that, miraculously, the fancy dive watch on her wrist was showing 5:50 am. I hadn't missed my 6 am yoga class.

No matter what went down on the island of an evening, I'd made myself a rule that I would haul my sorry arse to yoga the next morning. Perhaps it was a way to ensure that amid all the debauchery, I would still leave room for some sort of 'Eat Pray Love' spiritual experience. After all, I'd come here to figure out what the hell to do with my life, not just drink cheap booze with sunburned scuba divers.

That's not to say I got up to much debauchery. That was more Vanessa's domain, but I gladly allowed myself to get swept up in the madness. Even when we were thirteen, my proximity to my best friend's adventures made me cool by association.

I was voted class president, but Vanessa was the first one to have a boyfriend.

I was the entertainer, with a natural ability to make everyone laugh. But Vanessa was always the coolest girl in the room.

Seventeen years later and not much had changed, apart from the fact that the life I had built for myself was cooler than that of anyone else I knew.

Was. Past tense.

Now I was single and unemployed, while Vanessa led shark-diving expeditions in paradise and engaged in wild love affairs with the United Nations of scuba-diving lotharios. Balance had been restored.

I got to work rummaging through her drawers and soon commandeered a fresh T-shirt, baggy shorts, clean undies and a hair tie. I had amassed quite the collection of chic designer yoga gear. The kind of pants that made my arse look perkier than necessary, and tops that fell off my shoulder at just the right angle. But as I had no time to get back to my own room this morning, this random get-up would have to do.

Thankfully, the bikini top I'd drunkenly removed as I climbed into bed the night before had dried overnight. Bras were one of two things we never shared. I was a D cup by

Year 8. Vanessa's boobs, on the other hand, were perky and cute, and she could go braless without running the risk of treading on a rogue nipple.

The other thing we never shared was boys. Not because of some high-school pact; we'd just genuinely never found ourselves attracted to the same one. I went for guys who looked like they'd stepped off the set of *Pride and Prejudice*, or just finished going over your tax returns. Vanessa liked guys who may or may not have been in jail.

It was yet another reason we were destined to be best friends forever.

I set off to class, slightly miffed that my dead phone meant I couldn't listen to music. Every walk over three minutes deserves its own soundtrack, and today the island was giving me James Blake vibes. Maybe a bit of Bon Iver. But, for now, the island supplied its own symphony. Village dogs barked as they took advantage of the empty beach and enjoyed games of tag, while fishermen in the distance greeted each other on their way out to deeper waters to test their luck.

It was during the quiet moments of this daily pilgrimage that I loved Malapascua the most. The peace. The stillness. The possibility. It was like my own private little island. Soon enough, the harsh sun would force everyone into the shade, and the beachside hotels would be blasting dodgy Euro club tunes to set the holiday mood. But for now, I felt like some sort of reawakening might actually be possible. Like maybe today was the day I'd figure everything out.

My yoga studio back home was seriously bougie and membership cost an arm and a leg—it was one big sea of oversized

Chloé day bags and Lululemon. I loved overhearing the small talk between classes as the women around me complained about nannies, mothers-in-law and the quality of stone fruits at the local grocer. It was easy to find your Zen when your life was devoid of real-world problems, I often thought.

Here on the island, it was less of a studio and more of a hut, elevated above the village like a bamboo prayer tower. I made my way up the steps and was met at the top by Pinky, a tiny Filipina hippy, who offered me the same greeting I'd been given every morning since I arrived.

'Good morning, darling Alex.'

Each time it made my heart swell. I bowed my head with a wink. 'Good morning, darling Pinky.'

First to arrive, I chose my usual spot in the corner of the hut, rolled out a mat on the warm bamboo, and collapsed into child's pose, knees wide on either side, arms stretched out in front, forehead on the ground. Pinky was striking matches to light the incense behind her. I took a deep breath in, and let the smoky, sagey goodness fill my lungs and my head.

It took just seconds for the familiar tingly threat of tears to appear.

Quitter.

Loser.

Another deep breath. A single, stinging tear.

You're okay.

It's okay.

Just breathe.

᠁|᠁|᠁

6

Despite being the final morning of the year, I spent this one in the same fashion I'd spent the previous forty-nine on the island: lazily. I justified this easily thanks to the 6 am yoga session that I already had under my belt, which was one of the main reasons (apart from enlightenment etc., etc.) that I loved a morning yoga class.

As was our usual daily ritual, Vanessa met me after class for breakfast, and then we lay in a perfect little shady spot on the shore with bellies full of acai smoothies.

'I cried again in yoga today.'

Vanessa was lying on her back with her eyes shut, her legs in the air, feet resting on the trunk of the palm tree we'd plonked ourselves under. Her anklet glistened and the charms made a jingling sound every time she readjusted her legs. She opened one eye and shifted towards me.

'Again? Is this where I am supposed to ask if you wanna talk about it, or whatever?' Vanessa's face was both incredibly sincere and slightly disgusted.

'I'm fine. Just letting you know so that poor Pinky doesn't have to be the only one on the island who knows I'm a complete emotional mess.'

I smacked my bean bag a couple of times to fluff it up in just the right place, then lay back to relax in the little nook I'd carved out and took a sip from my water bottle. I rubbed my eyes and let out a frustrated sigh.

I had done enough therapy over the years to know that my problems would follow me wherever I went but I'd hoped the sting would have subsided by now. Instead, it popped up in moments of quiet reflection as a cruel little reminder that, despite my perfectly curated Instagram feed filled with sunset cocktails and bikini shots featuring *juuuust* the right amount of boob, I was still a little lost.

Vanessa stretched her neck from side to side. 'Well, if you're going to be an emotional mess you may as well do it in paradise.'

She was right in the sense that we really were in paradise. There was not a single stressful element to life here. Food was cheap. Booze was cheaper. I could do whatever I wanted, whenever I wanted, and nobody on the island expected a single thing from me.

Vanessa continued. 'Anyway, there's nothing wrong with running away from your problems for a little while.'

Vanessa had lived in ten countries since high school and changed cities more often than most people changed toothbrushes. 'No shit you think that, mate. You've made an art out of changing scenery every time you get even slightly bored or disillusioned.'

'Hey, I'd hardly call nearly dying from malaria a boring reason to leave Tanzania,' she quipped, eyes still closed.

She was right. I would have left too. Although, to be fair, I wouldn't have lived in a tent (or any dwelling) in Tanzania in the first place.

Vanessa heaved herself up and brushed the sand off her denim skirt. 'Speaking of Tanzania, remember I sent you a photo of the tiny-arse plane I was about to get on? And at that exact time you were in business class en-route to LA to interview one of the boys from One Direction or some shit. It was the perfect snapshot of how differently our lives had panned out. Man, I laughed.'

'I would have laughed too if I hadn't been so busy drinking all that goddamn free champagne. It was a tough life, I tell ya.'

We were now giggling the kind of giggles that only the truest, best memories can elicit. I took another sip of water, sat up and drew a deep breath.

'I think I'm gonna go shower then grab a massage. What time do festivities kick off tonight?'

'My last dive is at two so I'll be packed up and ready to hang by . . . five-ish. Which gives us seven hours to wreak one last bit of havoc on this island for the year. Speaking of which, that hot American I met at the dive school yesterday is joining the group so I might have company.' Vanessa winked and then wandered towards the dive school.

'I knew there was a reason you had the good bikini top on today. Your tits look great, by the way!' I yelled, a little too loudly, to my friend in the distance, as I gathered my things and trudged through the sand back to my room.

The American would probably fall in love with Vanessa and come out tonight. He would follow her around like a puppy dog for the remainder of the week, before boarding a flight home and becoming nothing but a Facebook friend memory that we'd one day laugh about on another beach in another country. It was the way things always had been and the way things always would be.

It only took me two minutes to get from the shore back to my room.

When I first arrived, I'd booked into the only five-star hotel on the island. My obsession with hotel booking and holiday planning was matched only by my love of Scandi pop music and buying hard-to-find designer shoes online.

The first week was spent lounging about in my king-sized bed, indulging in massages at the spa, and sipping overpriced cocktails by the pool while Vanessa was at work. I kicked off my daily yoga practice, journalled, and listened to copious amounts of happy music (everything from Chance the Rapper to Neil Diamond). When the seven days was up I was shocked to find that I was *still* depressed and the trip might extend a little longer than originally planned. With my savings account dwindling and the end date of Operation 'Get My Life Back Together and Stop Crying in Yoga Every Day' still unclear, I figured it was time to make alternative accommodation plans.

So, after seven luxurious nights, I rented a simple room near Vanessa's, with an air conditioner and a lockable door.

I walked into my little sanctuary, put my phone on charge, closed the blinds and undressed. The room was small, with a double bed, small set of drawers and an adjoining bathroom that housed a toilet, shower and full-length mirror.

Just as I was about to hop into the shower, my iPhone made a dinging sound, signalling its resurrection, followed by three new message tones.

I stood naked in the bathroom, both tempted to look and desperate to get under the shower and wash my crunchy, curly hair. I chose the hair. If this person really wanted to get a hold of me, they would call.

And call they did. By the third ring, I finally convinced myself that someone had died, rinsed out the expensive conditioner that I was fast running out of, and took three quick hops over to my bedside table, dripping water on the tiles of my tiny room as I went. By the time I dried my hands and picked up the phone, I'd missed the call. Although when I saw the caller ID I wasn't sure if I would have answered it anyway.

Ding. A text.

> Al. Call me back ASAP! I have news that might finally get your sorry arse home xoxo

A pang of guilt hit me like a punch in the gut. My curiosity was piqued, but I wasn't ready to face Tom just yet. I shut my phone off and hopped back into the shower.

⫶⫶⫶⫶

Despite the fact that I'd been on the island for seven weeks, I still hadn't so much as entertained the idea of a dive. I kept imagining that as soon as I got under the water my brain would explode from the pressure and my headless body would then have to be transported all the way back to Sydney.

What would they even do with a headless body? How would customs handle the blood? Would I have to be cremated first? Would there be an autopsy? So many questions. All that to say that, no, I hadn't been on a dive. While people from all over the world made the long and arduous journey to Malapascua, week in, week out, keen to dive in some of the best conditions on the planet, I remained safely on the shore, pottering about the island, sunbathing, reading and getting cheap massages.

There were also copious amounts of time spent feeling sorry for myself and wondering how exactly everything had unravelled so spectacularly. Five months ago I'd been deeply in love with my boyfriend, who looked like a tanned Australian version of Robert Pattinson, mentally planning a wedding (despite the fact that he was yet to propose). I had an incredible dream job, and my life was on a positive trajectory, coming together in the exact way I had always planned. Until five words caused it all to come crashing down around me.

I. Can't. Make. This. Work.

As if our relationship was a dodgy Airbnb Nespresso machine that didn't come with instructions.

Except he hadn't really tried. He hadn't googled it. He hadn't even turned it off and on again. He just stood there—shrugging his shoulders and avoiding eye contact.

How could he not make it work? I was quite literally the perfect girlfriend. I planned surprise holidays, always paid my way and had made all of his friends fall in love with me, one by one. In fact, most of them chose me in the break-up, such was my ability to crack people wide open and forge lasting bonds with everyone I met.

None of this changed the fact that *he* hadn't chosen me. His rejection was devastating and left me feeling weak and pathetic. Perhaps that was the worst part. My biggest fears had come to fruition, and there wasn't a damn thing I could do about it. I wanted him. He didn't want me back. He had decided that life would be better without me, and so he left.

And there it was. The kick in the gut. The wave of panic. I buckled down and let it wash over me, knowing that, as always, it would subside as quickly as it had come.

Deep breaths.
You're okay.
It's okay.
Just breathe.

I never knew getting dumped would feel so much like grief. Sometimes it felt worse. Grieving a dead person was one thing. But grieving someone who's still very much alive but just choosing to live without you? That sucked in its own very special kind of way.

The one consolation that I repeated to myself, over and over like a mantra, was the fact that if he couldn't make it work with me, then he was never going to make it work with anyone and would probably die alone. The girlfriend he procured three weeks later would no doubt learn the same lesson in time.

So, despite the fact that I knew a calendar date was nothing more than another notch in an ancient time measurement system and carried no real-world significance, I was still relieved that *this* particular year would be over in just a few short hours. And unlike every other new year's eve of my twenties, this one had required little to no preparation.

Tonight I wouldn't be partying at a harbourside VIP event hosted by some random vodka company with guaranteed views of the fireworks and a gorgeous boyfriend on my arm. And I wouldn't spend two hours in hair and make-up to guarantee I looked perfect when our photo was plastered all over social media. Because here on the island I was no longer that girl. I'd left her behind in a radio studio when, halfway through an Adele ballad, I'd burst into tears—become completely overwhelmed by crippling heartache—and simply walked out, never to return.

And now I was here. Shoeless at a (literal) dive bar, downing cheap rum like it was water; wearing frayed denim shorts, a worn-out bikini top and a ratty sarong that was currently wrapped around my head like a turban for no real reason other than that I couldn't be bothered carrying it.

It was five minutes to midnight when we stumbled out of the bar and onto the moonlit shore, bellies full of laughter and rum. Vanessa had ditched Mack the dumb American, who, I soon discovered, was pretty funny and had a PhD in biochemistry, and she and I were walking, arms linked, towards the water.

'You know, babe, what happened to you this year was shitty. But you've lived through shittier.'

Vanessa knew my life's history as intimately as her own—after all, she was there for most of it. She knew how hard it had been facing my teenage years without a father, grappling with the fact that, no matter how much I achieved, he wasn't ever coming back.

'I just don't want you thinking that any of this stuff defines you. Your life didn't end when your dad left . . . It shouldn't end now just because some arsehole broke your heart.'

'All right, Oprah,' I quipped back at her sarcastically.

'I'm serious! You've always kicked total arse, why stop now?'

Even in my boozy, happy state I knew she was right. I had to stop letting disappointing men dictate the trajectory of my life and how I felt about myself.

I took a long sigh. 'You're right. I guess shitty dudes are my kryptonite.'

'Yeah, well, you've still got a choice, ya know,' Vanessa mused. 'I mean, you didn't exactly get a choice in how this year ended, but you can choose how the new one starts.' She paused for a moment. 'Fuck, I really *do* sound like Oprah.'

I laughed as I walked beside her, taking a sip of rum.

'I've got an idea,' she said, as she stopped and crouched down ahead of me. A moment later she was dragging her hand through the sand.

'What are you doing?' I asked, confused.

'Drawing a line in the sand. Duh. It's both literal *and* metaphorical. Once that countdown is finished, you're gonna hop over it. And you're gonna leave your bullshit behind. Agree?'

I scrunched up my face. 'Babe, this is seriously lame.'

'No. Lame is you, the most talented person I know, rotting away on an island because you're sad you got dumped.' She tapped the dive watch on her wrist, then looked back at me. 'You've got one minute till the new year starts. It's your choice.'

I stared at her for a moment, and then down at the dodgy line she'd fashioned in the sand.

'Well, it can't hurt, I suppose,' I said, giving in. I sighed and placed my drink down then squeezed my eyes shut. A handful of people laughed as they made their way out of the bar and onto the moonlit shore, a sense of quiet anticipation in the air.

One last time, I let myself remember.

'Ten! Nine! Eight!' their loud screams echoed.

The nothingness on his face when he told me he was leaving. The deep ache of desperation as I wept on the kitchen floor, begging him to make me understand.

'Seven! Six! Five!'

The explanation that never came.

'Four! Three! Two! One!'

I drew on every ounce of strength I could muster and willed myself to let go of the year that had taken away so much.

The boy I'd thought I was going to marry.

The job that I'd thought defined me.

The life I'd thought was unfolding.

'HAPPY NEW YEAR!'

In one quick move, I hopped over the crude line in the sand. It was done. It had to be done. I had to find a way to move forwards alone. When I finally opened my eyes, Vanessa was running towards the ocean, her naked silhouette leaping joyously into the water as she looked back at me and squealed. Seconds later, I was ripping my clothes off and following her in. The cool water against my bare body rushed through every part of me as I dove in, cleansing me of the pain and regret that I was so desperate to leave behind. When I emerged back on the surface, I felt the warmth of deep, cathartic tears running down my face, the salt touching my lips as they fell. I looked to the sky, naked and free, with nothing to offer except a promise. A promise that I would never give up on my life again.

I was nobody's hero. I was nobody's girlfriend. I was nobody's. And maybe I never would be again. I was nothing but a girl swimming naked in the sea with a smile on her face the size of the moon, and for the first time in forever it felt as though that was enough.

Happy fucking new year indeed.

꧁꧂

Six hours later, I sat on the shore, hugging my knees into my chest and watching the sun rise over the water. I looked out at the calm blue sea, closed my eyes and slowly exhaled. The island was real, the sand and the ocean and the rum and the sea breeze were all real . . . but the life I was living here wasn't, and there was only so long I could pretend that it was.

I wanted my life back. And I knew that if I was given one more chance, I'd never throw it away again. Certainly not on account of love.

I reached over to check my phone. The message was still there. Still unanswered.

Al. Call me back ASAP! I have news that might finally get your sorry arse home xoxo

I stared out at the endless blue ocean until I felt a familiar sense of knowing settle into my gut. I knew what I had to do. It was decided. And once I decided something, it was generally always done.

2

Three days later, I stood nervously in the immigration queue at Sydney airport. I looked down at my dirty feet, pulling one out of my shoe to reveal a dark Birkenstock tan line and remnants of sand. In front of me was a well-dressed woman, holding a passport in one freshly manicured hand and a phone in the other, with a nondescript wheelie suitcase parked neatly in front of her. The boarding pass poking out of her passport indicated that she'd flown business class. I used to be that woman. Flitting in and out of overseas airports with the ease and familiarity that most people did their weekly grocery shop. There was no way she'd checked in luggage. Check-in luggage was for peasants.

'Excuse me, are you Alex York?' a voice sang out behind me. I swivelled around to see two teenage girls, hair braided, no doubt fresh off a flight from Fiji or Hawaii. They both looked at me, wide-eyed and excited.

'That's me! Hello!' I sang back kindly, slipping into my old routine.

One of the girls, a redhead, obviously the more confident of the two, readied her iPhone for a photo as she spoke. 'We love your radio show! We always listen on the way home from netball and we both follow you on Insta. Is Alex @ Night coming back?'

'Oh, that's so sweet of you! Would you like a photo?' I replied, without answering her question.

The girls arranged themselves on either side of me and I lowered myself down a little into the frame as they snapped away for twenty seconds, faces morphing into a variety of pouts and smiles.

'Thanks, Alex, we'll tag you!' the redhead said, once they were confident that the perfect shot had been procured. I winked and waved as they made their way back to their parents who were giving me apologetic looks from a couple of metres away.

'She looks different in real life,' I heard the other one say in the distance.

There were two reasons I felt sick with nerves as I slowly moved further forwards in the queue. The first was the obvious reality of the jobless life waiting for me on the other side of immigration.

The second was Tom.

Tom was more than just my producer, and more than just my friend. For four years he'd sat opposite me in a soundproof studio every night while we broadcast around the country from 7 pm till 10 pm. We existed in our own little world, full of inside jokes and insane memories. Like the time he had Starbucks-induced diarrhoea at Pete Wentz's house.

Our bandwagons were hitched to each other, and the unavoidable truth of the matter was that when I walked out on my job (and my life), I threw his life into disarray without much thought.

I had meant to apologise to him before I got on the plane to leave for the Philippines, but I didn't. And then I meant to call him when I arrived on the island, but I didn't. Next thing, seven weeks had passed and by then it was too late and too awkward and I avoided the situation altogether.

When I finally had the guts to respond to his text and let him know I had booked a flight home, he offered to pick me up from the airport. This response was confusing given he must have been upset with me. It was also confusing because he didn't own a car. He then sent a photo of himself posing topless in my Mercedes, informing me that he'd been using it since the day I skipped town. Because of course he had.

Once I finally cleared customs and collected my bags, I found myself nervously scanning the crowd of excited families and weary travellers in search of my ride. It didn't take long to spot him. There he stood, his blond hair perfectly combed into place, with a fresh fade on each side. He was wearing a sand-coloured tracksuit with matching Yeezy sneakers that made him look like he was part of a very fancy cult, with a black bumbag—Prada, I could tell from a mile away—draped diagonally across his front. He was holding something in his left hand that I couldn't quite make out. As I got closer, I realised it was a sign. A sign that made the knots in my stomach unravel as I laughed.

'WELCOME BACK DICKHEAD,' the sign read.

He had even drawn the 'i' in the shape of a dick. I picked up my pace and, once in earshot, yelled in his direction, 'I am a TOTAL dickhead! A selfish, losery dickhead who doesn't deserve you!'

He glared at me, the sign still prominently displayed in his hands. 'Go on . . .'

I was now standing in front of him. 'I'm an idiot. I shouldn't have left you high and dry like that. I was just too stuck in my own heartbreak to think about how my decision would affect your life. I was a shit mate. And you're the best producer and the best friend and just . . . the best everything. I'm so sorry.'

He looked back at me sternly with pursed lips. 'Hmm. Well, I got four parking tickets in your car and haven't paid a single one.'

'Is that your way of saying you forgive me?'

'No. It's just me saying that I got four parking tickets in your car and haven't paid a single one.'

'Right. Well. I'll pay the fines, that's fair. Thanks for picking me up.'

'Hmm. The sign idea was really only going to work at the airport, so my offer wasn't purely altruistic.'

We stood there in silence, me with my arms crossed and Tom still holding the sign. This was as close to 'serious' as he got, and underneath the paint and glitter, this was his way of letting me know that what I'd done had really hurt him.

I reached out and touched the sparkly penis on the cardboard. 'You did a good job on the cock.'

'Well, you know me, arts and crafts captain in Year 12.' He sighed. 'That kind of commitment to artistic expression doesn't just fade overnight.'

'No, it doesn't. I love you.'

He screwed up his face. 'Gross. Let's go. I want Maccas chips on the way. Your shout.'

And with that, Tom was off and walking towards the carpark as I scampered behind him, bags in tow, trying to keep up.

'Wait! You said you'd tell me what this news was when I landed!' I called after him.

He yelled back over his shoulder without slowing down. 'I lied. Kinda. Well there's news but it's not my news to tell. Expect an email tomorrow.'

Curiosity gnawed at my insides, but I still had grovelling to do and was in no position to make threats or demand answers. I made a face and decided to concentrate for the time being on getting to the car before my arms pulled out of their sockets.

᯼᯼᯼

We drove for the next half an hour eating fries and sipping milkshakes, blasting Rihanna while I regaled Tom with stories from my time on the island and promised to take him back one day. The thought of an island romance was almost as enticing as the cheap massages, he told me.

Soon enough, we pulled up in an all too familiar suburban street, and I felt a wave of hesitation as I looked out at the closest thing I currently had to a home. I hopped out and unloaded my bags from the boot.

'You all good?' Tom asked through the window, loudly slurping the last of his strawberry thickshake.

'Yep. Thanks for the ride. Just bring my car back at some point this week. I don't exactly have much going on, so no huge rush.' I sighed as I looked towards the house.

'Well, babe, if you ask me, your first priority needs to be a very long shower and a mani-pedi. You should be lucky I even *let* you in the car with those feet. Give my love to May! You know I love that bish!'

'I will. Bye, matey. Sorry again,' I called back at him as I dragged my luggage across the road.

'You'll find a way to make it up to me,' Tom said with a wink, and then he drove off, leaving me standing in front of the gate, the smell of the rosebush giving me a serious case of deja vu.

It was five months ago that I'd fallen arse-first into this very bush at midnight, tears streaming down my face as I watched my hastily packed suitcase roll down the driveway and narrowly miss flattening the neighbour's cat. The swearing had alerted May, who had appeared at the front door dressed in a silk kimono and moccasins, her reading glasses still perched on the end of her nose. That woman was always, always reading.

Loading myself into the taxi twenty minutes earlier, I had thought that it was possibly the worst day of my life. But lying stuck in a rosebush, while my seventy-year-old aunty tried to extricate me as delicately as possible, I knew that it most certainly was.

'Come inside, love,' she'd whispered once I was free. 'Nothing a cup of tea and some Savlon won't fix.'

It had soon become clear that a cup of tea and a bit of Savlon wouldn't even touch the sides when it came to eternal heartbreak and the crushing reality that the boy I loved had decided he didn't love me back and possibly never had. Instead, I needed to quit my job (and my life) and run away to a desert island, do yoga every day, drink my bodyweight in rum, and make a pact with the universe at midnight on new year's eve. And when I listed it all like that, I was pretty bloody proud of the effort I'd made to get my groove back.

And while my groove technically wasn't all the way back, I certainly felt like it was finally within my reach. This time, I made my way down the path in one piece, plonked my bags down and dug deep into my handbag, searching around for a key as the sensor light came on. I needn't have bothered as moments later the door opened and the familiar scent of May's Chanel Number 5 enveloped me.

'Welcome home, darling girl! Come inside! Billy made chicken soup!'

3

May and Billy had lived in the same house my whole life. A five-bedroom weatherboard, five streets back from Bondi Beach, which had always been a second home. When I was a child, it had seemed huge and loud, and always filled with visitors, which, when combined with the three kids already living there, meant there was always something fun happening. Or some sort of trouble brewing with my big cousins. Now they'd all moved out and started families of their own, rendering May and Billy empty nesters. Not that it was ever empty, as there was always someone crashing in a spare room. After the break-up, when everyone—including May and Billy—started referring to the front room as 'Alex's', I realised that I had technically moved in. I tried to give Billy an envelope of cash one day as a means of paying rent, and he was so upset he didn't speak to me for three days. I never made that mistake again.

It was still dark outside when I woke up the morning after I arrived home, and in a moment of clarity and inspiration,

I quickly jumped out of bed, found my yoga mat and headed to the beach in time for sunrise. I was no longer on a desert island, but I still had one of the world's most famous beaches at my doorstep and it would be a shame to let the routine slip away—especially as I'd returned home without any plan for my life and would need all the good vibes I could possibly muster.

Afterwards, I walked home via my favourite overpriced juice bar, and was having an in-depth chat with a random girl in line about her limited-edition crochet Prada beach bag as the email came through.

When I saw who it was from, I nearly passed out.

For twenty-five years Goldie Miller had been the G.O.A.T. of radio in Australia and everybody knew it. Goldie didn't just light up the airwaves, she set them on fire. Celebrities flocked to her. Listeners adored her. She was talented, electrifying, and I worshipped the ground she walked on. Goldie was probably also the first gay woman I'd ever known (apart from my mum's cousin Alia who divorced her weird husband when I was six and shacked up with her best friend DeeDee six months later). Goldie and Joanie had been together since their university days, and had always seemed like a perfect, unbreakable pair. Goldie, the effervescent rock star of radio, and Joanie, the understated human rights lawyer who inherited a large fortune from her wealthy parents years ago and now ran a charitable foundation in their name.

Hearing Goldie on the radio when I was thirteen years old was the sole reason I had been determined to have my own radio show one day.

Goldie did the Sydney breakfast show on my station, and it was then networked through to the entire country that afternoon. Hers was the jewel in the network's crown. In the four years that I'd done the night show, I had received exactly five emails from Goldie, all of which I had printed out, filed in a manila folder and hidden away in the locked top drawer of my desk at work. Everything from compliments (she loved a new artist I'd introduced and encouraged me to trust my ear when it came to breaking new music on the show), to advice (don't be scared to stretch out the break past five or six minutes if you feel the interview is going somewhere) and criticism (nobody cares that much about your life yet . . . keep it about the music until you've earned the right to waffle on about your day). I cherished these emails more than anything; not only because her advice was incredibly helpful, but also because they were proof that Goldie Miller knew I existed. And more than that: she sometimes listened to my show. Probably after dining with Hugh Jackman, or chain-smoking backstage with Elton John—although ruminating for too long on the fact that Goldie *might* be listening was a bad idea in the same way that nobody wants to do karaoke with Adele or cook a steak for Gordon Ramsay.

So now that I had left the network, not only did the finance team have no reason to pay me (devastating), but Goldie Miller also had no reason to contact me (soul-destroying). Which is what made the email even more surprising.

Greetings, Ms York!
A little birdie tells me you're back in town.
Would love to catch you for a little tête-à-tête in my office.

Thursday? 2 pm?

I'm assuming you're free since you have no job (and apparently no boyfriend? Geez, what a run!)

Chat soon,

x G

I sat staring at my phone, reading the email over and over. I even checked the email address to make sure it wasn't someone (most likely Tom) playing a prank. Upon confirming that the email address did, in fact, belong to Her Royal Highness Goldie Miller, I responded straight away with great enthusiasm and with absolutely no desire or need to play it cool.

So, this was the reason Tom had wanted me to come home so quickly. But why? Why the heck did Goldie Miller want to see me? Should I be excited? Should I be scared? So many questions. The most important of which was: what the heck was I going to wear? Tomorrow would obviously be dedicated to doing the thing I did best. The thing that brought me clarity and joy like no other. The perfect distraction. The perfect preparation.

Tomorrow, I would go shopping.

I would buy the perfect 'casual catch-up with Goldie Miller' outfit. One that would give me the confidence I needed to walk into a room with my hero and feel like I belonged there.

I pulled out my phone and dialled Tom's number. He answered after one ring.

'Did you get the email?' he blurted, not bothering with a hello.

'Yes! What does she want?'

'I don't know. All she said was that I had to get you home. And to text her as soon as you were on a flight. I swear. It's all so dramatic, I'm obsessed. What are you going to wear?'

'My thoughts exactly.'

'Don't forget the mani-pedi. You look like you've got talons and Goldie deserves better. We *all* do.'

᙮ᙁᙁᙁᙁᙁ᙮

I was so deep in my shopping spree haze the next day that I almost felt like I was having an out-of-body experience. The intoxicating sounds gave me life. The beep of the credit card terminal as I tapped my card, the steely crunch of receipts being stapled together and handed to me, the soothing thump of shopping bags hitting each other at my side as I walked. I was in my happy place, and while I didn't go as crazy as I normally would have (the peso-to-dollar conversion still had somewhat of a hold on me), I gave it a fair nudge, and once I got started it was hard to stop.

Mum FaceTimed me while I was in the dressing room at David Jones (our favourite department store) so I took the opportunity to catch up while getting a second opinion on potential purchases.

'I'm pretty sure I made you that exact dress when you were about six years old.' She laughed as I held up a silk and taffeta mini dress in blush pink. My grandmother had passed on her seamstress skills to Mum, which meant that while expensive shopping sprees were out of the question Mum could easily whip up anything I wanted without too much fuss. I still remember the sounds of her good sewing scissors cutting long strips of fabric against the dining room table, her sewing machine humming well into the night. Being a single mother to a precocious, fashion-obsessed ten-year-old couldn't have been easy, but more often than not, the morning after a trip to the shops I'd wake to find an exact replica of a top I'd lusted after waiting for me on the end of my bed. While I accepted that homemade versions of the latest fashions were my lot in life, I often did so with a distinct lack of gratitude, and by the time I was old enough to appreciate having a bespoke tailor on hand, Mum had packed up the machine and refused to make me another thing. I didn't blame her.

I always promised myself that one day I would buy myself all the pretty things I wanted, and for the better part of my adult life, I'd kept the promise. I wasn't ashamed to admit that it felt good to be envied for once, to know that I had built the kind of life that would shield me from pity. There was a certain kind of satisfaction that came from a complete stranger eyeballing my outfit from head to toe as they walked past, though I knew it was altogether vacuous and represented everything that was wrong with the world. I worked hard, I had no dependants and no debt (apart from a credit card, the balance of which I checked only when I was feeling supremely brave). I had also earned a shit-tonne of money over the years and had nothing to show for it other than a world-class collection of designer shoes and handbags, but hey. Fiscal responsibility could wait.

'I wonder what Goldie wants? I've got half a mind to call Tom myself for an interrogation,' Mum said as I squeezed myself into a leather mini skirt.

'He's told me everything he knows. We'll find out tomorrow, I suppose.'

'Okay, darling. But you'll let May and I know as soon as possible, won't you?'

'Promise, Mama. Love you!' I waved at the phone as she blew a kiss back.

The martini craving hit sometime between the purchase of the Aje leather dress and the Golden Goose sneakers, and because I very rarely stopped myself from doing what I wanted at exactly the moment I wanted to do it, I soon found myself walking up George Street to the QT hotel, shopping bags in hand, salivating at the thought of my favourite drink and a gossip with Malik.

I loved this bar for many reasons, but perhaps the most obvious was that it was four minutes' walk from my radio studio, which made it the perfect late-night spot to come down off the high of broadcasting live. Then there was the fact that the bar was in a hotel. Something that, even after years of travelling, I still found intoxicatingly romantic. The transience. The idea that everyone was from somewhere else and tomorrow they might all be on different continents. The reason I loved this bar the most, however, was that it was home to the world's best cucumber gin martini, as judged by yours truly.

I lifted myself up onto a high stool and dropped the countless shopping bags I'd acquired to the floor, ignoring the urge to calculate how much I'd actually spent. That kind of behaviour was for rookies, and I was no rookie when it came to quietening the rising tide of anxiety with pretty new dresses and shoes. Why ruin a lovely day with those kinds of details?

In any case, this was less of a 'feel better' shopping spree and more of an 'I need a very specific outfit for a very specific meeting' kind of shopping spree. Which made it totally okay.

A familiar voice sang out from across the room, getting shriller as it got closer.

'Heeeeere she is!'

Malik was gliding towards me, tea towel over his left shoulder, his hands waving excitedly in the air. He leaned in for a long hug.

'I missed you!' I said into his aproned chest.

Malik was tall and slender with a shaved head, a gorgeous angular face and a thin gold nose ring. In four years, I'd never seen him wear anything but black.

'I missed you too. Every time I make a cucumber gin martini, I think of my big-mouthed little barfly. And here it seems I've wished you into existence,' he cooed, as he reached for the bottle of Four Pillars gin.

'And not a moment too soon. I've been drinking dark rum for two months.'

Malik pretended to dry-retch as he got to work, and a minute later the perfect gin martini appeared in front of me. It felt like it had been both days and years since I'd been here last. I took a sip and let out an exaggerated moan as Malik spoke.

'So, tell me everything. The island looked incred on Instagram. Please, tell me you got that arsehole out of your system?'

'Affirmative. I've sworn off men altogether. I will never let myself be that pathetic ever again. I shall be forever alone with my shoes and my bags and my martinis. And I shall be happy,' I declared dramatically, taking a long sip of my drink.

'Love to hear it!'

We were interrupted by a cough at the other end of the bar. And not a real cough. The kind of fake cough people do when they want your attention. We both looked over to the man sitting on his own four empty seats down from me.

'Oops. God knows how long he's been sitting there waiting for a drink. Be right back.' Malik winced as he ducked off.

I wondered what this guy was doing alone at a bar at 2 pm on a Wednesday. After all, I had the excuse of unemployment, but unemployed people didn't wear Breitling Navitimers. (Most girls instinctively check for wedding bands; I check for watches. Because I'm classy like that.)

'Gin martini, please. With cucumber.' His voice was calm and deep.

Well, this was interesting. His taste in drinks was as good as his taste in watches. I had a real knack for chatting to strangers (or perhaps it was a compulsion). My ex used to roll his eyes as I'd launch into deep conversations with check-out chicks, strangers in the line at the post office, and literally anyone on the street with a dog of any description. I had another subtle look, trying to take in as much of him as I could in one quick glance. He would have been in his mid-thirties, with dark chestnut hair pulled back into a sort of man-bun situation. Ponytails on a dude were high up on my 'ick list' but I'd always considered the man-bun in an entirely new category altogether. This one in particular was not only acceptable, but also . . . kind of hot. He had stubble (not too neat) and wore a crisp black tee that looked like he'd just taken the tags off, and dark jeans rolled up at the ankle to reveal chunky, worn-in

Redwing boots. The kind of boots I imagined Bradley Cooper or Ewan McGregor might wear while riding a motorbike into the sunset. Oh, and of course, the $15,000 watch. There was no two ways about it, this guy was gorgeous.

A watch says a lot about a man, in my opinion, and his choice was intriguing not because of the expense, but because of how understated it was. Douchebags spend that much money on a Rolex. But this was the kind of watch that flew under the radar altogether. Unless I was in the room.

'Does this bar offer two-for-one deals, oh, handsome bartender?' I called to Malik as I downed the last of my martini and motioned towards my empty glass.

'For you, anything,' he cooed as he pulled out a second glass from the rack, widening his eyes at me in a way that showed he too was vibing on our handsome interloper.

The man and I watched in silence as he muddled the vermouth with the cucumber, and added it to a cocktail shaker with the gin and ice. I raised my voice to contend with the sound of the shaker. 'Has Malik ever made you a martini?'

'Uhhh, no, actually. My first time here,' he replied broodily, glancing very quickly at me, then back towards Malik's hypnotic arm movements behind the bar. He sounded tired.

Malik passed us both our drinks. I raised mine in the direction of Watch Guy. He returned the gesture while making a very distinct effort to avoid eye contact. Was he being shy? Rude? Or did he just want to be left alone to enjoy his martini in peace? None of these possibilities deterred me.

'Well, welcome. I've had approximately twelve thousand over the years and I've never had a bad one. So, good choice.'

'I won't need twelve thousand. Just one, and then I'll head upstairs to my room.' He said, more to himself than me. 'I'm a little jet-lagged. I'm guessing you're tired too . . .?'

I was confused for a moment, the penny dropping as I followed his gaze towards the shopping bags at my feet.

'Oh . . . right. The shopping. I actually have a meeting tomorrow that I'm super nervous about. Well, I don't even know if it's a meeting. She called it a "tête-à-tête" so . . . yeah, look, I have no idea. But I'm shitting myself. And when I'm nervous, I shop.' I was now officially rambling. 'Which is dumb because I quit my job and I'm unemployed and shouldn't be spending money on designer clothes . . . or martinis. But questionable life choices seem to be somewhat of a theme in my life these days.'

At first he said nothing, then after a moment he asked, 'Do you always share this much information with strangers at bars?'

Malik interrupted and answered on my behalf. 'She does. Every time.'

'Yep. I do. It's a compulsion,' I added, swigging back the last of my martini and pulling out my wallet (vintage Gucci purchased from the most amazing store on the planet in Florence). 'And now I shall leave you to finish your drink in peace.'

Malik held the EFTPOS terminal out and I tapped my credit card on top, a dance we'd both done hundreds of times. Only this time, a very loud and very unfriendly buzzing sound rang out from the little machine. It gave us both a fright. Malik squinted at the screen.

'Well, babe, it was bound to happen eventually. Declined.' He was trying to force a sad face but couldn't through the giggles.

Mortified, I grabbed the terminal in my left hand to check for myself. 'What? How? What do you mean?'

I pulled out my mobile phone with my free hand and saw a text on the screen. From the bank. Shit. I looked up at Malik, who was still giggling, and glanced over at Watch Guy, who was grinning and looking directly down at the bar.

'My card got cut off. I . . . think the Aquazzura slingbacks may have tipped me over the edge there.'

Malik reached across the bar and patted my head as if I were a small, helpless dog. 'Well, that makes sense. You have many strong areas but personal finances is not one of them.'

'I suppose.' I sighed. 'I didn't even know the card *had* a limit . . .'

Watch Guy stood up, put his phone in the back pocket of his jeans (classic Levi's) and slid a fifty-dollar note across the bar. 'Since we got a two-for-one deal, this should cover it.'

I defensively put my hand across the bar, pushing the note back towards him. 'Oh God, no, it's fine, I practically live here . . . I can pay next time!'

'We can consider it an IOU for when our paths cross again,' he replied, finally making proper eye contact. His eyes were a deep honey shade of brown and his lashes were thick and dark. This only made me more embarrassed.

'But . . . it's . . . it's fine!' I spluttered back.

'I know. The martini was excellent, mate, thanks.' He tipped his head at Malik as he strode towards the door, checking his watch (it was definitely a Navitimer). 'See ya, Alex,' he called as he walked.

'Um, bye.'

Malik and I looked at each other, confused. Perhaps both realising at the same time that I had never actually told him my name.

᭜ᥲ᥊᭜᥊

Vanessa Blake, 8:01 pm: Adjusting to life in the big smoke?

Alex York, 8:02 pm: Yes. I went shopping today. ☺

Vanessa Blake, 8:02 pm: What's the occasion? Hot date?

Alex York, 8:03 pm: Work meeting. I think. It's complicated. But I did share a martini with a hottie at a bar today.

Vanessa Blake, 8:03 pm: Work meeting sounds interesting . . . Wait, so you did have a hot date?

Alex York, 8:04 pm: Not really. He was at the bar at the same time as me. And we had a drink at the same time.

Vanessa Blake, 8:04 pm: That's not really 'sharing a martini' but fine. Did you get his number?

Alex York, 8:05 pm: As if. I'm not you.

Vanessa Blake, 8:10 pm: No you're not babe. I would have closed that deal in twenty minutes tops.

Alex York, 8:12 pm: He didn't seem that keen. He was obviously blind. Or gay. If I ever see him again I'll let you know. Bedtime for me. Love you. Miss you.

Vanessa Blake, 8:12 pm: xoxoxooxox

4

I walked through the lobby and into the lift with the kind of confidence that can only come from thirty minutes of HAIM blasting through my AirPods. Their music always makes me feel like I could single-handedly dismantle the patriarchy wearing a leather mini skirt and nipple tassels. I got out of the elevator on the thirteenth floor and immediately searched through my handbag for my swipe pass as I'd done thousands of times. The lobby walls were adorned with giant posters advertising the network's marquee talent. Goldie Miller, of course, was first. Staring down the barrel with an electric smile, her arms crossed in front of her. I recognised the blazer immediately as current season Dolce, which meant the photoshoot must have been recent. Next to her, the network drive show hosted by monumental flog Darren Chase and his latest co-host, an ex–reality-TV star he was no doubt sleeping with, and who would (as with all of his co-hosts) soon find themselves unable to spend another moment in his presence and quit. The neon-lit frame on the wall that once showcased the 'Alex @ Night' photo was now empty, which I suppose was a good thing given that I'd hated that photo from the minute I saw it. My teeth had been whitened and some idiot in marketing had done a complete hack job of my hair, photoshopping around my curls in a way that made it look like I was wearing a cafeteria lunch lady hairnet.

It still hadn't clicked that I was no longer in possession of a swipe pass—and hadn't been since I resigned from the network two months ago. I was elbow-deep in my giant handbag, rummaging through a swarm of tampons, USB cables and bobby pins, when the door in front of me swung open, narrowly missing my head. I didn't have to look up to know who was in front of me. The scent hit me first.

The scent had a story. Nine months ago, I had interviewed Tinie (the hot British rapper) in a hotel in downtown Sydney. Tom had asked about his cologne, and, after the interview wrapped, we detoured via David Jones to pick some up, only to return to the office empty-handed due to the $600 price tag. But even at the age of twenty-five, Tom was milking his father's post-divorce guilt for fancy Christmas presents, and soon enough the Creed Aventus was his.

'Oh God, there you are. I couldn't get through to your phone and I prayed to Cher that it meant you were just in the elevator, not doing one of your three-hour phones-off meditation classes run by that hippy man I abhor downtown.' Tom was panting furiously, one hand around my arm as he dragged me down the hall, his new (and hideous) Balenciaga sneakers squeaking as we raced through the office.

'You mean Phil?'

'Ugh, Phil. He smells like sage. And I DETEST sage.'

'I admire many things about you but your ability to really, truly hate is impressive.'

'It's part of my personal brand. That man needs a haircut and a steak. Anyway. You're here now, which is a relief because I spent the last two minutes convinced that without me organising every minute of your day, you'd got the time wrong for your meeting with Goldie.'

'How useless do you think I *am*?'

'Bitch, you once missed an interview with Katy Perry because you got stuck bingeing *The Real Housewives of Orange County* and lost track of time. I have *every* reason to doubt your ability to be here on time.'

I felt somewhat self-conscious walking through my old office. I made quick and friendly eye contact with old colleagues as I passed, thankful for Tom's quick pace, which made it clear we had somewhere to be. We stopped outside Goldie's office on the executive floor. Tom spun me around, put both hands on my shoulders and looked into my eyes as he spoke. 'Okay. You're on your own from here. But just remember, you ditched me once, you can't do it again. You're nothing without me and I make you infinitely more organised, successful and cool. Got it?' He pressed on. 'Got it?'

'Babe . . . what is going on?'

'I *told* you. I don't know. Well, I kind of know. But I don't fully know. So go in there, have the chat, and I'll be waiting in our spot for a debrief afterwards.'

He gave me a little shove towards Goldie's office and slinked off. I took a moment to smooth out the creases on my mini dress (I'd gone with a light pink Alaia dress with fuchsia mid-calf socks and Miu Miu kitten heels), reapply a bit of lip balm and give my curls a quick shake. I took a calming breath and knocked confidently on the door.

'Come on in, Ms York!' I heard the familiar voice call out from inside.

Sitting in a lush velvet armchair, basking in the sunshine of her corner office, was Goldie in all her magnificent glow. She was wearing denim bellbottom pants that I recognised instantly as Stella McCartney, and an oversized embroidered sweater with the word SMILE stitched into it. Her platinum bob was sharp as a razor, and her huge blue eyes were framed by oversized fire-engine-red glasses. She stood up and greeted me with a quick hug, and pulling away, directed her attention to the desk on the other side of the room.

'I don't think you've met my dear friend, Leo. Leo Billings, this is Alex York.'

I clocked the man-bun before I even saw his face. Sitting at Goldie's desk, straight-backed, stern, and looking altogether uncomfortable, was none other than Watch Guy from the bar. He was wearing an outfit almost identical to the one he was wearing yesterday. Crisp black tee, Levi's, boots.

He stood up slowly and extended his hand to me across Goldie's desk. I was absolutely flummoxed.

'Actually, weirdly enough we have met,' I spat, doing my best to sound confident and not at all confused. 'In fact, I owe Leo twenty-two dollars fifty.'

'I told you we'd meet again,' he replied, barely looking at me.

'Well, Leo, you could have been a *liiiiittle* more specific about the what, when and where of our next meeting, but here we are. Good to see you again.'

My tone indicated that it was most definitely *not* good to see him again. Why hadn't this dude mentioned that he knew exactly who I was when we were in the bar yesterday? What kind of psycho would let me sit there like an idiot while I blabbed on about how nervous I was about this very meeting? My utter mortification was interrupted by Goldie ushering me to the spare lounge seat opposite hers and sitting back down.

I still couldn't believe I was actually sitting inside Goldie Miller's office and was momentarily distracted by the photos that adorned the walls. Goldie with every celebrity, musician and person of remote significance over the last two and a half decades. Everyone from the Backstreet Boys to Bono was there, beaming alongside Goldie and her signature bob, which only made me even more confused about why I was there and—more importantly—why Watch Guy (I was too angry to use his real name) was too.

'Well, my dear, I suppose you're wondering why I've summoned you,' she said.

I slowly raised my eyebrows as I exhaled. 'That is exactly what I'm wondering, to be honest, Goldie. I didn't think I'd ever set foot back in this building again . . . Oh my God, is that Paul Simon?'

Out of the corner of my eye I'd spotted a gold-framed photo of a twenty-something Goldie Miller with her arms around arguably my favourite songwriter of all time. 'Oh my lord. I'm guessing that's from the 1983 tour. I wasn't even born yet but man, what I would have given. I saw Simon & Garfunkel in 2009 but they barely made eye contact on stage, which made me kind of sad. I also saw him with Sting a couple of years ago, and when they closed the show with "Bridge Over Troubled Water" I cried and an old lady next to me handed me a tissue and it was all pretty magical.'

Goldie beamed back at me, then glanced towards Leo, who was staring out the window, utterly emotionless.

'Sorry, Goldie. Continue.'

'You never have to apologise to me for getting excited over Paul Simon, my dear.' She laughed. 'Now, I'll get straight to the point.' Goldie leaned forwards, put one hand on my knee and fixed her sparkling blue eyes on me. 'I've decided to retire. Go out on top. On a high. Before anybody decides I'm too old or too out of touch or too . . . whatever adjective they'll inevitably use to get rid of me.'

Sorry, what?

'Goldie, you can't retire!'

'Oh, I can. And I have. And it's done. Just ask *him*.'

I looked over to Leo, who was still sitting quietly behind the desk. I noticed he was fidgeting with something on his left hand. Something gold and shiny. Something that, upon closer inspection, I realised was a wedding band. One that he had definitely not been wearing yesterday at the bar.

I liked this man less and less by the second.

This discovery did nothing to quell the rage that was now becoming more and more existential in its fury. I was angry that this stupid, married man had the audacity to embarrass me the way he had. I was angry that he was just sitting there silently while the greatest broadcaster I knew was telling me she felt the need to retire. But most of all, I was angry that Goldie of ALL people felt like she didn't have the freedom to age. After *everything* she had achieved.

I took a deep breath. 'So . . . what does any of this have to do with me?'

Leo spoke first. 'Well, Alex. Goldie has agreed to a seamless transition, giving her blessing to only one successor. A successor she has chosen and remains—much to our confusion—unmovably set on.'

I was getting dizzy. What was happening? I centred myself by putting my hands on my knees and staring at the ground.

'Alex,' Goldie said gently. 'I want you to replace me. You're the obvious choice. It will be you. And only you. Unless they want me to kick up a fuss, which I can guarantee will not end well.'

At this point I was half expecting a laughing Tom to open the door and shove a camera in my face, screaming with glee à la Ashton Kutcher in *Punk'd*. An elaborate prank would be far more believable than the reality that was unfolding before my eyes.

Goldie Miller, my most revered hero, was retiring. And she wanted me to replace her.

'But why me?'

'Why not you?'

'Because . . . I . . . I'm not . . . I could never be . . .'

'No, Alex, you're not me. But the world has had me! It's had all of me for twenty-five years and now it's time for them to have you.'

'How long have you known? When did you decide?'

'Well, I've had an inkling for a while. But when you quit, that's when I really knew for sure.'

Leo exhaled through his nose and made a strange sound that was somewhere between a sigh and a groan.

'You having the guts to walk away from a job you loved, in a strange sort of a way, proved to me that you'll never let this job own you. You go with your gut. You do what you want without waiting for permission. It makes you a brilliant broadcaster. Well not brilliant just yet, but one day. Your gut will never let you down, which is why, after years of trusting mine, I'm so sure that you're the right person to replace me.'

'So let me get this straight. You're handing me one of the most coveted gigs on radio in the country . . . because I wasn't too scared to quit?'

'Precisely. Oh, and I think you're the most talented interviewer I've heard since, well, me at your age.'

The three of us sat in silence while I tried to bring some order into my racing mind.

'I have a thousand questions, but I guess the main thing I want to know right now is—' I looked at Leo. 'Who are you? And why are you here?'

He swivelled his chair towards me.

'I can answer that simply, Alex. I'm your new boss.'

If my jaw could have physically reached the ground, then it would have. Instead, it just hung open.

He clocked the shock on my face and pushed on. 'To be fair, we all know that the talent is always actually in charge, so you could say that you're my boss. But I've been tasked with overseeing the new show and making sure it's a success. In fact, I'll be over-seeing the whole station. We'll be working together over the coming weeks, and then we'll look to launch in February.'

'February? That's three weeks away!' I swallowed. 'And I haven't even accepted the role yet.'

Goldie scoffed. 'Alex York, you've just been offered the job of a lifetime. In what universe are you going to say no? Don't be silly.'

'What about Tom? I've left him once; I won't do it again. I'll need him by my side . . . and . . . he'll need a pay rise.'

'I understand. Of course,' Goldie replied. 'As broadcasters we are only as good as the team around us, and he is one hell of a team to have around you. I've lost great producers in the past and, trust me, they're hard to replace.'

I couldn't help but notice Goldie holding Leo's gaze as she said this. He looked embarrassed and fidgeted with his ring again.

At this point there was too much going on for me to even think straight. I was both devastated that Goldie was retiring and giddy with excitement at the prospect of my entire life changing in three short weeks.

'Goldie, I don't know what to say. Five days ago I was lying on a beach in the Philippine islands with no prospects, no plan and no money. And now—'

'Now you're about to be 750 grand richer. Per year,' Leo inter-rupted. 'With a guaranteed thirty per cent pay rise in year two if you maintain the number one spot in the market . . . which nobody expects you to do, don't worry.' Leo looked over at Goldie and continued, 'You can thank Goldie for that. I certainly wouldn't have offered you such a good deal if it was up to me.'

Goldie lifted an eyebrow in his direction. 'Well, my dear, lucky it wasn't up to you.'

An awkward hush fell over the room. I was jumping between spending the money in my head and trying not to throw up. At least I'd be able to finally take care of my credit card bill.

Goldie clapped her hands. 'That's enough business for me for one day. I'll leave you two kids to get to know each other.'

And with that, Goldie disappeared in a quick haze of colour and light, leaving me alone in her office with Leo. He cleared his throat and stood up. 'I'll be in touch ASAP about the contract,' he said.

I glared at him. 'I can't believe you didn't tell me who you were yesterday. You just let me babble away like an idiot!'

He just shrugged, fiddling with his ring again. 'What difference would it have made? I'll see you soon, Alex.'

Then he walked past me and out of Goldie's office without another word. So much for getting to know each other.

I headed downstairs to find Tom, who was waiting for me exactly where I knew he would be.

There are few places on Earth I would rather be than inside a radio studio. Those places include: front row at Royal Albert Hall seeing Ray Lamontagne live in 2007; sipping on an Aperol Spritz on the Amalfi Coast; and making sweet love to Ricky Martin in an alternate universe where he is not a gay man and I am fifty per cent hotter.

Our radio studio was our own sacred little world. A soundproof wonderland full of microphones and buttons with the ability to broadcast to anywhere in the world, live.

My night show had been three hours long and broadcast weeknights, with a couple of weeks off for Christmas and mid-year break. That's 720 hours spent in my little glass box every year. All 720 hours pure bliss. That is until I was too depressed over the break-up to function and all of a sudden the glass box felt more like a cage, where every love song I played made me want to scream 'LOVE ISN'T EVEN REAL' into the microphone.

I pushed open the heavy soundproof door like I'd done thousands of times and sat on the floor as Tom quickly made sure all of the mics were off, the faders were pulled down and ensured that there was no power running to the desk.

'So, please tell me Goldie has convinced you to come back?'

'Well . . . yeah, but she doesn't want me doing our old show.'

He gasped as he sat up straight. 'Oh my God. Dramatic. Tell me everything right now.'

And so I explained everything in detail to Tom, who continued to gasp, scream and at one point pretended to pass out.

'Oh, and you're getting a pay rise.'

And with that, he pretended to pass out for the second time in fifteen minutes, before opening one eye and looking up at me. 'Okay, now tell me more about this Leo guy that you inexplicably have run into twice in twenty-four hours.'

'Ugh. I have no idea what to think of him. First of all, the wedding ring thing is kind of a dead giveaway that he's a schmuck. But I trust Goldie. And she called him her "dear friend". Surely she'd know if her "dear friend" was a lying, cheating philanderer.'

'Or she's just so used to working with lying, cheating philanderers in this business that she's grown immune. And in any case none of this changes the fact that you think he's hot. Or at least, you thought he was hot when you saw him at the bar yesterday,' Tom said.

I shot him a shocked, disgusted face. 'I never said that!'

'Babe, you didn't have to. You've told me he's brunet, has a man-bun, stubble, and kinda looks like he might ride a motorbike. He is to you what Shawn Mendes is to me. The prototype of your type. If you had to describe your type to one of those artists they get in on *CSI* to draw a mugshot of the perp, he would hand you back a headshot of Leo in perfect detail. Framed.'

'Since when do you use the word perp?'

'They've had me working on that pre-recorded weekends show since you left and it's been woeful. Let's just say I've been watching a *lot* of *CSI* at my desk during work hours. I'm waiting on someone from the IT department to report me to HR.'

'I'm sorry, babe. Wanna go to Starbucks?'

'Depends. Is your credit card working again?'

'No, but now that I'm rich again I'll be able to pay it off! Oh, and I'm going to return the Aquazzuras today. They gave me a bit of toe cleavage anyway. In the meantime, I've got a tiny bit of savings left. All is not lost.'

We were walking arm in arm towards the lift when I felt Tom's body tighten.

'Well look who the cat dragged in,' a voice hissed.

My head snapped up to see Darren Chase leaning against the elevator door.

I suppose everybody, no matter what line of work they find themselves in, needs a work nemesis. Darren Chase was mine.

His drive show had always been on air directly before mine, and in the years that I did 'Alex @ Night' he never once mentioned my name on air. Sometimes he purposefully went late to throw me off. The guy made my skin crawl. Producers and co-hosts came and left faster than the B-grade celebrities he dated. Darren had taken an intense disliking to me the day I started at Star FM, and the feeling had been mutual.

None of this changed the fact that he was a brilliant broadcaster. His shows were tight, punchy and slick in a way that mine never would be, and, when he wanted to be, he was absolutely hilarious, but always at the expense of someone else.

I groaned, forcing a saccharine smile in his direction.

'I was hardly *dragged*, Darren. And while the reason for my reappearance must be eating you alive, I can't tell you why I'm here or on whose behest. Top-secret stuff.'

He scoffed, rolling his eyes. 'Oh I'm *sure*. No doubt here begging for your job back.' He looked me up and down slowly with more than a hint of disgust. 'Anyway, gotta run. Some of us have radio shows to prepare for.'

'The only thing he should be preparing for is the syphilis I've been wishing upon him for the last four years,' Tom muttered as Darren sauntered off towards his studio. 'I can't wait to see his face when he hears about you taking Goldie's gig.'

'Hmm. He's gonna be a real bitch about it, isn't he?'

'Oh yeah. Take it from me, the biggest bitch in this building. Darren Chase is going to lose his fucking mind.'

᠁᠁᠁

Alex York, 5:00 pm: You. Are. Not. Going. To. Believe. This.

Vanessa Blake, 5:01 pm: TELL ME NOW!

Alex York, 5:03 pm: The guy at the bar.

Vanessa Blake, 5:03 pm: You saw him again????

Alex York, 5:04 pm: He's my new boss.

Vanessa Blake, 5:05 pm: I'm calling you right now.

5

Unsurprisingly, that night I had the carpark dream. The long and short of it was that I'd be in a carpark, going about my business, and my father would appear, nonchalantly claiming he hadn't left after all . . . He'd just been hanging out in the carpark waiting for me. He'd act cool and calm, as if he hadn't up-ended my family's whole world and changed the trajectory of our entire lives with one single decision. I'd be shocked and angry and, just before I started yelling at him, I would wake up.

The reason I wasn't surprised that I'd had the carpark dream was because it usually visited me on momentous occasions. Perhaps a reminder that he would always be missing from every big celebration or commiseration in life. It's not like I ever really missed him, because he was never really around in the first place, even before he abandoned us for good. But in big life moments, I suppose I missed what I imagined the 'idea' of a good father would be, and how it might feel to make him proud. Lucky for me, Mum was generally proud enough for the both of them.

I'd been lying in bed at May's house, staring at the ceiling, thinking about the dream for a couple of minutes when Leo rang, bang on 9 am. Our phone call was short and to the point. He had my contract and wanted to hand it to me directly. Three hours later I was sitting at a cafe down the road on Bondi Beach, waiting to have my third encounter with this man in as many days. In some sort of power play move, I had pretended I had a busy day and suggested he come to my neck of the woods for a catch-up 'in between meetings'. There were no such meetings. I suspected he knew there were no such meetings. I committed to the bit anyway.

A taxi pulled up in front of the cafe, and through the rear window I could see a jovial Leo, laughing with the cabbie as he passed his credit card over to the front seat. He didn't exactly strike me as the type of guy who liked to engage in friendly banter with strangers . . . or with anyone, to be honest. On the other hand, it was entirely possible that he just didn't engage in friendly banter with *me*, which was even more unsettling due to the fact I am the QUEEN of friendly banter.

A minute or so later he stepped out of the cab with an A4-sized envelope under one arm and scanned the cafe. He looked perfectly at home among Bondi's beautiful people: a sea of long-legged twenty-somethings in Lululemon, topless surfers and middle-aged men with dubious incomes and luxury cars. I'm not sure why I was so surprised that he was once again wearing his uniform, although today his tee was a midnight blue. Same jeans, same shoes, with his hair pulled back into that signature man-bun in a way that looked both messy and neat at the same time.

'Hello again.' His tone was polite. The sunshine against his skin illuminated a couple of soft wrinkles around his eyes. On anybody else, I would have called them laugh lines.

I was immediately hit with a scent I couldn't quite put my finger on; one I had definitely smelled on one of the countless rich and/or famous men with whom I'd spent time over the years.

I went in strong and friendly. 'Hi Leo! Thanks for coming to my side of town!'

Tom Ford. Tabacco Vanille. Of course. I didn't know much about him yet, but I did know he had impeccable taste in watches, cocktails and now cologne.

I passed him a menu straight away. I had no desire to let this catch-up extend any longer than it needed to.

'All good. It's been a while since I've seen an Aussie beach.' He looked out at the ocean.

'Oh, right. Where have you been?'

'In the UK. For the last ten or so years,' he replied matter-of-factly.

'So the job brought you home after all that time?'

Leo shuffled around in his chair for a moment, an uneasy look on his face. It was clear he didn't share my interest in long-winded, highly detailed monologues about one's personal history.

'I love living by the water. I swam every day on the island,' I told him.

'You didn't get bored?' His deep, serious eyes finally made contact with mine, sending a tiny jolt of surprise through me. It was the first question he'd asked me since he sat down, and I couldn't tell whether his tone was judgemental or just direct.

'Uh, no, to be honest.' Heat rose on the back of my neck. I'm not sure if it was shame or embarrassment, but I was suddenly incredibly self-conscious. 'I'd spent the last four years working my arse off twelve hours a day in a freezing cold studio and was in desperate need of some sunshine. Plus, how could you get bored when the massages cost ten bucks, the rum costs two and the ocean is free? It was paradise.'

Leo's attention turned to the ocean for a minute, a light breeze sweeping a couple of rogue strands of hair off his face. 'Well, when you put it like that, it makes perfect sense, I suppose. Coffee?' I guessed he was just as keen to not drag this out as I was.

'Almond piccolo, please.'

He walked up to the counter to order and returned a minute later, reaching into the envelope he'd placed on the table and pulling out a pile of papers stapled together.

'Your contract. I'm assuming you've got a lawyer or business manager to look over it in the next forty-eight hours?'

I most definitely had neither of those things. I nodded anyway.

'I also had Tom's contract drawn up and delivered it to him at his desk.' He looked at me, deadpan. 'He didn't read a word of it; he just made me take a photo of him signing it for his Instagram and then handed it back.'

This made me chuckle. In turn, Leo followed suit, his face softening, the crinkles around his eyes coming to life.

Maybe they *were* laugh lines after all. I felt my shoulders relax a little.

A young waitress appeared with a tray of coffees. She was universally stunning with legs up to her neck, the kind of cleavage that you only get until you're twenty, and huge doe eyes that she fixed on Leo as she spoke.

'I've got an almond piccolo and a long black.'

'The piccolo is mine, thanks,' I responded, reaching out to give her a hand.

She ignored me, swapped her hands around and placed the long black in front of Leo with the kind of adoration in her eyes that I usually reserve for dogs on the street that I want to pat. I wondered if she'd missed the wedding ring on his finger or just didn't care.

'Can I get you anything else?'

'Alex? Did you want to eat?' Leo asked.

I shook my head. The waitress widened her enamoured gaze, attempting to illicit a response from a completely oblivious Leo, who instead took a sip of his coffee and quickly checked his phone. She walked away like a lovesick zombie, and even turned to look back at him on her way to the kitchen. Nada. Zip. Nothing. This girl was a sucker for punishment.

'So, Leo, what exactly is your role going to be in all of this? Like, day to day.'

'Well, you, Tom and your team will take care of the ins and outs of the show. But I'd like to be in your daily planning meetings at least for the first month, and we'll need to have weekly check-ins to make sure everything's on track. And, of course, I'll be heavily involved over the next couple of weeks as we figure out the DNA of the show. I've already got the head of audio mocking up some ideas for the show's sound and imaging, which we'll get you across by the end of the week, if you're interested.'

My stomach dropped. Of course I was interested. This was my bloody show! With my name on it! In what universe would I not care about every single detail? I took a deep breath and counted to five as I attempted to swallow my anger and reply in a manner that didn't make me sound as murderous as I felt.

'Leo, I would have liked to brief the audio producer myself. Or, at the very least, have been part of the conversation.'

He looked genuinely taken aback by my response, uncrossing his legs and re-crossing them on the other side.

'Right.' He mused, tapping a finger meditatively on his knee. 'I can easily CC you in. Any thoughts on everything else?'

I had a thousand thoughts on everything else. Most of which went something along the lines of 'piss off and leave me and my show alone' but instead I chose something a little more vague.

'I'm sure we'll figure it out as we go.'

And there it was. The first awkward silence. Leo stared back at the ocean and fidgeted with his wedding ring. Why did he always do that? I took another sip of my coffee and did my best to commit to the silence between us. This was an almost impossible task as I never did well in situations where nobody was talking. My job was quite literally to talk into a microphone and avoid silence at all costs. I only had another ten seconds in the tank before I was going to start rambling and truly embarrass myself for the second time this week, so I was thankful when a familiar voice boomed out from halfway across the road.

'Good morning, my darling heart!'

Aunty May was approaching, dressed in her walking gear. Her brunette locks were up in a short ponytail, held in place by a bright pink visor as she waved happily and took her AirPods out.

'I missed you at home this morning and wondered where you'd got to! And here you are!'

'Here I am! May, this is Leo, my new . . . work colleague. Leo, this is my Aunty May, who I live with.'

May raised her eyebrows and stood back to take him in as he rose from his seat to shake her hand. She looked back at me with a face that was, for lack of a better word, pretty damn horny. Since moving in with May I had discovered that women get to a certain age where they consider themselves exempt from the kind of social norms that deem gawking at somebody with a look on your face that says 'you should have sex with this one' as inappropriate.

'So, Leo, what do you think of our girl so far?'

I prayed for a tsunami to swallow us all whole, wincing apologetically towards Leo.

'You don't have to answer that, May is just being a shit-stirrer.'

Leo looked relieved to have been let off the hook, as May giggled heartily.

'Would you like to join us, May?' Leo asked politely.

I gave her a look that implied she was most definitely not welcome to join us. She understood and responded accordingly.

'A lovely offer, Leo, but I've got twenty minutes left on this podcast and then a yoga class so I must be off. But I do hope to see more of you in the future. Perhaps you can come over for tea one night? My husband Billy is a chef, which I think is half the reason Alex still lives with us so long after the break-up.'

Again, I prayed for the tsunami as Leo tightened his mouth in order to stifle a smile.

'Okay, May, off you go. Enjoy yoga. Namaste.'

May, satisfied that an appropriate amount of humiliation had occurred in her short encounter, winked at Leo, gave me a kiss on my forehead then popped her AirPods back in and waved goodbye. We both watched as she walked into the distance, and it was Leo who spoke first.

'So, you live with your aunty and uncle?'

'It's a long story. And to be fair, Billy really *is* a great cook.'

Leo broke a half-smile, checked his watch and knocked back the last of his long black.

'Well, you can certainly afford your own place now. You've got your contract; take a look and we'll be in touch in the next day or two. Coffees are all paid for.'

As he stood up, I caught myself noticing the distinct way that his shirt clung to his shoulders, which were surprisingly broad. In the midst of scanning the street for a cab, he glanced back at me. 'Oh, and by the way, Mark Holdsworth wants to meet you, so expect an email.'

'The CEO?' I called back.

A cab appeared on the other side of the road and he lifted his arm into the air to hail it. My gaze fixed itself on his strong bicep as it flexed in the sunshine. I hastily reminded myself that the jury was still out on this dude, and I may still have to hate him. The cab pulled over as he yelled back. 'Yep! The CEO. Good luck.'

I watched him drive away and realised I was no closer to actually figuring out anything about this man. He didn't seem to be a complete arsehole, but he also wasn't exactly warm. Or maybe he was warm to other people and not me. Maybe when he got home he was a perfect, adoring husband who bought his partner flowers and offered up foot massages. Doubtful.

My phone dinged with an SMS notification.

Leo! Wow! Hubba hubba! Xoxo May

᎐᎐᎐᎐

Victoria Milligan was a terrifying woman. In her role as executive assistant, she had outlasted four CEOs over a period of twenty years and commanded more power over the staff than all four of those old white men combined. She had short grey cropped hair, fabulous glasses and ran marathons in her spare time. Everything about her was sharp. A sharp memory, a sharp tongue and a sharp sense of style. It took mine and Tom's keen eye for detail and obsession with French luxury brands to discover that everything this woman wore was outrageously expensive. Hers was the kind of wardrobe that was not just thrown together but 'expertly curated' over many years. I worshipped and feared her in equal measure.

An email from Victoria only ever meant one of two things, neither of which were pleasant. Option one was that you'd broken an office rule (I once lit a Dyptique candle that had been sent to me by one of the record labels. The lavender hibiscus scent wafting down the hallway was enough to alert Victoria of the fire safety breach). Option two, however, was one that I'd never had to face. Option two was a meeting with the CEO, and even with forewarning from Leo I was a little unsettled at the thought.

When I arrived outside Mark Holdsworth's office the next day, Victoria gave me a curt smile as I sank into a chair to wait. My mouth felt dry but my armpits were suddenly swamps. It was absolutely ridiculous that I was sitting there feeling like a naughty schoolgirl. I was the new host of the goddamn breakfast show for goodness sake—I should be sitting there holding my head high. Like Goldie would have been. Instead, I was half expecting Victoria to hold her palm out and ask me to spit out my chewing gum. I wasn't even chewing any.

A friendly voice boomed from inside the office.

'Come on in, Alex.'

I pushed open the heavy door and walked through to a huge corner office, with a large mahogany desk in the middle and a spectacular view of Sydney behind. The walls were completely empty and the desk was sparse, apart from a computer and some family photos. A lone Peloton bike sat in the corner. The office was entirely insipid. Mark stood and smiled warmly, pointing to the chair on the other side of the desk. It couldn't have been more different to Goldie's office on the same floor—hers was full of colour and light and life. After a polite handshake, I settled in and placed my bag on the floor. I wouldn't normally place a vintage Louis Vuitton rucksack on any floor, but this carpet looked like it had never been walked on and I decided it was a safe bet.

'Thanks for stopping by, Alex. I thought it would be a nice idea if we had some face time ahead of the big announcement.'

He was about fifty-five years old, with a head that looked as though it had been shaved at the first sign of balding, which was a decision I respected in a man his age. He wore rimless round spectacles, a crisp white shirt with the top button undone and a slim-fit grey suit jacket. I'd seen him hundreds of times around the building, but never alone and never this close up. If he were a stranger in the street I would think he ran a bank, not an entertainment empire. Although to be fair, I imagined there was a fair bit of boring money stuff involved in the old CEO gig. More boring money stuff than Lady Gaga concerts, at least. I supposed I could forgive him for not looking particularly cool.

'No worries, my pleasure. I'm glad we're finally meeting!' I chirped.

He narrowed his eyes towards me. 'If you don't mind me asking, how old are you?'

His face told me the question was a serious one, to my surprise. He went on, 'I only ask because I've got a twenty-eight-year-old daughter.'

'Oh, right.' That made a little more sense. 'I'm thirty later this year.'

'Lovely. Hannah is a physiotherapist. She lives in Brisbane with her boyfriend.' He picked up one of the framed pictures from his desk and passed it over to me, pointing to one of three girls. 'Three daughters! That's Abbey next to her, and Harper on the other side.'

It would appear I wasn't going to be getting the interrogation I'd imagined. Perhaps I should have brought tea and scones.

'Do you have any siblings, Alex?'

'Uh, nope. Only child, I'm afraid. I grew up listening to the radio for company, so it makes sense that I ended up here!'

At this point I realised the forced politeness on Mark's face was perhaps more condescending than kind. Were we actually going to talk business? Or did he want me to draw him a family tree?

'And where are Mum and Dad?'

Mum and Dad? I shifted awkwardly in my seat. 'Um. Mum's in Melbourne and Dad could be anywhere, really. He could be dead for all I know!'

Mark's eyes grew wide and then flicked from me to the desk. He took the framed photo of his daughters back and returned it to his desk.

'Right. And how are you feeling about the new job? As you know, it will be lots of pressure.'

I grinned confidently. 'Yep. Lots of pressure, but I'm certainly up for the challenge and I'm going into this with my eyes wide open. Goldie is my hero and I'll forever be indebted to her. I'm going to make her proud.'

'Right. Yes, of course, we all love Goldie,' Mark said with a disingenuous tone that made me think he didn't love Goldie at all. 'Oh, speaking of Goldie, we've decided to turn her office into an executive retreat, but you'll be glad to know you can have your old desk back, which should make settling in nice and easy.'

'Oh, right. That's fine,' I replied. I hadn't presumed I'd get her office, but now that he'd made a point of letting me know I wouldn't, I felt a little miffed.

'Well, Leo tells me the paperwork is all taken care of, and from the sounds of things you're in very good hands, so if you need anything, you know where to find me.'

One thing was clear. I absolutely would not ever need anything from Mark Holdsworth.

'Of course. Thanks, Mark.'

I picked up my rucksack and headed for the door, wishing to God I'd chosen a more grown-up bag for the meeting. It had set me back three grand at an exclusive vintage store in Harajuku, but I doubt he knew that. I swung it over my shoulders and felt his eyes burning a hole in my back as I left, with the distinct and unwavering sense that there wasn't a single bone in Mark Holdsworth's body that took me seriously.

I walked out the door and past Victoria's desk, numb and increasingly dejected by the brisk and shallow encounter I'd just had with my new boss.

'Nice bag, Ms York,' she whispered under her breath as I passed.

I gave her a grateful look. She mouthed the words 'chin up' as she lifted her own chin with her index finger.

I raised my chin and took a deep breath.

She gave me a satisfied nod in return.

⑴⑴⑴⑴⑴

As if I hadn't already had my fill of mediocre white men for the morning, I found myself face-to-face with Darren Chase in line for coffee downstairs not twenty minutes later. My assumption that we were going to simply ignore each other and caffeinate in peace proved to be ill-founded as he collected his iced long black and made a beeline for the corner booth I'd hidden myself in.

'Are you stalking us now?' he asked. 'You're kinda reminding me of one of those sad girls who hangs outside her ex's workplace hoping to run into him.' His face was smug, high on some sort of imagined superiority.

'Yeah and you're kinda reminding me of Zac Efron in *High School Musical* with that hair—go easy on the blow waves, Darren, it's not 2006.' I committed the insult to memory word for word, knowing I'd be retelling this story verbatim to Tom later.

He scoffed. 'I just don't know how you have the guts to come within a kilometre of this building after your embarrassing little performance. And it was all over what? A break-up?' He laughed.

'Yeah, well not all of us have a break-up every eight weeks,' I snapped back. 'My boyfriend at the time may have turned out to be an arsehole, but at least he stuck around long enough to learn my middle name, unlike every girl you've dated since, well, forever.' The insults were coming free and easy, presumably due to the fact that I knew I'd already won. That soon he'd find out I was getting his dream gig. If it were anyone else I'd go easy, humble in the knowledge that I had nothing to prove, maybe even feeling a hint of pity. Darren's attitude, however, was making humility far too hard.

'You know you could always come and work on my show, Alex. I've been saying for weeks we need someone to get coffees . . .' He cocked his head to the side, studying me with a look of disdain as he took another sip of his iced long black.

The irony was too much. I downed the last of my piccolo and picked up my rucksack, extricating myself from the booth so that Darren and I were face-to-face.

'Great. I'll send my CV to you today. Is your email address still lonelyguy69@gmail.com?'

Obviously far more used to being insulted than I was, his face didn't flinch. 'Gmail is for unemployed bums. I still have my official *company* email address since, unlike you, I have a job here.'

'Yes you do, Darren. And you're *soooo* very good at it. I can only hope that one day I can climb to such illustrious heights!' I bellowed, my eyes wide with faux wonder. 'And now, I must be off. Very important unemployed bum business to take care of, but I might see you around. Sooner than you think, maybe. You never, never know . . .'

His bottom lip twitched as I gave a dramatic wave and disappeared into the crowd of coffee-hungry office workers.

6

The next week or so was a blur. It's not often you find yourself smack bang in the middle of your dreams coming true, and so far I was giving the experience a solid ten out of ten. We'd managed to keep the news well under wraps externally, but keeping the rumours in check at the office proved a little harder. Tom eventually took things into his own hands and planted a story on the office grapevine that I'd be resurrecting 'Alex @ Night', which at least gave me a decent excuse to roam the halls occasionally. With two weeks to go until the show launch, the PR team had been called in to figure out the best way to announce Goldie's departure and my debut. Goldie had been insistent that the announcements were made together, which I was grateful for. As far as I was concerned, it gave less time for people to speculate about who her replacement would be, and then be shocked/disappointed/angry when they found out it was little old me. It also meant that Goldie could control the narrative, which I assumed was the bigger motivation at play.

Every big PR campaign starts with a photoshoot, and every photoshoot begins with an outfit. The stylist had pulled a full rack of designer looks for me to try, and I squealed with utter glee that my first choice, a stunning Jacquemus blazer with matching pants in lilac, fitted like a glove. When teamed with the insanely high Louboutin stilettos I'd brought from home, my legs looked far longer than they ever deserved to. This was one act of deceit I would happily be complicit in. Once my outfit was locked in, I headed towards hair and make-up where Carla was waiting for me.

Carla was five foot three, Spanish, and the biggest rock and roller I knew. She'd started out her make-up career as a teenager working in music TV, and twenty-five years later was a treasure trove of insane stories, adventures and wisdom. On her first day of work experience as a fifteen-year-old, she met Dave Grohl. He remembered her two years later. That was the kind of effect she had. She rocked a jet-black mullet and a nose piercing like nobody's business. She took zero shit from anyone and was completely unfazed by the world of celebrity (which is probably why so many celebrities wanted to party with her). We hit it off the day we met, and she'd taken me under her wing early on. Five years later and she was like my big sister. My big sister who was really, really, really good at hair and make-up.

I lay back for what felt like twelve hours (probably closer to two) while Carla worked her magic. I'd heard somewhere that Kim Kardashian spent two hours every single morning 'in glam', and wondered if she ever regretted all the time spent sitting in a chair, but then again I probably spent the same amount of time scrolling Instagram every day, and that had made me neither a sex symbol nor a billionaire.

Carla and I chatted while she worked, and I happily outlined every detail of my escapades on the island. And then, as was her custom, she encouraged me to close my eyes and meditate while she finished off my hair. This last ten minutes of quiet was a tradition she'd started with me early on, and it meant that I was always calm and focused by the time we finished and I was whisked off to perform whatever duties lay ahead. I loved Carla for it. I loved her even more when I opened my eyes and saw how hot I looked when she was done.

Once I was dressed, I took a couple of selfies in the mirror and sent them straight to Vanessa, which is what every self-respecting girl does when she knows she looks insanely good. Her response was to tell me to put my new-found face to good use, go out tonight and get laid. But, if I'm honest, that would have felt a little like catfishing.

Now, no woman likes being upstaged at her own party, but when Goldie walked on set five minutes later looking cooler and more beautiful than any woman her age (or twenty years younger) has ever looked in the history of the universe, I couldn't help but clap. She was radiant. And she knew it.

For the next twenty minutes, we sat side by side on a chaise longue under bright lights, with Goldie at the forefront and me off to her left, while a team of photographers, stylists and make-up artists fussed about in our orbit. I hoped to God that my armpits weren't sweating onto the borrowed blazer, and was halfway through a subtle pit check when I noticed Leo silently observing me from the shadows, arms crossed. The photography studio was on the same side of the building as his office so it wasn't altogether surprising to see him there, and even less surprising that he was yet again wearing the same outfit. Did he have multiple pairs of those jeans or was he wearing the same ones every day? Would it kill him to mix it up a little?

Goldie clocked him at the same time as I did. 'So how are things with the two of you? A little less icy than they were last week, I hope?' she whispered in between camera flashes.

'We'll be fine.'

'That doesn't exactly answer my question, my dear. But I'll take your word for it.' She paused, as if she were thinking. 'You know, I'd never set you up to fail.'

'I know. Like I said, I promise we'll be fine!'

'But?'

'Well. There is just one thing. And I hope you don't mind me asking.' I moved closer towards her and lowered my voice to a whisper. Goldie leaned in. 'You see, when I first saw him at the bar, he wasn't wearing a wedding ring. And the next day he was. I just—'

Goldie pulled away and put her right index finger in the air as if to hush me, her piercing blue eyes looking directly into mine. 'Are you asking me whether he's a cheating, lying bastard?'

My face was deadpan. 'Well, to be fair, this industry is full of them.'

Goldie raised her eyebrows knowingly. 'True. But Leo Billings is not one of them. You have my word. I think in time you'll find a perfectly reasonable explanation. In the meantime, I wouldn't make any more assumptions.'

My heart sank. I felt like an idiot for bringing it up.

'Right. Sorry, Goldie, I shouldn't have said anything.'

'None of that, my dear. Now let's hurry these clowns along. My armpits are three flashes away from sweating through the Valentino silk.'

Minutes later we gathered around the monitor as the photographer's assistant scrolled through hundreds and hundreds of images, any of which I would gladly have printed on my tombstone. Goldie picked her favourites, I agreed, and we were done.

As I began the retreat back to my dressing room, Leo emerged from his spot in the corner and whispered something to Goldie. A moment later he was jogging towards me to catch up.

'Alex, can I grab you for a second?'

'Of course.'

'Great. We can do a *West Wing* walk and talk,' he replied.

I sure as hell wasn't going to let him know that *The West Wing* was my all-time favourite show (thanks to Uncle Billy forcing me to binge it with him one Christmas when I was twenty). Bonding over a favourite show was something you told someone you wanted to be friends with, and despite Goldie assuring me in a roundabout way that he wasn't a horrible person, I wasn't ready to be friends with the guy.

'What's up?'

'A trip to London. This week. For an exclusive with Tilly Roy. We'll air it during show launch week.'

I nonchalantly pulled out my phone and scanned my calendar app. 'Hmm, I've got quite a bit on this weekend, so I think I'll have to pass. But thanks for the offer.'

Leo stared at me in silence. I tried my best to look as serious as possible as I held his gaze, but it only took a moment for him to realise I was pulling his leg. This time I squealed twice as long and twice as loud as I did when the Jacquemus blazer fitted perfectly and without thinking threw my arms around him, squeezing him in a bear hug as I jumped up and down gleefully. I quickly remembered the twelve litres of foundation that had been applied to my face, and also the fact that he was my boss (who I had just decided not to be friends with), and let him go.

'London is my favourite city on the planet and I love Tilly with unending passion. And if you need some entertainment, you can come with me to see Tom's reaction when we tell him. He does this really elaborate fake pass-out thing, which always goes down a treat.'

'I'll take your word for it. Just so it's all clear in your mind, the Goldie announcement will be made to press tomorrow at 9 am, so it's going to be a big day. You'll have a lot of press calls, which the PR girls will sit in on. Then we fly the following evening. We arrive Wednesday night local time, and the interview isn't until the following night so we've a bit of time to settle in and prepare.'

We? Did he mean he was . . . coming with us? I took a step back, surprised.

'Leo, this isn't my first Tilly Roy interview. And Tom and I have done dozens of these trips . . . it's nothing new.'

'Don't worry, I'm not coming to babysit. I've got some network business to attend to anyway, the timing was just lucky.'

I gave him a quizzical, disbelieving look. 'Sure, Leo. Well, I can assure you I'm not going to ditch Tilly Roy and go on a thirty-six-hour ketamine bender with some randoms I meet in Soho. I'm a pro.'

He furrowed his brow, still trying to figure me out. The ketamine call may have been a step too far. 'I promise I won't get in your way. I'll just be . . . there if you need me,' he replied, his forced casualness both obvious and awkward. Like a parent chaperoning a Year 12 formal.

'Which I'm sure we won't,' I quipped matter-of-factly.

'Even better. Hey, Goldie also mentioned you had some sort of a friendship with Finley Stark? Might not hurt to see if you can tee up something there too?'

'Of course. I'll shoot him a text once I scrub all this off,' I replied breathlessly, pointing to my face.

'Yep, good idea.'

I looked back at him, puzzled.

'I mean, you look good. I just can't imagine it feels nice to have all that stuff on your face.'

I continued to stare. He was looking more stressed by the second.

'I'm going to stop talking and head back to my office. The photos of you and Goldie look great.'

I decided to ignore the implication that I was an ogre who'd been magically transformed into something more palatable, instead making a beeline for Tom's desk, where half the office was treated to one of his best fake pass outs yet.

That afternoon, I sat at Tom's desk mentally planning my London wardrobe. He sat next to me booking tickets to

West End musicals and loudly serenaded us all with his rendition of the *Dear Evan Hansen* soundtrack, complete with original choreography. An email appeared in my inbox from a somewhat familiar name. Intrigued, I opened it straight away.

Hi Alex!

You absolutely don't know me, and I hope to God this email isn't weird BUT I'm Georgia Jones. I'm a senior producer on Darren's show. (I know. Stick with me!)

I won't beat around the bush. If the rumours are true about you coming back then I want in. I don't care if I need to be the coffee-run girl in order to make that happen. Which would be a massive waste of my talent but a demotion I would gladly take if it means working with you (badass, talented woman) instead of He-who-is-none-of-those-things.

I know it ain't kosher to email talent directly, but in this instance, I figured I'd shoot my shot.

Tell me what I gotta do and I'll do it!

Again, hope this isn't weird.

x Georgia (the brunette with the sharp bangs who sits by the window)

I tapped Tom on the shoulder, beckoning him to come and read the email. He scanned it quickly.

'I mean it's gutsy. I'll give her that,' he said, slightly amused.

Another email notification appeared on my screen. Georgia had emailed me again.

PS: Yesterday I caught Darren searching his own name on 'celebrity foot finder'.

'Hire that bitch or I'm quitting,' Tom proclaimed, before returning to his showtunes. Famously impossible to please, his instant acceptance was an encouraging sign. He'd once had someone moved to another show because their perfume 'smelled too cheap'.

I raised my head above the cubicle and scanned the room in search of a brunette sitting near a window. I caught Georgia's eye straight away. She looked unsure. It had been a risky move. A risky move that was about to pay off.

Georgia. Gutsy move. Give me twenty-four hours.

᪲᪲᪲

Alex York, 2:33 pm: Remember that time we went to London and I got so drunk I fell in the gap at the tube station?

Vanessa Blake, 2:50 pm: LOLLLLLLL. And you spewed all over BOTH our beds.

Alex York, 2:51 pm: I'm going there for work this week. Come! You can bunk in at my hotel!

Vanessa Blake, 2:52 pm: Ugh. My boss is away so I'm running the dive school for the next fortnight. Lame. What's in London?

Alex York, 3:00 pm: Tilly Roy.

Vanessa Blake, 3:01 pm: Your fucken life, man. Speaking of bosses—is Leo coming?

Alex York, 3:05 pm: Yep.

Vanessa Blake, 3:06 pm: Boo. Don't spew on his bed.

Alex York, 3:06 pm: We were nineteen! My tastes are far more refined now.

7

I had known Finley Stark since the early days of his career—when he didn't have a security detail and happily handed out his number to music journalists he met on promo tours. He was twenty-two, and I was twenty-seven, and initially I'd done the interview as a favour to my mate Miles who worked at the record label. Finley had just been signed and didn't have a hit on his hands yet, but the label was 'sure he was on the verge of something huge' so Tom scheduled him in for a fifteen-minute interview.

These gambles rarely paid off, and usually the kids they wheeled in on the promise that they were 'about to be huge stars' did not make a second appearance.

The morning of the interview I pressed play on the advance copy of his single while brushing my teeth. I knew by the first chorus that Finley Stark might just be the exception. I was right, and within six months he was the biggest pop star on the planet.

We hit it off straight away. He had banter as strong as his musical chops and a cheekiness that instantly cemented him as the annoying but extremely lovable little brother I never had.

Finley was tall with thick, auburn hair that he slicked back and tucked behind his ears, the kind of guy who could make a Gucci silk shirt look strangely masculine. The morning we first met, he wore big chunky rings on each finger and contrasted his big black Alexander McQueen boots with a raw silk shirt that made his green eyes sparkle and caused everyone to stare as he walked through the radio station and into my studio. He had the kind of presence and swagger that should have come across as dicky but somehow didn't. We bonded over a mutual love of Paul Simon and Stormzy. We laughed at jokes no one else understood. I took the piss out of him and he revelled in the banter. By the time we'd stopped recording we both knew that we would be friends for a long time.

That night after the radio show wrapped, Tom and I had headed to a chic hotel downtown for drinks with Finley, Miles and a couple of their crew, where the banter flowed as freely as the expensive booze. The hangover I endured the next day was worth it for the friendship that blossomed that night and continued in a rush of WhatsApp messages, random drinks in random bars around the world when our schedules aligned, and a whole lot of love.

I sent Finley a quick voice message to see if there was any possibility of a London crossover, knowing full well that my chances were low. He was so rarely at home these days between the touring, the recording and the general duties that came with being one of the most famous people on the planet.

By some miracle, we discovered a one-night overlap between us arriving and Finley leaving for Los Angeles, and plans very quickly swung into place. While I suspect that Leo was envisioning a fully filmed and recorded sit-down interview, Finley had more of a rager in mind. I was confident I could make both work.

⸱⫾⫾⸱⫾⫾⫾⫾⸱

On my insistence, Georgia Jones was very quickly hired as the show's new senior producer, although after a quick perusal of her CV and a five-minute chat, Leo didn't need much convincing. She'd started on Darren's show the week before I left, so while I was lounging about in paradise attempting a life-reset, she was spending her days brokering peace deals between Darren and his new co-host Skye (I was right, they'd had a fling and things had soured quickly). She was a couple of years younger than us but was such a radio nerd that she'd skipped university and started doing station internships straight out of high school, scoring a full-time job at nineteen and working solidly in the industry since. I must admit, it was great to have someone so even-tempered on the team, given that Tom and I often gave in to our more dramatic urges. On the morning of the announcement, I was making myself a cup of tea when she walked purposefully into the office kitchen and stood beside me.

'Soooooo. How are you feeling?' she asked as she scooped bright green protein powder into her tumbler.

I poured a tiny splash of cold water into my piping hot chamomile and brought the mug to my lips. 'About the announcement?'

'Yep. I mean it's exciting, but . . .'

'. . . but it makes it real and it's so much pressure and it would be understandable if I wanted to vomit when thinking about everyone finding out that I'm taking over the biggest radio job in the country?'

'Ahhhh, I wouldn't worry too much. Since when do people give women in media a hard time?'

I let out a loud cackle, placing my tea down on the bench to avoid a spillage. 'I mean in many ways the gig is like a poisoned chalice. It would be so much easier to replace someone who sucked. But Goldie? She never sucked. Not even for one second.'

She gave me a thoughtful look. 'True. But people are going to have opinions regardless.'

'Yeah and now they have 500 ways to share them. Back when Goldie started, if someone didn't like you they'd have to take the time to write a letter and pop it in the post. Now they can tell me how utterly crap I am before I've even gone to a commercial break.'

I'd never harboured much self-doubt in my life. It's not that I normally had a false sense of self-confidence, I just always backed myself pretty hard. The break-up had temporarily rocked my confidence (and confirmed my lifelong fear that the men in my life would eventually leave), but when it came to work, I generally had a pretty unshakeable belief in my ability to nail it, which is why the trepidation that kept creeping in felt so unfamiliar. I suppose in a way it was like I'd been playing in the little league all these years and now I was being promoted to play with the big boys (I say boys because radio is largely dominated by them).

'Yeah, I get that.' Georgia sighed. 'But the internet isn't real. The only thing that's real about it is how shitty it can make you feel. So, maybe stay off it today?'

Obviously her advice was correct. Obviously I was going to ignore it.

֍֎֍֎֍֎

It took about thirty minutes for my phone to start blowing up once the press release went out. Friends, colleagues and randoms whose numbers I no longer had stored in my phone but who were suddenly elated for me and keen to catch up. There were emails from management companies asking if I needed representation, journalists looking for quotes and even an old boss who had made me cry nine days out of ten offering his services. I deleted that one before I'd read halfway. How short did he think my memory was?

So far, I'd managed to avoid reading the *Daily Mail* comments section and anything on social media. The attention certainly felt exciting, but now that it was all out in the open I couldn't deny that I was even more terrified. Tributes to Goldie read like obituaries, spanning decades and decades of her career, reminding me just how big the shoes were that I was expected to fill. The press's reaction to my new gig was overall pretty positive, and the general consensus was that it was a brave decision by the network to pass on the torch to a 'young gun', and time would tell whether I could cut it. I wasn't sure whether 'brave' was code for 'stupid' but was thankful that any true disbelief was vaguely masked. The press could often be cruel, and I suspected that they were showing me kindness because of Goldie.

Then there was Darren Chase.

I'd mostly been working from home, avoiding the office whenever possible to keep rumours at bay, which meant I'd not seen him face-to-face since our coffee shop encounter. In the past, every now and then word would filter back to me about some insult he'd hurled my way or an off-colour comment he'd made about me to some colleagues, but I didn't care enough to be offended. This week, however, he hadn't been at work, and rumour had it that his absence was a form of protest. I knew Darren would have *something* to say about my new gig, especially since he always assumed himself to be Goldie's natural successor, but I didn't think he'd care enough to say something publicly. Evidently, I was wrong. He'd supplied a quote for a news article, which wasn't surprising given that he had made a point of staying chummy with the press. Tom had screenshotted it and sent it through, accompanied by a turd emoji.

'Goldie Miller was a once-in-a-lifetime talent who cannot be replaced. She will be sorely missed.'

Given that we *technically* worked together and he couldn't flat-out publicly insult me, he'd obviously figured that the next worst thing he could do was not mention me at all. Tom was absolutely right. Darren Chase really was a top-rate turd.

That night, May sat on the edge of my bed, rollers in her hair, FaceTiming Mum as I packed for London, the two of them oohing and aahing over the outfits I was laying out for the trip. May was my mother's sister, and for as long as I could remember our relationship had always been a special one. As a kid I'd often fly up to Sydney for visits during school holidays, especially after Dad left. I never got homesick because she was so much like my own mother. The two of them were best friends, and their daily FaceTimes meant that as long as I was living under May's roof, I never had to remember to call Mum. The two of them spoke so often that Mum may as well have been living with us too.

'May told me your new boss is quite the looker! Send me his Instagram name so I can have a look!'

'Ma . . . in what universe am I going to do that? Plus, he's married! And we work together! Enough of that. Now: McQueens or Chloés?' I held up a chunky black Alexander McQueen boot in one hand, and a more formal Chloé boot with a small heel in the other.

'The McQueens,' they both replied in unison. At least I could always trust them to agree. I stuffed the boots with socks to help them keep their shape and then zipped them away in the top compartment of my suitcase.

'Darling, still no word from "he who shall not be named" I hope?' Mum called out, her face drawing closer to the camera.

'Not a word since the day we broke up. I don't even know if he's still living at our place or not, and to be honest I don't care. I've got more important things to think about—like the fact that I'm taking over Goldie freaking Miller's breakfast show.'

It took two and a half seconds for tears to appear in Mum's eyes.

'Oh, my darling. I'm *sooooo* proud of you! I still can't believe this is happening!'

To be fair, she would have been proud of me even if I spent all day locked in my room playing *World of Warcraft*, but this new job had pushed her over the edge and there had been a lot of emotional outbursts this week. The fact that she hadn't alerted the entire family tree and broken the news early was a miracle.

Mum's sob-fest was interrupted by a phone call. I picked up to hear a breathless Tom on the other end.

'Babe. We are horrible people.'

I took a moment to scan my memory for any recent behaviour that could warrant such an outlandish claim and found nothing. 'What are you talking about?'

'He's not a lying, cheating philanderer.'

It took a moment for me to figure out who he was talking about. 'Leo?'

'Yes. He's not a cheater. He's . . . a widower. As in, his wife died.'

My stomach dropped. I stood up and hurriedly walked into the study to be alone, leaving Mum and May chatting away.

'Fuck. That's horrible. We are horrible. Oh my God. Fuck. How do you know?'

'I was chatting to Caroline, the PR girl. You know, the brunette with the bangs? She told me. She didn't know any details, but it was two years ago. I suspect she's got the hots for him and did a bit of snooping. I mean, come on, have some respect.'

It all made so much sense. Why he got weird when I mentioned his move home. Why Goldie shut me down so quickly when I brought it up with her. Why he always fiddled with his ring when he got nervous.

We both sat on the line in silence. Tom eventually spoke first.

'I suppose we don't really have much of a reason to hate him, do we?'

I looked up at the ceiling and rubbed my forehead with my free hand. 'Maybe not.' I sighed. 'I feel like an arsehole.'

'Go make yourself a gin. Wanna share an Uber tomorrow morning? I'll swing past May's on the way to the airport.'

'Sounds good, babe. Thanks for letting me know.'

'Hey, keeping up this many relationships in the office is exhausting but ultimately has its benefits. See you tomorrow. I hope there's at least one hot flight attendant on the plane. If I'm in business class they contractually have to flirt with me, right?'

'Definitely. Night, darling.'

By the time I'd hung up, May had gone upstairs. I went back into my room, hopped into bed and pulled the covers up. I felt sick. And sad. And then, before I knew it, there were tears in my eyes. I didn't even know who or what the tears were for.

Sleep wasn't an option, so instead I put on my José González playlist and let myself fall into a spiral of online shopping, purchasing approximately half of the Sephora website's stock and a pair of silk pyjamas with feathers on the cuffs. They felt like something Audrey Hepburn would wear in *Breakfast at Tiffany's* and were entirely impractical but fun. I set my alarm for 7 am and finally fell asleep around 1 am, praying to God that I wouldn't have the carpark dream again.

Spoiler alert: I had the carpark dream. And, as usual, I woke up before I got the chance to yell at Dad. Rude.

˙ılııˈıllıˈıllıˈ

When you host a music radio show in Australia, and most of the action happens on the other side of the world, you spend a lot of time travelling long-haul. Work usually paid for seats at the pointy end of the plane, and the copious amount of travel also meant that I had top-tier frequent flyer status. As such, Tom and I had spent many an hour drinking fancy champagne in fancy lounges all around the world. This time, however, Leo the babysitter was tagging along and we had to be on our best behaviour.

Tom and I checked in quickly, got through immigration and made a beeline for the lounge, where we would spend forty-five minutes eating our way through the entire menu. 'Free is me' was a notion that we had truly taken to heart, and even though work would be paying for everything over the next week, it still felt right to take advantage of any menu on which every item was entirely complimentary.

I loved the First-Class Lounge for many reasons, but my favourite was the people watching. I once witnessed an eight-year-old-child wearing a blazer summon a waiter over and ask if the calamari was back on the menu yet. I both loathed and loved that child in equal measure and remember him often.

As was tradition, Mum had called for a quick pre-flight chat, which I'd taken in a quiet nook near the lounge entrance. (She also tracked on her phone every single one of the flights I took and would text me the second I touched down, no matter the time of day. It had started as a cute little ritual, but soon became oddly superstitious.)

En route back to the table, I spotted Leo sitting in an armchair across the room, writing notes in a Moleskine notebook. As usual, he was wearing his uniform, this time with a dark, olive-green jacket resting on top of his carry-on bag. I suppose while I wouldn't necessarily call it a 'splash of colour', it was an improvement. I'd never seen anyone in my life who consistently looked so well put together. Nothing ever out of place. Even as he stared down the barrel of a twenty-four-hour transit.

I, on the other hand, was wearing harlequin-print knitted flares, yellow crocs and an oversized Beyoncé tour sweater (as a rule I never wore artist merchandise, but Beyoncé defies all conventions). Next to him I probably looked like a kinder-garten kid on mushrooms who'd dressed themselves for the first time.

I felt horrible for assuming what I had about Leo, but it was still clear that he was less than excited at the prospect of us working together. I thought back to my two options. Make him see how fantastic I am, or hope that he quits. The latter was still the preference, but I supposed it wouldn't hurt to turn on the Alex York charm a little.

I walked confidently in his direction. He noticed me straight away (the outfit was hard to miss) and took his AirPods out.

'Ready to spend twenty-four hours in a metal tube flying through the air?'

Why did I say that? Why was I being weird? Why was I talking like I'd never taken an aeroplane before?

His face was polite, calm. 'Ready indeed. Hoping I can finally get some sleep. Are you guys all set? How did you go with Finley?'

Could this man talk of nothing but work?

'Yep, we're going to see him a couple of hours after we land, before he heads to LA to do some recording. I'll be sure to get ten minutes of audio in the can before things get out of hand. Which they always do with him.'

'Sounds like you've got it all under control.'

'Yep. And, Leo . . . I need to apologise to you before we go.' I paused a second and crossed my arms nervously. He must have noticed my change in tone and sat up a little straighter. Like clockwork, he began to fiddle with his ring. 'I'm sorry for getting defensive about you coming. We're just used to kind of doing our own thing and flying under the radar. But this show is a big deal, and I get that there's a lot more at stake now. So. Yeah. I understand why you're here. And sorry I was weird about it.'

His eyes narrowed. 'Right. Thanks.' His brow furrowed a smidge, before relaxing back into place. 'I'm glad we sorted that out before spending twenty-four hours in a metal tube flying through the air together.'

'Great. I'll try to refrain from offering you any more drugs for the duration of the trip. And for the record I don't actually do drugs. Mainly because I'm a hypochondriac and I'm convinced I'd have a stroke the first time I try them. And then someone would have to call my mum and explain that I died from taking drugs.' Oh God. I was talking about dying. I didn't know how to stop. 'Anyway, that's enough of that. Wow. I swear I don't ramble like this on air.'

'I know. I've spent a better part of the last week listening to old episodes of your night show.'

I looked down at his notebook just as he closed the cover, obscuring my view.

'Is that what those notes are about? Oh man. Is that what you were listening to?'

'Ah, no. I was actually listening to music. Don't give yourself too much credit. And before you ask, I'm not going to tell you what kinda music I was listening to because if I've learned anything from a week of listening to your show it's that you have a near encyclopedic knowledge of all popular music. And I am old.'

'So, what did you think?'

'Of the show? I think we're going to be fine.'

And then he gave a look that I could not for the life of me figure out. It was resolute, but it also could have been the kind of look you give when you flat-out lie and want to shut down the conversation entirely. 'Fine' was hardly a glowing review. But for now, it would seem that 'fine' was all I was going to get, and I should probably exit the conversation while I was ahead.

'I'll take "fine". See you up there, Leo.' I gave him an awkward wave and walked back towards Tom, who had already caved and ordered himself a glass of champagne. As I got closer to the table, I saw a second glass waiting patiently for me too.

Five hours into the flight, I was a little restless, having decided to save my big sleep for the second leg of the journey. Tom, on the other hand, had spent most of the trip so far watching *The Twilight Saga*, drinking Bollinger and flirting with a Dutch flight attendant named Hendrik. I'd headed to the business-class bar at the rear of the cabin and was nursing a gin, animatedly regaling two of the flight attendants with some of my most memorable celebrity encounters. They were lapping up a particular favourite from my early days as a music journalist about a time I threw up on myself five minutes before an Usher interview, when all of a sudden they stifled their giggles, acknowledging a passenger behind me. I swivelled my chair around as Leo appeared through the curtains looking just as tired as I'd left him hours before. He clocked my performance and shook his head, half-chuckling.

'What can I get for you, Sir?' one of the flight attendants asked politely as he approached.

'Whisky, please. On the rocks,' he replied with a weary smile as he sat down next to me, stretching his neck from side to side. 'So, who told you about my wife?'

I sat up quickly, panicked. 'What?'

'People always act differently towards me once they know. Human nature, I suppose.'

I'd been found out, and there was no denying it now. 'Tom told me last night.' I swallowed. 'He heard from someone at the office.'

'Well, I managed a full week before it became office chit-chat, so that's not so bad, I suppose.'

'I hope it doesn't sound like we were gossiping. It's just that—' I paused. 'Ugh, I don't know if this is going to make it sound better or worse.'

'Try me.'

'Okay. When I first saw you at the hotel bar, you weren't wearing your wedding ring. And then the next day at the office, you were wearing it. And I had mentioned that to Tom . . .'

His face told me he understood. 'Right. You thought I was some sort of—'

'I believe the words we used were lying, cheating philanderer.'

He chuckled. And I chuckled. And the tension lifted ever so slightly. I took a sip of my gin and gave him an apologetic look.

'Well, if we're going to work together, I suppose I'd better just get it all out on the table. Her name was Laney. We met ten years ago at a bar in Sydney—she was out doing a gap year and I was working with Goldie. It was love at first sight; you know the drill. I was enamoured. I followed her home to the UK. We got married. And then she got sick. We had some great years, some tough years and then some even tougher years. She passed away two years ago.'

It was a lot of information all at once, but it sounded as though it was a script he'd recited hundreds of times.

'I'm so sorry, Leo. I don't think I have the right words for how incredibly shitty that is.'

He shrugged. 'Shitty is right. Thank you.'

'So now . . . you're back in Australia?'

'I am. I thought a fresh start might be nice. Anyway, when Goldie calls, you answer.'

I leaned in, intrigued. 'What did she say, exactly? To get you home?'

'That she had a huge idea for her show. That it was going to be the next big thing. That she needed me home to help her.'

I was starting to understand.

'And when exactly did you find out that the next big thing was . . . her quitting?'

'About two hours before you saw me at the bar that day.'

Right. This changed everything.

'I don't normally drink martinis alone in a bar on a workday, Alex. I was coming to terms with the fact that I'd moved my entire life back to Australia to work with Goldie Miller. And instead . . .' He paused.

I put him out of his misery. 'You don't have to finish that sentence. I'd need a drink too, after that.'

Leo smirked into his glass as he took another sip.

'So, Alex. Tell me. I know the marketing spiel and our positioning in the market already, but on a personal level, have you thought about what *you* want this show to be?'

'Hmm. I've only been thinking about it for around twenty-five years.'

'Well, you should have the pitch pretty well ironed out then— hit me.'

I raised an eyebrow. 'What, now?'

'I've got nothing else to do for the next seventeen hours or so.'

I put my gin down and sat up straight.

'It's simple, Leo. Joy.'

He gave me a curious look. 'Care to elaborate?'

'I just want the show to be joyous, without being condescending. I want to use it as a tool to celebrate music without being exclusive or snobbish. Like an awesome party that everyone is invited to. Life is complicated and stressful for most people, so I want keep the show accessible and easy and fun. Not just a distraction from the shittiness of life, but a reminder that even in the shittiness there's joy and wonder and fun to be found. And for so many of us that wonder is found through music.

'I want to connect tired, stressed people with the magic of music again. I want exhausted mums to win trips to Vegas to see the Backstreet Boys, and dads to surprise their kids with tickets to their favourite pop star's sold-out concert. That's the kind of radio I love to hear, and I think it's the perfect antidote for the world we're living in now. Our competitors aren't doing it, and I know it's what I do best.'

Leo's narrow gaze focused in on me even more, as if he had been reading my dialogue in subtitles and needed a moment to catch up. After ten seconds or so he still hadn't spoken. There was a whole world of conversation happening in his mind, I just had no idea what it was about.

'Well? What do you think?'

'I think . . .' he mused, the corners of his mouth beginning to curl up.

Oh, for the love of God, would this man please hurry up?

'I think . . . you know exactly what you want to do, Alex York. You've got stars in your eyes, and the audience will be drawn to that. It's infectious.'

I stifled a grin, slightly embarrassed.

He stiffened a little, as if switching into business mode. 'I'll have a think about some concepts that we can incorporate that help bring that vision to life practically, and more importantly, how we can monetise it in a meaningful way—which is really the only thing the board will want to hear about.' He paused. 'Sorry, I'm aware of the fact that you just poured your heart out and I'm talking about dollars and cents but—'

'I get it. Go for it. You do your thing. I'll do my thing. Who knows, we might just end up being a good team after all.'

'Stranger things have happened,' Leo quipped as we clinked our glasses together and knocked back the last of our drinks.

Ten minutes later I was back in my seat, fully reclined and peacefully drifting off to sleep with a glimmer of hope that maybe I might not want Leo to quit after all.

ıļ|ıı|ļ|ıı

By the time we arrived at the hotel in London it was 8 pm, which left an hour before Finley was picking us up downstairs. Leo headed straight from the airport to dinner with friends and we all agreed to regroup over breakfast the next morning.

The handsome blond on reception beamed as we approached. 'Welcome back to The London EDITION, Ms York. Both your and Mr Winter's rooms are prepared and have been paid for, I'll just need a signature here and a credit card for any incidentals.'

I handed over my Amex and gave Tom a look that said, 'This had better not be a repeat of New York.'

How anyone could rack up US$800 worth of champagne and lobster mac 'n' cheese on a four-night stay was beyond me, but I had asked no questions and instead lied to the finance department about the meals being a 'specific request' from an 'A-list celebrity' we were interviewing.

Thankfully they bought the lie and the expense request was approved.

The concierge passed us our room keys and motioned towards the elevator.

'Both of your rooms are on the sixth floor. Enjoy your time with us!'

I had stayed at this hotel the year before for two nights after a trip to Amsterdam, and while my memory was as hazy as you'd expect after a trip to Amsterdam (I never did drugs, but everyone knows weed doesn't count as it's basically a salad), I did remember that the rooms were small but incredibly chic, (what else would you expect when the cheapest option was 500 quid a night?).

The elevator doors opened and we followed the signs down dimly lit hallways to our rooms. At the final corridor, I went right and Tom went left.

'See you downstairs in an hour,' he called out as he walked away, waving behind him.

I found room 608, scanned my card and pushed the heavy door open.

The room awaiting me on the other side was nothing like the one I had stayed in last time. Dark wooden floors, soft fur rugs and pendant lights exuding the most gorgeous warm glow. A thick velvet throw lay across the perfectly made king-sized bed, and fresh flowers added a splash of colour to the bedside tables. Glass doors by the bed led to a terrace that overlooked the busy London street below. Past the bedroom there was an entirely separate area with a large Chesterfield sofa, a reading nook and a full-service bar that was built into the wall.

There was no way this was the room my company had booked. My room phone rang, and I quickly picked it up.

'Is your room insanely bougie?' asked Tom. 'Or does the blond on the front desk want to fuck me?'

'I was just about to call you and ask the same question,' I replied, confused and delighted.

It was then I noticed a bottle of Bollinger resting in a bucket of ice with a small note attached. I opened it with my free hand and read it out: '"*Enjoy the suite life. So good to have you both here x Finley*". Did you get a note too?'

After some huffing and puffing down the line, Tom finally responded. 'Sure did. Same thing. I gotta go and take pics of the room for TikTok.'

And with that, the line was dead and I was left to swan about the palace I would call home for the next three days. I pulled off my shoes, removed my bra and collapsed into the huge puffy cloud of a bed, letting the soft mattress and expensive linen envelop me. I pulled out my phone again and opened my emails, quickly scanning for anything important, and as I did a new WhatsApp message popped up on my screen.

> Hi Alex. It's Leo. Hope you made it to the hotel safely. A thought. iPhone audio is fine for the Finley chat if it's too hard for Tom to lug a mic out to dinner. See you in the morning.

I threw my phone back onto the bed and laughed at the idea that Leo thought we'd be having some sort of civilised dinner with Finley Stark. He was too famous to sit at a nice restaurant for more than fifteen minutes without some sort of a kerfuffle. A dark nightclub suited him much better. I did a speedy unpack and headed into the huge marble bathroom. Before long I was standing under the shower, exhaling as the hot water hit my shoulders and the steam filled my lungs. There is quite simply no better feeling on Earth than a hot shower after a long flight and I found myself half-wishing I could crawl straight into bed.

Instead, I dried my hair, pulled out my make-up and toiletries bags, and got to work transforming myself into a somewhat presentable version of the bleary-eyed traveller in the mirror. Half an hour later, I headed through the lobby looking pretty damn good in a Maje muted green sequin mini dress. It was off the shoulder, with a small cut-out on the right side of the waist. I pared it back with my black McQueen boots and a casual black leather jacket. The pièce de résistance was a silver Miu Miu clutch that Tom had never seen, which meant a dramatic reaction was more than likely.

A dark spaceship-esque vehicle that looked like it could fit an entire football team was parked directly in front of the hotel entrance with the lights on. If Finley wanted to go incognito on the streets of London, he was doing a bloody horrible job of it. I knocked on the window and waited for the door to open.

'Come on, Finners, open up!' I yelled as I continued to knock.

Twenty seconds later there was still no movement from inside the car.

'Real funny, you little shit, let me in—people are starting to look!'

The window of the spaceship-esque vehicle slowly rolled down to reveal a car full of Japanese businessmen in identical suits staring back at me with looks of utter confusion. I quickly spun around, mortified to find Tom a couple of metres away, filming me on his iPhone and laughing.

'Stop filming me, you idiot! Have you been there the whole time?'

'Yeah, but I only started filming like five seconds ago.'

A loud beeping sound rang out from the street, as a matt-black Mercedes G wagon approached in the distance, with one Finley Stark at the helm, right arm out the window waving frantically. If I'd thought the spaceship car was an unsubtle approach, then this was about as conspicuous as humanly possible. This guy truly gave zero fucks.

I ran around the front of the car and hopped into the passenger seat, squealing as Finley leaned over and kissed me on the forehead. Tom closed the door in the back just as the commotion kicked off on the street—iPhones were out, pedestrians were yelling and even the hotel concierge was craning his neck to have a look. Within seconds, Finley's foot was on the accelerator and we were on our way, leaving a trail of excitement and hormones in our wake.

'My two favourite people! Right here before my very eyes!' Finley yelled as he reached his left arm towards the back seat to playfully punch Tom in the chest, only for Tom to swat him away with faux annoyance.

There was something about Finley's energy that made my heart burst. He was joy and fun and fearless youth all wrapped up into one human being, and he instantly made me feel like anything could happen. A ball of sunshine dressed in a fuchia hoodie with black shorts, Converse All Stars and odd socks. On anybody else the get-up would have been ridiculous, but he truly looked like he'd just walked off a catwalk at Paris Fashion Week.

'Thank you for the rooms. Tom thought the receptionist must have wanted a piece.'

'And the room is so nice that I probably would have obliged,' Tom quipped.

'I couldn't have my Aussie mates in anything less than a suite. And, if I'm totally honest, they didn't even charge me. Isn't it weird that the richer you are, the less you have to pay for shit?'

'Weird is one word, babe,' Tom scoffed.

Finley caught his eye in the rear-view mirror and gave him a wink. I could have sworn I spotted a quick grin flash over Tom's face before he broke eye contact, and then Finley was looking at me with a wildness in his eyes that made my liver shudder in anticipation of the night ahead.

'Okay, Finners. Three or four questions. Nothing crazy. Let's just record it before things get hazy so I don't get fired. And I'm pretty sure for legal reasons you can't mention that you're operating a car while we do the interview.' I knew from previous experience that it was best to get business out of the way as soon as possible.

'I am but your humble servant, Ms York. Proceed.'

Tom pulled two small USB microphones out of his bumbag and passed one to me, then reached over the middle console and held the second under Finley's chin.

The next ten minutes contained so much hooting, hollering and colourful language that I couldn't decide whether it was incredible or altogether unusable. Tom gave me a nod, which indicated that he could work magic with the edit. Which he always did. He zipped the recorders back into his bag, and with that it was time to let the good times roll.

And roll they did. They rolled so hard that I still don't actually remember how we got back to the hotel. In fact, everything got a little blurry after the tequila shots. When was I ever going to learn that things always get blurry after the tequila shots?

8

I woke to a cacophony of sounds including but not limited to my iPhone alarm, the hotel phone ringing and somebody banging on the door. I checked the clock next to my bed. It was 11 am. I was meant to meet Leo three hours ago. Fuck.

'I'm coming! I'm coming! Hold on!'

I jumped out of bed, stumbled over to the door and on the way caught a glimpse of myself in the mirror. My hair looked as though a wild ferret had been run over and then strapped to my scalp, and my dress was on sideways. How was that even possible? And why was I still wearing it?

Flashback memories of me spinning around in circles trying to reach the zip and giving up the night before came flooding back. I pulled open the heavy hotel door.

Leo was standing on the other side, mobile phone in one hand, looking altogether panicked.

'How much trouble am I in?' I winced, leaning my head against the door and closing my eyes. At this point, I was too nauseous to be embarrassed.

He sighed, crossed his arms and looked at me with utter exasperation. 'Alex, I'm not your father.'

'Well, that's a relief. I haven't seen the guy in twenty-five years but I'm pretty sure he didn't look anything like you.'

'I'm not joking. I was worried about you. I've been knocking and calling for twenty minutes. You assured me you were taking this trip seriously, Alex.'

The implication made me furious. 'I *am* taking it seriously, Leo. In two days we'll board a flight home with incredibly well researched and executed interviews with the two biggest artists on the planet, both of which are exclusives. This is what I do. And this is how I do it.'

'Well I hope you got the chat with Finley in the can *before* you knocked back the three tequila shots and attempted to do the worm on the top of a bar somewhere in Shoreditch.'

I glared at him, confused, exhausted, hungover and, well, mainly confused.

'That would explain the throbbing hip bones. But how do you even know that?'

I couldn't tell if he was finding all of this funny or pathetic.

'Tom uploaded a play-by-play on his Instagram stories, which kept me across your movements until about midnight. I expected you'd miss our 8 am, to be honest. Thankfully this morning the hotel let me know you'd had the wherewithal to order room service at three, so I knew you'd come home; I was just worried you'd choked on it in the bathtub or something.'

I scanned the room, spotting a tray of half-eaten club sandwiches on the floor next to my bed. Nice.

'I love 3 am drunk me. What a clever gal she is. Anyway—' I resumed my previous serious tone. '—I'm sorry I missed our meeting, that was shitty of me. But can you please just trust me? I've got this. I promise.'

Leo looked at me hesitantly, then peeked over my shoulder.

'Please tell me the network is not paying for this room?'

'Oh. Yeah. No, they're not. Friends in high places. Wanna come in?'

'I might get drunk on the fumes. Why don't you have a shower, freshen up and go eat something greasy. We've got a couple of hours until we need to head to the interview, so that should be enough time for you to return to the land of the living.'

I rubbed my eyes and gave him a sarcastic thumbs up. He walked back towards the elevator without saying goodbye.

᛫ᛁᚢᛁᚢᛁᚢᛁᛁ᛫

Alex York, 11:10 am: London has destroyed me once again.

Vanessa Blake, 11:15 am: I know. You FaceTimed me from a bar somewhere. How's the head?

Alex York, 11:15 am: I've felt better. You should be here.

Vanessa Blake, 11:15 am: Damn straight. Finley Stark is so fkn hot. When's the big interview?

Alex York, 11:16 am: In a couple of hours. Leo just berated me for getting drunk last night and missing our meeting this morning.

Vanessa Blake, 11:17 am: Well at least one of you knows how to have fun.

Alex York, 11:20 am: His wife died. He's allowed.

Vanessa Blake, 11:21 am: Still can't believe you thought he was a cheater. Sooooo awks. I think he's the one who needs a couple of tequila shots.

Alex York, 11:23 am: You're probably right. I better get in the shower. Love you. Miss you x

Vanessa Blake, 11:23 am: Love you too. Wish I was there x

ılıılııll⊩

A little while later I was showered, fresh and ready for bacon as I waited for Tom in the lobby of the hotel. My phone made a dinging sound that, due to the delicate nature of my current state, nearly made me fall over with fright.

York! How's the head today? Still keen for dinner tonight? Would love to see you again X teddy

I closed my eyes and strained, trying my hardest to piece together the memories from last night that would help me figure out who the heck Teddy was.

Before I had time to respond, Tom appeared behind me in a pair of Versace sunglasses that I was pretty sure even Gianni himself (God rest his soul) would classify as 'too much'. He moved them down to the tip of his nose, squinted and stared at me with a mixture of intrigue and disgust.

'Why is your face doing that thing? What's happened?'

I showed him my phone screen. He quickly scanned it, then removed the monstrous sunglasses entirely and shrieked, 'PLEASE tell me you got a wax before you came.'

'Babe, who is Teddy?'

'How drunk were you? Teddy! The Canadian guy that Finley knows. Owns all those ski lodges. We told him we'd definitely come visit next ski season. I think at one point you got your phone out and started looking for flights.' Tom snorted as he laughed, pulling out his phone and scrolling.

I groaned and reached into my handbag—Fendi, baguette, black embossed leather with a gold chain—for some gum, as Tom let out a loud 'a-ha!' and showed me a blurry picture of myself next to a tall, mixed race demigod with a shaved head and kind eyes. It all started coming back to me.

'Ohhhhh, Teddy! Nice guy!'

My mind was racing through the contents of my suitcase, trying to remember if I'd packed any good undies before I reminded myself that this was a work trip and there was no way I was going to let myself fall in love with some kind-eyed lothario who lived on the other side of the world.

'Have you packed some nice lingerie or do we need to do a quick La Perla stop?'

'How do you do that?'

'Read your mind? We spend more time together than most couples. Plus, I have access to your emails and your socials and occasionally read your text messages.'

Alarmingly, none of this was news to me.

'Also, how much do you think I earn? I haven't got a spare 300 pounds for a new lingerie set.'

'Yes, you do. Don't fake poverty with me, it's not classy.'

I also knew with 100 per cent certainty that he would have read my employment contract. I didn't bother fighting him on this one. What made the whole situation even more infuriating was that despite Tom's intricate knowledge of every detail of my life, he'd managed to keep his own private life off limits. To everyone. Especially me. He was a closed book. He could have been married to an Italian billionaire for all I knew. He could technically be straight for all I knew. He never ever told, and I'd given up asking long ago.

Both of our phones buzzed in unison with a message from Georgia including a link to a news article. The headline read 'Finley Stark on a wild bender with Aussie radio host and swag of attractive revellers'.

Tom gasped, furiously scrolling through the article, breathless with anticipation. 'OMG, AM I THE ATTRACTIVE REVELLER? SHOW ME RIGHT NOW!'

'Morning, again.'

My head snapped up from my phone to see Leo standing in front of us. He was freshly showered, and his hair was wet and out nearly to his shoulders. He ran his fingers through it self-consciously when he noticed me staring. I instinctively wanted to look away but it was as if I'd just seen my schoolteacher out in public. Tom hid his phone behind his back with as much subtlety as he was capable of (absolutely none). Leo cocked his head to one side and glared suspiciously. Tom looked at the ground. I felt nauseous (and not just because of the hangover). Of all the big nights we'd had with Finley, the only one that appeared in the press the next day just so happened to be on the same trip that my new boss decided to come on? My new boss who still isn't really sure I deserve the gig? It felt particularly cruel.

Leo gave Tom a knowing look. 'If this is about the article, I've already seen it. Caroline from PR sent it through a couple of minutes ago.'

At the mention of Caroline's name, Tom pretended to spit on the ground. He had obviously chosen a new office nemesis, which meant George in HR was off the hook. 'I just wanted to clarify that when the article said "attractive revellers" they were referring to me . . .'

Leo gave Tom a confused look. 'Right. Well, luckily for you, Finley's label shut down some of the more salacious images that were snapped so the pictures in the article are all pretty tame. Can we all agree to just focus from here on in? No ragers. No hangovers.' He focused his attention on Tom. 'No grainy images surfacing of what may or may not be illegal substances being snorted off the chests of exotic dancers.'

Tom winced. 'You can just call them strippers, Leo. No one uses the term "exotic dancers" anymore. Plus, if my memory serves me correctly, he was from Essex, which isn't exactly exotic.'

'I don't think that's the point,' I whispered.

My stomach grumbled loudly. 'Okay, interrogation over. I got us a table at Dishoom where I will be ordering every fried item on the menu.'

I could tell Leo was trying to look legitimately exasperated by me but was still somewhat amused. 'We'll leave here at 3:30 pm. Do I need to attach some sort of ankle-monitor hardware to you both or can I trust you to stay sober for the next few hours?'

I shook my head. As Leo walked off towards the lifts, I pulled my phone out and composed a message as Tom peeked over my shoulder.

Teddy my friend! Head is okay thanks to a perfectly timed club sandwich from room service. Working tonight so might miss you, sorry. Hope the rest of the trip is fun! X

'No need for the lingerie, sorry, darl,' I told Tom. 'The last thing I'm gonna let myself do is get entangled in some cross-continental love affair; in any case, no one that rich or that handsome turns out to be good news. Let's just nail this interview, prove to Leo how effortlessly talented and wonderful we are and go home.'

An hour later, with my belly full of bacon naan and strong black coffee, I felt ready to do exactly that.

᭑᭠᭑᭠᭑᭟᭑᭟

Sometimes when you're getting ready for a special event, no matter what you do you just can't seem to make it work. The outfit doesn't fit right, your make-up looks weird and your hair refuses to cooperate. And then sometimes the universe shines down on you and you look back at yourself in the mirror genuinely convinced you could seduce George Clooney. Thankfully, this particular afternoon I was firmly in the latter category. I looked good. Really good.

We were thankfully ahead of schedule as we zoomed through the streets of London in the back of a taxi, Tom wearing more beige, Leo in his usual uniform (this time with the olive-green jacket) and me in a tight Acne tie-dye mini dress, black chunky Versace heels I got on Facebook Marketplace and an oversized lilac coat that looked altogether edible. Taking inspiration from Dua Lipa on the *Rolling Stone* cover I'd passed at the airport bookshop, I did a kind half-up half-down thing with my hair, and while she is at least seventeen times hotter than me (even on her very worst day), I still looked great. When her latest single came on the radio in the taxi, I took it as a sign that the pop music gods were on my side.

As we pulled up at the venue, the boys got out of the cab first and Leo held his hand out to help me as I shuffled over to the door. I wondered if he thought I looked good too. I wondered if he even noticed how women looked. I remembered how he'd paid the hot waitress in Bondi absolutely no attention even when she fawned over him so hopelessly and decided that if he didn't notice her, he certainly wasn't going to notice me.

Not that I wanted him to. I just . . . wondered. That's all.

A rep from the record label was standing on the street waiting for us. He looked as though he must have been quite junior—not more than twenty-one—holding a clipboard in one hand and a phone in the other. Before long we were being ushered through the fire exit, directly to the backstage area. There were busy men and women everywhere, dressed in black with headsets on; crew eating lunch; and lots of American voices talking loudly into their mobile phones. We were given a dressing room to set up in, and Tom was quickly in work mode, unpacking gear, running cables and connecting power boards. I set up two chairs opposite each other, sat in one and went over my notes one last time as Leo chatted outside with someone old and important from the UK label. They were talking and laughing as if they were old friends and I wondered if they'd known each other when Leo was living here. I moved towards the door where I could hear the conversation a little better.

'We miss you terribly, mate. No one could ever run that place like you did, and believe me they're bloody trying,' the older voice was saying.

'They'll be right, Benj.'

'And how's Goldie? I couldn't believe the news.'

'I was just as surprised, mate, trust me. But you know Goldie, she'll do what she wants.'

'Ahh. If only we all had the luxury. But you're going to keep the gig?'

'Well, I tried to quit when she first told me, but it obviously didn't work because here I am. So, we'll see.'

'It's good to see you looking so well, Leo. Next time let me know and we'll make a night of it, eh?'

I jumped back across the room and sat down in my chair, notes in hand. It occurred to me then that I'd never even really bothered to find out about Leo's work history. Perhaps I'd been too busy mistakenly hating him for being a cheater.

I pulled out my iPhone and typed the words 'Leo Billings radio' into Google.

Holy shit.

'Tom!' I hissed.

He looked up from the ground, with a cable in one hand and a roll of gaffer tape in the other.

'He was the network head of Pulse.'

'Huh?'

'Leo. He was the network head of arguably the best fucking radio brand on the planet. It says here he's the one who got them back to number one after all those years.'

Tom stared back at me. 'Ohhh. He's *that* Leo.'

'You knew?'

'Yeah, but I didn't know that Leo and this Leo were the same Leo. Wow. That makes sense, I suppose.'

Leo's voice grew louder outside the door. Tom snapped back to work and I closed the screen on my phone. He reappeared in the room just as Tom had finished setting up, giving us both a brief thumbs up, clearly impressed at how quickly it had all come together. Little did he know, Tom's all-time record for setting up a two-camera, two-mic shoot with lighting was one minute and fifty-three seconds. For big interviews like this one, however, he preferred precision over speed and I knew better than to ever offer to help. He liked things done just so, and I couldn't be trusted to not make a mess of his precious cables and cords.

Soon enough we heard a hustle and bustle outside, which was a sure sign that things were about to kick off. People like Tilly Roy are always surrounded by a hustle and bustle.

For the first couple of years of Tilly's career, I wasn't much of a fan. She'd started out as a country singer and before long had ditched the ethereal long dresses and cowboy boots for sequin leotards and absolutely catapulted into the very upper echelons of all-out pop stardom. The whole schtick felt contrived, and her fans were so obsessive that I found it all a bit overwhelming. I enjoyed her radio hits but had never bothered to listen to an album in its entirety. That all changed the first time I interviewed her, around seven years ago. I walked in a sceptic and I walked out ready to run the Australian arm of her fan club. She was utterly enchanting. Freakishly smart. Unassuming. Hilarious. She was the kind of girl everyone wants to be best friends with, and for that eight-minute interview she made me feel like that's exactly what she was. My best friend. Every encounter we'd had since had been exactly the same. She'd achieved the level of success that means press tours aren't even really necessary, and yet she still did them, and treated everyone she met with familiarity and respect. She made the kind of effort that no other star on Earth did, and for that I'd always been grateful.

The energy in the room automatically shifted as a handful of her team walked in, did a quick check of the set-up and then signalled to those waiting outside.

A short woman holding three mobile phones looked towards me with a face that meant business. 'Alex, thanks so much for coming all this way. The set-up looks great. Tilly is about two minutes away. She wants the chat to be as intimate as possible so it will just be you three, Tilly and one person from her team. You've got a strict fifteen minutes. All sound good?'

'All sounds perfect. We're looking forward to it.'

I winked at Tom, took my seat and revelled in the nervous energy that was coursing through my veins. It was my favourite feeling in the world.

The most important part of any interview is the first two minutes. That's all the time you have to win an artist's trust, so it's in those initial two minutes that I would have to prove two crucial things. The first? That I'd done my research and was familiar with the music. The second? That I wasn't going to ask dumb questions. Once an artist knows these two things, they relax into the chat and start to open up. And that's when the fun begins.

Seconds later, Tilly appeared in chunky stilettos and an acid-green mini shift dress that looked like something Twiggy would have worn in the 1960s. She was the epitome of pop-star glam and I was instantly obsessed.

'Alex! It's so great to see you again, thanks for making the trip out from Sydney!' she cooed as she leaned in for a hug before taking the seat opposite me.

I know with 100 per cent certainty that one of her team had, not two minutes ago, told her I'd flown in from Sydney, and I appreciated the effort on all parts to make it seem like she knew anything about me. This was classic Tilly Roy. She went the extra one per cent when she didn't have to.

'Well, it was this or stay home and help my aunt prune back her roses, so . . .'

She laughed wildly and heartily in a way that would have seemed insincere from anyone but her. 'I'm sure that would have spared you the hangover you're no doubt nursing after last night's Finley Stark debauchery!'

I looked back at her with a mixture of laughter and shock. 'How do *you* know about that?'

'Finley texted me a video of you doing the worm at, like, 2 am and said to go easy on you.'

I put my head in my hands. 'I'm gonna kill him!'

Tilly's raucous laughter burst out again. I looked up at her, shaking my head with faux embarrassment. She reached over and patted my knee lovingly. 'I love a woman who can party hard and then kick ass at work the next day.'

I flashed Leo a quick, triumphant look. He caught my eye quickly before shifting his focus to the ground, hiding a grin.

'Well babe, it takes one to know one,' I sang back, refocusing on Tilly. I took a deep breath and bent down to press the start button on my phone timer, letting everyone in the room know we were ready to kick it off. I gave Tilly a wink as I did so, and then sat up straight and dove in.

'Well, the album is amazing, my friend, congratulations!'

And we were off . . .

᠁᠁᠁

When we finally made it back to the hotel, I collapsed back into bed and checked my phone.

Hello Ms York. How's London? Leo said you absolutely nailed the big interview. Go girl! Sounds like you're getting along better? Hmm? xx Goldie

I knew I had killed the interview. Tom knew I had killed the interview. Even Tilly's team came back to thank me for killing the interview. But Leo had remained his usual calm, stoic self and not said a word, so Goldie's text gave me a quiet sense of satisfaction.

> Goldie! So happy to hear from you. Tilly made it easy . . . but yes, I nailed it! Leo isn't as bad as we thought . . . you were right. London is still my favourite city on the planet. Big love Xx

Satisfied and happy, I grabbed the remote control and was surfing the room service menu when my phone buzzed again, presumably from Goldie. With one eye still on the menu, I looked down to see Leo's name light up the screen in a group message with Tom and me.

> Brilliant job today, team. Shall we head out for a bite to celebrate?

Tom already had tickets to *Les Mis*, and I didn't want Leo to feel obliged to have dinner alone with me. I stared at my phone for a while, not knowing what to say. Tom messaged a second later.

> Awww cute. Soz got cheap tix to see a show so I'm out. Don't go anywhere expensive/chic without me! Have fun.

It would appear as though Tom had decided that we would be going out without him. Unless Leo was about to retract his offer, which would be even more awkward. Oh God. Why did it feel like everything was getting awkward?

A couple of minutes passed and neither myself nor Leo replied. It was like an SMS Mexican stand-off. In London.

I decided that the best course of action was to make an excuse and let him off the hook. Only before I pressed send, another text came through. This one was from Leo, sent directly to me.

> Shall we? Or are you planning another round of room service club sandwiches?

Was Leo Billings . . . serving up the banter? I honestly didn't know he had it in him. I returned serve.

> I prefer my club sandwiches at 3 am while stuck in a sequin mini dress and reeking of tequila.

Seconds later he replied.

> Downstairs in ten?

Well, I supposed we were having dinner then.

> Sounds good. But I'll need twenty. Unlike you, I don't wear the same thing every day.

And then Leo showed his age by replying with the thumbs-up emoji.

⑊⑊⑊

I exited the lobby elevator twenty minutes later wearing high-waisted black silk pants with a matching oversized blouse tucked in, a gold vintage Gucci belt, my McQueen boots and last night's leather jacket, which was somehow still in pristine condition despite the bar-top dancing. Very moody and London-y, and as understated as I could muster— I didn't want to look completely overdressed next to Leo in his uniform. Only this time, when I spotted him across the lobby, the uniform was nowhere to be seen. Leo Billings was wearing . . . proper trousers. Kind of. The denim jeans had been replaced by charcoal pants in what looked like some sort of very chic wool blend, secured on his hips with a mustard-coloured drawstring. On his top half he wore a black tee with a chunky grey sweater over the top. And on his feet were sneakers.

Well, I'll be damned. I didn't know he had it in him. Leo Billings looked . . . cool.

'Well, well, well,' I mused in an exaggerated tone.

Leo looked embarrassed.

'I do own other clothes, you know. I just don't see the point in wasting time on a work day figuring out what to wear.'

'Working out what to wear is literally the highlight of my day.'

'Yes, well that's obvious. You always look cool. Although I never want to see your credit card bill. I think it would give me a premature stroke.'

'Says the guy with the Navitimer on his wrist! Don't think I haven't clocked that baby.'

'This . . .' Leo sighed happily, '. . . was a gift. Let's walk, I know a place that's not too far.'

He held out his left arm, ushering me to follow. Were we just going to skip over the fact that Leo said I always look cool? I concealed my grin as we stepped out into the crisp London air and made a right turn.

'Does dinner mean I'm forgiven for last night's antics?' I goaded.

Leo let out a short 'ha', which didn't really answer my question. He just continued to walk, as if there was a conversation happening in his mind that I wasn't privy to.

We walked in silence for five minutes, until we reached a quaint and incredibly busy little Italian bistro with a long line of people out the front. I was grateful I'd worn boots instead of precarious heels that would have made the wait unbearable. Leo craned his head to peek inside.

'Wait here for one second, I'll be right back.'

And with that, he disappeared inside. I pulled out my phone only to see a message from Teddy. I'd completely forgotten that I'd even palmed him off.

I understand :(Enjoy your last night in London and come visit soon. You promised! x

'Alex!'

I looked up as Leo poked his head out from inside the busy restaurant. I shuffled towards the entrance, somewhat self-consciously passing the lines of London's beautiful people waiting patiently for a table. Leo held the door open for me, and I followed him inside, slightly bewildered. The smell of garlic made my tummy rumble. An old Italian man stood at the front desk with a head of curly grey hair, a bushy moustache and incredibly kind eyes. He looked positively delighted by Leo's presence as he barked orders in Italian to the waitstaff, who scurried around busily. Seconds later, he was ushering us to a secluded corner table, where he continued to beam at Leo.

'Marco, this is my work colleague, Alex, from Australia.'

'*Buona sera*, Alex, welcome!' Marco took me in his arms for a bear hug before patting my cheeks gently. '*Che bella!*'

He looked back at Leo joyously and repeated the cheek pat on him.

'*Grazie*, Marco!' I replied, using up the entirety of my Italian vocabulary.

'The pleasure is mine. A friend of Leo is welcome always. *Sempre, sempre*! Sit down, I bring you drinks? *Vino rosso* for you, Leo, and for you, *bella?*'

'I'll have a gin martini with cucumber, please, Marco!' I said.

'Of course! And I will choose the food. Happy?' Marco clapped his hands gleefully and disappeared into the crowded restaurant.

'I keep forgetting that you used to live here. Ten years is a long time.'

'Sure is,' Leo mused.

'Was this your regular?'

'It was Laney's favourite. They have a strict no takeaway rule, which they broke when she was too sick to go out. Marco was very good to her.'

I felt a pang in my gut. It was still so hard for me to believe that he'd lost Laney just two years ago.

'What was her go-to dish? If you don't mind me asking.'

'That's easy. The lasagne. If I wanted even a spoonful, I'd have to order my own. Laney was generous to a fault but not with Marco's lasagne. Even when the chemo took away her appetite . . . it was a sure thing.'

I could tell by the contentment on his face that he liked talking about her. It was the kind of nostalgic look that made every part of his face open up. It was the most human version of Leo I'd seen.

'Did she work in radio too?'

'Oh God, no.' He laughed. 'She was a paediatric nurse. The best in the world. She instilled a sense wonder and awe into the lives of sick six-year-olds, while I sold my soul to the fast-entertainment gods so I could make enough money to keep her alive and comfortable for as long as possible.'

I leaned forwards and rested a hand under my chin. 'You're lucky to have found your person.'

'Yeah, well some people never have what we had. I just wish we had it longer,' he replied, staring at the table. 'So, what about you? Your aunt mentioned a break-up.'

The question was jarring and I was immediately embarrassed. Bloody Aunty May and her big mouth.

'Oh my gosh, my ex does not deserve to be discussed in the same conversation or even on the same day as your wife. Yeah. No. He's a nobody. He . . . yeah, he sucks.'

'So I take it you're not holding out hope for a reunion anytime soon?'

I screwed up my face and made a gagging sound. 'Correct. I mean, for a while I was hoping for one. Obviously the whole . . . break-up hit me pretty hard. I mean, hard enough to make me quit my job and run away to a desert island. Which sounds pretty lame compared to what you've endured . . .'

Leo shrugged. 'Pain is relative. I get it.'

'That's kind of you to say. I think I'm only just starting to get enough distance from the relationship to see that I never really *had* him. No matter what I achieved, what I did. No matter how delicious a meal I cooked or what holiday I planned. It was never enough. It's almost like . . . keeping me on a string made him feel like he had power.' I started to worry that I was oversharing but the interested look on Leo's face told me he didn't mind.

'It sounds to me like maybe he was jealous of you.'

I'd never thought about it that way, but his words instantly made sense. I remembered a time I'd been nominated for a huge media award, and on the night of the ceremony he realised he'd double booked himself. I won that night but still cried in the taxi on the way home because he'd ditched me. My big night had been ruined. 'I think maybe you're right. It's like the things that I thought he loved about me turned out to be the things that he resented. I dunno. Maybe he never actually loved me at all.'

Leo leaned back in his chair a little. 'And were you? In love with him?'

I thought for a moment. 'Maybe. Perhaps I was just too infatuated to see things clearly. In fact, the night he dumped me he was acting weird and . . . oh gosh this is super embarrassing to admit . . .'

Leo's eyes widened. 'Go on . . .'

'I actually thought he was about to propose.' I buried my face in my hands, stifling a fake, mortified scream.

I looked up as Leo mouthed the word 'eek'.

'Yeah. I don't often read the room that badly.' I chuckled.

Moments later a waitress appeared with our drinks. She passed Leo a glass of red wine, and handed me a perfect-looking gin martini with a twist of fresh cucumber. I held it up to Leo for a toast. We clinked glasses as I spoke.

'I feel like I'm cheating on Malik ordering this here.'

Leo chuckled. 'Speaking of Malik . . .' He paused. 'There's a reason I wasn't wearing my wedding ring that day.'

I took a long, dramatic sip of my martini and winced. 'Go on.'

'It was a test run. The first time and only time I'd ever taken it off. It's why I bolted for my room so quickly. I think I lasted twenty minutes.'

Once again, all signs pointed towards me being the arsehole. Not him. I was getting hot and sweaty, trying to suppress tears that I had no business shedding. Certainly not in Leo's presence at least. I took a big gulp. 'My God, you absolutely do not need to explain a single thing. I feel like such an idiot for presuming what I did.'

His eyes were serious. 'Please don't apologise. I just wanted to explain. That's all.'

I made a mental note to never presume anything about anyone ever again, knowing full well this was an impossible task.

He continued, 'Wanna hear something weird? I don't actually drink cucumber martinis. They were Laney's favourite drink and I thought ordering one might help me through the shitty day. When I looked across and saw it was you of all people next to me at the bar, drinking the same thing, I knew Laney was up there somewhere, laughing. It actually cheered me right up.'

'I'm sure my credit card getting declined was the icing on the cake!'

He guffawed as I buried my head in my hands, reliving the mortification all over again.

Conversation flowed freely for the next half an hour as we gorged on fresh burrata, prosciutto, the best focaccia of my life and melt-in-your-mouth octopus. I told him exactly how I came to live with May and Billy, and stories from the island (some sanitised for my own self-respect). He asked questions about my shopping addiction and looked like he was about to genuinely have a heart attack when, three martinis later, I filled him in on my most lavish purchases.

'So you're telling me you've never seen a financial planner? An accountant? No one is across your spending?' he asked incredulously.

I pretended to fall asleep. He laughed heartily into his wine glass.

'I know, I know. It's bad.' I sighed. 'And I know there's only so long I can continue this whole *go shopping every time I feel any sort of negative emotion* thing. But hey, sometimes I do yoga instead!'

'Well Alex, it's your life. It's your money. You can do what you want with it. I'd just recommend you at *least* know when you've hit your credit limit so your card doesn't get declined in front of a stranger who turns out to be your boss . . .'

I rolled my eyes sarcastically. 'Hey, if I remember correctly you told me that I was the real boss in this relationship . . .'

'I did say that. You're absolutely right.' Leo chuckled.

It was hard to believe this was the same man that just one week ago I'd found so irritating. In this light, Leo was easily someone I could see myself being actual *friends* with.

He leaned forwards, resting his chin on his hands. 'Part of me envies you, you know . . .'

'Me? Why?' I asked, shocked.

'Because you can be . . . reckless. I don't have a reckless bone in my body. I've always done the responsible thing, even before Laney got sick and I had to be . . . properly responsible. I mean, following her to London was pretty crazy, but soon enough I got a job and committed to it, worked my way up and stayed there. For eight years.'

'But you loved it, right?'

'Not like you love it,' he replied warmly.

'So what *would* you do, if you could do anything?' I asked.

Before he could reply, we were interrupted by Marco appearing alongside our waitress, who was carrying a large tray laden with plates. One by one, he filled the table with dishes, each more amazing than the last, leaving space in the middle of the table for one final plate. Slowly he lowered onto the table the lasagne of my dreams. Gooey and crispy and melty. I looked at Marco, whose eyes were wet. He grabbed Leo's hand and squeezed as a single tear rolled down his cheek.

'*Grazie*, Marco.'

'*Buon apetito, amico mio.*' He winked, patting Leo's shoulder, then made his way back to the kitchen.

Leo stared at the plate of lasagne, his face wistful but at peace.

I shuffled in my seat. 'Are you okay?'

'I am.' He raised his eyes to mine. 'I just hope you're ready to be ruined for all other lasagnes.'

The lasagne really was the best I had ever had. As was the course that followed. As was the tiramisu. When we finally made it back to the hotel, I wanted nothing more than to unzip my pants and lie on the ground unhindered, basking in the glory of my carb coma. Leo walked me to my hotel room door, animatedly regaling me with stories of the good old days working with Goldie. He told me how, all those years later, she and Joanie had flown to the UK to attend Laney's funeral in person, filling the church with thousands of pink peonies. Soon after, the hospital ward Laney worked at received a hefty donation in her name, courtesy of Joanie's foundation.

I swiped my key and walked in, holding the door open for him. 'You may as well come in for a second and see what £1000 a night will get you in central London.'

Leo followed me into the room and raised his eyebrows as he looked around. 'Friends in high places, hey? Are you ever going to tell me who this mystery benefactor is?'

'Oh, it's no secret. That would be Finley. He's too generous for his own good.'

Leo hesitated for a moment. 'So. You two . . .'

I furrowed my brow, confused. 'Us two?'

'You two . . . um. Are you . . .?' Leo stumbled.

'Are we?'

'Come on, Alex, are you really going to make me ask?'

And that's when the penny dropped. 'Oh, I'm gonna make you ask all right. Please proceed with your line of questioning.'

Leo leaned against the back of the Chesterfield in the lounge room and looked at me as I sat on the edge of the bed. 'Are you and Finley . . . more than friends?'

I crossed my arms dramatically as I stared back at him. 'You do know that these days you don't have to be more than friends to fuck, right?'

Startled, Leo looked at the ground and made an awkward chuckling sound. It was clear I'd really flustered him.

I continued, 'But in this case, we are most definitely just friends. He's like a brother. A very, very generous and very, very rich brother. In fact, he organised the same room for Tom. One big happy family. Nothing debaucherous going on, sorry to disappoint you.'

As I spoke, I noticed the suite had been made up by house-keeping while we were out at dinner. The bed was pristine, and one corner of the duvet had been folded back into a triangle shape with two chocolates on the pillow. I casually popped one in my mouth and chucked the other one towards Leo.

'Sorry for asking. I should have known you two weren't dating. I don't think you'd date someone like him.'

'Like him?'

He popped the chocolate in his mouth. 'Famous.'

'What, you don't think someone famous would date me?'

'No, that's not what I said. I don't think *you* would date someone famous.'

I sat back on the bed, intrigued. 'Why is that?'

'You care too much about your reputation. Your credibility. I can't imagine you'd do anything to give people reason to doubt it.'

I stared at Leo. He was absolutely right. I may occasionally party with famous types, but I took my work far too seriously to ever date one.

'Yep. Maybe I care too much. Who knows. My best friend Vanessa always says that she should have had my job because she would have done it justice in the old "sleeping with pop stars" department. I've just never even been tempted.'

'Well, I'm sure many have tried. You're Alex York, for goodness sake.' The words tumbled out of his mouth, and even he looked surprised by them. 'I mean, if you can charm Tilly Roy as well as you did today, I'm sure you can charm anyone.'

'Oh, so you think I did a good job, hey? I was hoping to get some feedback,' I teased.

'Oh, come on.' Leo rolled his eyes. 'You know you were brilliant.'

A kick of adrenaline surprised me; I was about to blush, which would be mortifying for both of us. I gave him a sarcastic look and wandered into the walk-in wardrobe.

'Take a seat,' I called out. 'That Chesterfield is as comfortable as it looks. I'm just gonna get my comfy socks on!'

I took a couple of moments to compose myself, then pulled my boots off and slid the warm fluffy socks on. A minute later I returned to the lounge room to find Leo sitting on the couch with his eyes closed and his head resting on the soft brown leather headrest.

Tom had been right when he'd said that Leo was my type. Physically speaking, he was absolutely my type, with a quiet masculinity that wasn't obvious at first. If I was completely honest, I'd known he was my type the second I laid eyes on

128

him at the bar. The fact that he had zero ego when it came to how good-looking he was made him even more attractive.

I sat on the ottoman opposite him. His eyes were still closed. I looked at his clothes. Strangely enough, I missed his uniform. There was something comforting about it. Like I always got what I expected. No surprises. And while he could be as straight as an arrow and unwavering in his need to put business first, it made me feel like everything was going to be okay. Predictable. Safe.

He stretched and opened his eyes again, catching me staring directly at him. I held his gaze in silence for a moment and said nothing. I wondered who would speak first. But neither of us did. I smiled at him slowly. Kindly. Calmly. Because that was exactly the thing: I didn't feel awkward or embarrassed or like I needed to fill this silence. I was happy and content to just be. Be here. Staring at Leo. Saying nothing.

His honey-coloured eyes were on fire all of a sudden. And they were staring directly back at me. Through me. I wanted so desperately to reach out and touch him. To let him know that I wasn't scared. That I wanted to be here with him. That I wanted him to see me and to know me and I wanted so much to know him.

And then he stood up. Holding my gaze, he took a slow, deep breath and let his arms fall, moving towards me until he was just centimetres away.

He reached out his hand and ever so gently brushed it against mine. The contact lasted only a moment. It was utterly electrifying.

'Goodnight, Alex. I had a wonderful dinner.'

And before I could reply, he moved past me and was gone.

ılıııllılıı

Alex York, 11:05 pm: Are you up? I need to talk!

Alex York, 11:07 pm: Hellllooooo?

ılıⵏⵏⵏⵏⵏⵏ|ⵏⵏ|ⵏⵏⵏ

The next day was our last one in London and I spent the hours between 6 and 8 am lying in my stupidly large and stupidly comfortable hotel bed, staring at the ceiling, listening to Bon Iver in an attempt to settle my mind as it raced between two possible scenarios. The first was that I'd imagined whatever the hell had happened last night, that Leo never actually looked at me like he wanted to rip my clothes off, and I never actually for a moment maybe wanted him to. The second was that I hadn't imagined any of it. I wasn't sure which scenario was preferable, given the fact that up until three days ago I kind of hated the guy. Then there was the complicated working relationship situation. And the fact that he was a grieving widower.

I wondered how long someone had to be a 'grieving' widower before they could just become a 'widower'. I started googling it on my phone before realising how utterly insane I was being and burying my head under one of the fourteen pillows that surrounded me. This was certainly not a situation I'd been in before. In fact, I wasn't sure I was even in a situation. Maybe I was just being dramatic (so unlike me, I know). I decided that the only option was to send Leo a friendly message that let him know I certainly *wasn't* spiralling about whatever did or didn't happen last night. I pulled out my phone and started typing out the kind of nonchalant message that someone would send to a work colleague after a perfectly aboveboard and not confusing or emotionally charged evening.

Morning! Dinner was great thanks for the invite. Regretting not shoving some tiramisu into my handbag . . . How'd you pull up today? Ready to fly?

There. Yep. I was happy with that. I pressed send, stretched out and rolled over on the bed, opening up Instagram and preparing myself for a solid block of mindless scrolling.

I was less relaxed an hour later when I still hadn't received a reply. Eventually my phone dinged, interrupting my brain's fourteenth go around the 'grieving widower slash boss' hamster wheel and snapping me back to reality. It was a message in the group thread from Tom.

How was dinner, kids? Anyone around for breakfast?

At what point did he decide that communication would now happen in the group thread? In what universe did Tom include Leo in our social plans? I was pretty well convinced at this point that Leo had ignored my earlier text, which meant he certainly wasn't going to reply to Tom in the group thread. I picked up the phone, called Tom direct and told him to put on the most chic daytime outfit he'd packed. I sure as hell wasn't going to spend my final morning in London in an emotional shame spiral.

An hour or so later, the two of us were perched at the caviar bar in Harrods with a bottle of Veuve on ice, nibbling away at two dozen rock oysters, Prunier caviar and a lobster roll that I simply couldn't *not* order. Whatever feelings of confusion or self-loathing I'd had earlier that morning had disappeared as I let the incredibly overpriced champagne soften my edges and the zingy oysters bring me back to life. Once Tom had taken sufficient photos for the 'gram and topped up our champagne glasses, he leaned in, narrowed his eyes in my direction and began the interrogation.

'So, last night. Tell me everything. Was it awkward? What did you guys even talk about?'

I knocked back another oyster, followed it with a swig of champagne and leaned back in the most relaxed fashion I could muster on a bar stool.

'It was fine! Nothing awkward but nothing special to report. We had dinner at an Italian bistro around the corner and then came home.'

I certainly was not going to tell Tom about the 'moment' in my room afterwards. In fact, I wasn't going to tell him that Leo even set foot inside my room, otherwise he would soon be joining me in the spiral and we'd lose the next twenty-four to forty-eight hours trying to figure out what had actually happened. Whiteboards would probably be involved. He might even have called Toulla, his very expensive but eerily spot-on psychic from Western Sydney.

'So, no goss at all? Nothing? You just had dinner and then came home?'

I nodded as I took another sip. 'Yep.'

Tom sighed. 'He really is boring, isn't he? I'm kinda glad he never wrote back in the group chat; I only involved him in breakfast plans because it's our last day and I felt bad for ditching you guys last night.'

And then, in some sort of spooky coincidence, both of our phones dinged. Tom flipped his over and swiped across to unlock it, revealing a message from Leo in the thread.

Sorry Tom, catching up with some friends before we leave. I'll see you at the airport.

I took my phone out, hoping he'd written back to my message too, but there was nothing. Not even three dots to let me know he was typing.

Leo Billings had left me on read. Ugh.

I called for the waiter and ordered the bill, tapped my card without even looking at the total (the Veuve alone was 135 quid, I didn't need to know how much the rest of it cost), and we both finished off the last of our champagne. I grabbed Tom's hand and gave him my most devilish grin.

'So, it's our last day in London. We're at one of the best luxury shopping destinations on the planet, we've just smashed a bottle of French champagne, and I'm probably never going to earn as much money as I'm currently earning ever again. Let's go spend the last of my savings on some insanely over-priced shit.'

Tom closed his eyes, made the sign of the cross, blew a kiss to the sky and, with a shriek, we were skipping arm in arm in the direction of the handbags.

After a pleading call to the hotel to extend our check-out time even further, three dizzy hours later, an Uber dropped us back at the hotel lobby with enough shopping bags to put an Arab oil magnate's long-suffering wife to shame. I had shopped like I'd never shopped before. I was unabashed, I was free. I was fearless and shameless and I justified it all by the exorbitantly large monthly pay cheque that would soon land in my bank account. I knew that buying pretty things wouldn't always fix life's hiccups, but the shopping-induced adrenaline had now replaced the Leo-induced confusion and I'd momentarily been able to forget the fact that he still hadn't bothered to respond to my text. That was, until I spotted him sitting at the hotel bar writing in his Moleskine note book as we gleefully traipsed through the lobby.

His eyes caught mine the second I spotted him, before darting back to his notebook. My first instinct was to simply keep walking, but instead I strode in his direction, with Tom scurrying quickly behind.

'Hi Leo!' I chirped as he looked up, feigning surprise.

'Hi, you two,' he replied, his eyebrows raising as he eyed the dozen or so shopping bags at my feet. I remembered that last night I'd confided to him that I shop when I'm sad or upset, and felt very exposed all of a sudden.

'You know . . . the right limited edition Chanel handbag appreciates at a greater rate than most houses in Sydney,' I quipped, despite the fact that he hadn't said a thing about the shopping bags.

'So you . . . bought a limited edition Chanel handbag?'

'Oh God, no, I'm not sixty years old, I don't use Chanel handbags.'

'Ew,' Tom whispered under his breath in solidarity.

'Oh, by the way. Sorry I didn't write back to your text; I was . . . on the tube when it came through and lost reception.'

His response was stiff and awkward. Tom looked sideways at me. I didn't let my expression drop for a moment.

'Oh, I forgot I'd even sent that! No stress. Anyway, we'll leave you in peace. I know you've got plans.'

Leo stared back at me blankly.

I pressed on confidently. 'With some friends? Which is why you're going to meet us at the airport?'

Leo shifted awkwardly in his seat, looking over my shoulder as he replied. 'Oh right. Yep. Yeah, of course. I do, yeah.'

Oh my goodness. He had totally lied about having friends to catch up with. It was obvious that he just didn't want to see me today. I felt as if someone had kicked me in the gut. I became hot and sweaty as I frantically searched for the name of the emotion I was feeling.

It didn't take long to hit the nail on the head.

Rejection.

At this point my cheeks had begun to hurt from the forced smile, so in one polite but swift movement I said goodbye and quickly made a beeline for the hotel lifts, Tom trailing close behind. Once the doors closed behind us, he spun around, dropped his shopping bags and put his hands on his hips.

'What the *hell* happened with you two last night?'

9

A week had passed since London and neither Leo nor I had said a word about the moment in the hotel. The warmth and ease I'd felt during dinner had disappeared, and instead Leo had turned into a kind of polite robot.

I wondered if I'd overstepped the mark somehow; missed some sort of sign that I was making him uncomfortable. Maybe I never should have invited him to my room in the first place? But nothing had actually happened between us, and 'staring at each other intensely' was hardly salacious. In the end, I had put the whole thing down to my imagination, convincing myself that the jet lag, exhaustion and sheer magic of being halfway across the world had made me feel something towards Leo that had never been there.

I wondered what Leo had put it down to. Had he spent the whole flight home going over and over it in his head like I had? I wondered if he looked at me differently now, in the same way that every time I looked at him I remembered the colour of his eyes as he stared at me that night. How the air had been sucked out of the room.

Instead of talking about it, we threw ourselves into work. Tom and I lived in our studio for the better part of the week, recording mock shows, planning segments, recording intros and perfecting interview edits. Tom on his side of the desk, and me on my side. Just like it had always been. It felt like being home again. From a logistical point of view, he always did the button pushing and I did the talking. Although he often did a bit of talking too, much to our listeners' delight. The technical term for 'pushing the buttons' is 'panelling', and while I knew how to do it, it never came as naturally to me as it did him. It came to him so naturally, in fact, that he'd been known to engage in a litany of non-work-related activities while simultaneously panelling a live radio show to millions of listeners without missing a beat. These activities included but were not limited to: ordering Uber Eats, watching YouTube dance tutorials, and even sexting. He'd also developed a quick way to figure out if a male caller who 'sounded hot' was actually hot IRL (plug their phone number into Facebook to secure a headshot). More often than not, this all happened while the caller was still on air trying to win tickets to P!nk.

The show had my name on it, but everyone knew Tom was as much a part of the on-air product as I was.

And so, like an old Gucci loafer (they age beautifully and get more and more comfortable over time), we slid back into our old routine—this time with a much bigger budget and a lot more pressure.

Leo came in sporadically, usually with forms that needed filling out or documents that needed signing. He'd never once got in our way as I'd initially suspected he would, but instead gave insight when it was appropriate, all the while looking *past* me and never *at* me.

It was hard not to take it personally. If nothing else, I'd thought we were becoming friends. There'd been such an ease between us that night at dinner in London, and I'd seen a side of him that was soft and funny and pretty likeable. All of that seemed to have disappeared now, and I found myself wishing that I'd never met 'fun Leo' in the first place. It would have been easier to ignore him completely if I really did still think he was an arsehole.

I had filled Tom in, of course, but to protect my sanity we'd agreed in the lift that morning to never discuss it again. I was glad he knew, and equally glad that we'd put it to bed and were getting on with more important things. Like the fact that our career dreams had come to fruition ten years early and we had a radio show to launch in a matter of days.

The rest of the team fell into place. It only took a week for us to realise that Georgia would one day run the place, such was her immense proficiency. Her jumping ship from Darren's show to mine was yet another excuse for him to hate me, but I'd soon learned to completely ignore the scowls that emanated from his annoying face every time our paths crossed in the office. Our audio producer was a quiet (they're always quiet) Scottish guy called Ferg who spent even longer in his studio than we did. He had worked on Goldie's show for five years and was as impressive as he was understated.

On Friday morning, three days before the show launch, Tom and I held hands as the screens were turned on in the studio, revealing our shiny new show artwork. This time my teeth had been left as is, my hair looked natural, and I looked like myself. I was wearing a simple denim mini dress, cinched in at the waist, with a single gold bangle on my wrist. It was classic, but it was me. Above the image were the words 'The Alex York Breakfast Show'. Tom squeezed my hand. The whole thing felt completely surreal.

The heavy studio door opened behind us, and I breathed in a subtle hint of Tom Ford. I want to say that my heart didn't do a teeny tiny little jump, but it absolutely did. Not that anyone would have known, because I didn't so much as flinch.

'Well done, guys. It looks good. It sounds good. You should be proud.'

I opened my mouth to give Leo a polite thankyou, and was overjoyed to find Goldie gliding in behind him. She was beaming at me, but I could see the shimmer of tears emerging. I tried to imagine what it must have felt like for her to see my face on that wall after twenty-five years. I opened my mouth to speak, but I knew I would cry if I dared. Instead, I reached out and hugged her. She felt tiny in my arms.

'Thank you, Goldie,' I whispered into her ear as I held her.

'Thank *you*, my girl. This is how it was meant to be. I promise. You belong here,' she whispered back.

Goldie stood back and cleared her throat as she looked around the room at us all.

'Now. Joanie and I are off tonight. To Italy. And then France. And Switzerland. And wherever else we decide to go.

The joy and freedom of unemployment awaits! Maybe we'll just stay there forever. Who knows?'

'What? You won't be here for the launch?' I asked, surprised.

Goldie smiled warmly. 'No, my dear. And nor should I be. It's not my show anymore. It's yours. And I mean it with all the love in the world when I say that I absolutely won't be listening. I'll be too busy eating pasta and drinking limoncello with the love of my life, who has waited a very long time to have me all to herself.'

Of course, Goldie had earned the right to never turn the radio on ever again, and I suppose knowing she wasn't listening took some of the pressure off. I imagined her and Joanie reclining on deckchairs in the Cinque Terre overlooking the bright blue ocean below, without a worry in the world. For some reason in this specific daydream Goldie was in a Dolce & Gabbana leopard-print bikini, which, to be honest, could have been real.

'I think Europe sounds perfect, Goldie. I'm just gonna need you to text me photos of any outrageous designer purchases because you know that no one on this planet will appreciate them more than Tom and me.'

Goldie's face lit up as she chuckled, and she lifted up her long, flared trousers to reveal patent silver brogues with diamanté-encrusted buckles.

'Get me a d-fib—stat,' Tom gasped.

I held a hand to my chest. Leo craned his neck to see what all the fuss was about. 'Okay. Someone enlighten me?'

I whispered as I approached the shoe, in reverence. 'Roger Vivier. I've had them in my shopping cart for weeks but not even

I had the guts to follow through. These shoes are handmade in Italy and, as you can see, they are arguably the perfect loafer.'

Leo stood in silent confusion with his arms folded across his chest, trying to make sense of the scene unfolding in front of him as Tom and I got down on all fours, taking in every magnificent detail as Goldie spun around slowly, showing off the shoes to a chorus of 'oohs' and 'aahs'.

After a couple of twirls, Goldie bowed and bid us a quick farewell, then her tiny frame disappeared into the office, with Leo following close behind.

I didn't know then that this would be the last time I would ever see Goldie Miller. But I'm glad I spent our final moments together admiring her shoes.

ılı·ıl|ıl|ıı·

I filled the weekend with my favourite activities in an attempt to get myself in the best possible headspace for Monday morning. I swam in the ocean, did lots of yoga, walked at sunset, made nachos with extra jalapenos and binged *Schitt's Creek* on the couch. I got a mani-pedi and stuck around for an extra half an hour to help Sally the manicurist set up her new Bumble profile. Vanessa and I FaceTimed for a solid hour and she took me through the sordid details of her latest love affairs. As expected, Mack the American had fallen head over heels and she'd ended up blocking his number.

Sunday night finally rolled around, and I was lounging in bed listening to Simon & Garfunkel and debuting the silk and feathered pyjamas I'd shame-purchased before I left for London when I heard a knock on the door.

'Come in,' I sang.

My bedroom door slowly opened as May's head appeared behind it, book in hand with her reading glasses on the tip of her nose. She looked worried.

'Darling. Oh, nice pyjamas! Very Audrey Hepburn.'

I kicked a leg in the air and blew her a dramatic kiss. Her face snapped back to serious mode.

'Sorry, there's . . . someone here to see you. I haven't told him you're home; I wanted to check first.'

A wave of relief washed over me. I wasn't sure how Leo had got my address but I was glad that he wanted to clear the air before the show started.

'Thanks, May, I'll come out in a second,' I replied, grabbing a hair tie and a robe.

She stood in the doorway, blocking my exit. 'I don't think you understand. It's . . . Jax. Jax is here.'

My stomach lurched. I hadn't heard his name spoken out loud in months. Why the hell was my ex-boyfriend at my house? And why now?

'I can tell him to go. I'll tell him to go!' she whispered.

I shook my head no and glanced at the mirror, tying my hair up and rolling my shoulders, willing myself to relax.

'Thanks May. Let's see what he has to say, I suppose.'

'We'll just be in the kitchen if you need us, darling.'

She brought her palm to my cheek and kissed me on the forehead as I walked past her through the door and down the hallway.

I inhaled and exhaled deeply, and confidently opened the door. There, standing centimetres away with a smug look on his face that was instantly infuriating, was the man who had unceremoniously dumped my sorry arse and gone golfing, thus sending my life into a complete tailspin. He had not said a word to me since. But there he was. Standing on the doorstep. Holding a box of my stuff. I stood in silence, taking him in. He looked skinnier than I remembered, and he'd grown the kind of wiry beard that not even Robert Pattinson could have made hot. His eyes were as blue as ever, but they didn't sparkle like I remembered.

Or maybe they never had. Maybe I had just imagined it the whole time.

'What's this about?' I asked curtly.

He looked down at the contents of the box as he replied, 'I thought I'd just drop over the rest of your stuff. I'm moving and didn't know what else to do with it.'

'Right,' I spat, frustrated. 'And you thought that tonight was the best time to do that? Of all the nights?'

He paused, confused.

'What do you mean?'

Two possibilities occurred to me in that moment. Both of which proved once and for all that this guy was a top-tier douchebag. Either he knew I was starting my new show the next day and came around anyway. Or he had no idea. He was either purposely throwing me off or hadn't bothered to keep tabs on me at all. I didn't want to give him the satisfaction of knowing either scenario upset me, so I changed the subject entirely.

'Nothing.' I reached over and grabbed the box. 'Thanks. Good luck with the move.'

'Yeah, thanks. I'm actually moving to Portugal. With Ana. We fly out in a couple of days.'

He was so nonchalant. So calm. I was beginning to seethe. He'd up-ended my life with no real explanation, no excuse. And just as I was beginning to find my feet again, here he was on my doorstep smiling, announcing his plans to move overseas with his new girlfriend. Anger swelled in my gut. All of a sudden, I wanted to rip his fucking head off.

He continued, 'So, you're still living with May and Billy?'

Unmoving, I just stood there. Despite my rising fury, the words weren't coming. The silence was deafening. He was winning. Again. Why was I letting him win?

'Yeah. Still here,' I managed to respond.

For someone whose entire job revolved around quickly finding clever words to say, I was having a rough go of it tonight. The smug smile crept back across his stupid, ratty little face. 'Crazy, hey? I'm off overseas and you're living with May and Billy. Funny how things turn out.'

I stared back at him and, all of a sudden, something within me snapped. And the words began to flow.

'You know what, Jax? Living here is actually great because it means I can save most of the exorbitant amount of money I get paid to host my new show. My breakfast radio show. Arguably the best radio job in the country. A job that I start tomorrow. Which you obviously already know about, otherwise you wouldn't be here trying one last time to make me feel small in order to make yourself feel big.'

He furrowed his brow, taking a step back.

'Don't feign confusion. It's not cute. And also, you're not the only one with a passport. Work just sent me to London. I flew business class. And now that I don't have you stealing my frequent flyer points all the time for your lame golf trips, I'll probably head to New York in July. So, unless this box contains the three years of my life that you wasted, I don't want it back.' I chucked the box at his feet and grabbed the door handle. 'And please shave. That beard is making me nauseous.'

I'd never actually slammed the door on somebody before. In fact, I didn't think it was even something people did in real life. Kinda like how in movies people walk off in a huff. I'd never walked off in a huff. But slamming the door in his face felt as satisfying as I'd hoped. It also felt a little dramatic and over the top, which I wasn't entirely angry about.

I was still standing in the hallway when I heard slow, careful footsteps coming towards me from the kitchen. Uncle Billy appeared wearing a Pink Floyd T-shirt, flannelette pyjama pants and Ugg boots that looked like they'd been worn every day since World War II.

'I'm making grilled cheese toasties. I've even got a bit of leftover truffle. Want in?' he whispered. He had a block of cheddar cheese in one hand and a grater in the other. I could tell May had forced him to come and coax me into the kitchen.

My head was still spinning and I was unsure whether I'd imagined the entire encounter as I dazedly followed him up the hallway to find May leaning against the oven, sipping a cup of peppermint tea.

'The cheek of that spineless little weasel,' she hissed, much to my amusement.

Billy immediately shushed her. 'That's enough May. I doubt that's helpful.'

I interjected, 'Actually, it is.'

Billy raised his eyebrows towards me and resumed the mammoth job of grating the cheddar as May continued. 'He's had, what, three months to give your stuff back? And he chooses the night before you're due to start the biggest show of your career? I mean, how pathetic is that? At one point I was going to barge in and sock him one. I'm glad you got yourself together in the end there.'

'You don't think it was petty?'

'There's nothing wrong with a bit of pettiness every now and then, love. Especially when it comes to spineless weasels. Beat him at his own game. I'm proud of you.'

I smiled graciously as she passed me a cup of tea. 'Thanks, May.'

Billy wiped off the grater and chucked it into the sink, turning the tap on. 'I've got a question for you.'

'Shoot.'

'How much money would you classify as "exorbitant"?'

May gasped, whacking him with a tea towel.

I giggled as I covered my face with my hands. 'Do you really wanna know?' I peeked out at him through a gap in my fingers. 'Because I'll tell you. But you can NEVER tell Mum. Or anyone.'

Billy's eyes were wide with anticipation. 'I've never wanted to know anything more in my life, kid.'

I grabbed an old takeaway menu and a pen out of the drawer and scribbled down a number. 'This is what will land in my account every month. After tax.'

He lifted up the paper to the light. His eyes grew wide as he clutched his heart with his left hand, before staggering around the kitchen pretending to have some sort of a seizure. May snatched the menu out of his hand, took a look and burst out laughing.

I was laughing too. 'I suppose you're going to start charging me rent, now.'

Billy calmed himself down and took a sip of May's tea. 'Don't be ridiculous Al, we're family. What I am going to do, however, is insist that you sit down with our financial planner because if you're anything like your aunt over here—' he was now waving a slice of sourdough at me '—you'll soon have $62,000 worth of feather-trimmed pyjamas and no savings.'

May scrunched up her nose at him, then slowly looked towards me with guilty eyes. 'He's right, my darling. You've got an opportunity to really set yourself up here. You could even buy your own place.'

'Is this your way of kicking me out? Have I not suffered *enough* tonight?'

'Of course not. But you know we won't be here forever . . .'

'May—you're fitter than I am!'

'Darling, I mean in this *house*, not on Earth. This place is too big for us, and . . .' she looked towards Billy, 'we have been talking about downsizing. Maybe an apartment . . . with an ocean view.'

Billy cleared his throat and raised a finger in the air. 'Side note, how much do you like truffle?'

'Very much. Keep going.' I turned my attention back towards May. 'So . . . when you say you're *not* kicking me out you mean . . . not just yet.'

May continued, 'Oh calm down would you. It's just a discussion we've been having lately. Anyway, you don't wanna get stuck living here forever. We can make an appointment for you with our friend Henry. Just get a bit of advice. See what your options are. Would you do that? For us?'

The very thought of sitting opposite some old nerdy guy in a suit and admitting that I'd quite literally spent every dollar I'd ever earned on shoes (and feather-trimmed pyjamas) made me sick with dread.

'Of course I'll see him.'

There was no way I was going to see him. Not until I had something to show for my life that couldn't be worn.

A sizzling sound crackled through the air as Billy pressed another grilled cheese toastie into the skillet. The scent of cheesy, truffley goodness filled the room.

'Funnily enough, Leo suggested the same thing to me when we were in London.'

May's head popped up like a meerkat's as the words came out of my mouth.

'Leo? The hot boss?'

'Like I said, he's not *really* my boss, but yeah. Him. Actually, when you came to my door I thought you were trying to tell me that *he* was here.'

May looked confused as I pressed on.

'I'm glad it was Jax though, otherwise I wouldn't have been able to tell him how utterly disgusting that beard is.'

She raised her tea towards me as if it was a pitcher of beer and we were ten drinks down at Oktoberfest. 'Hear hear! Now, do I want to know why you thought your married boss was knocking on the door on a Sunday evening?'

'Oh. He's not married after all. Well, he was. But he's not now. And yeah. We're just . . . very different. I dunno.' I was now rambling, which would only encourage her more.

'You know, Billy and I have absolutely nothing in common other than the same wedding date.'

'Oh, and the kids,' Billy chimed in as he passed me a toastie.

I'd heard this schtick a thousand times, but it was undeniably true. They had nothing in common. May drove a brand-new European car and Billy drove a Corolla that didn't even have electric windows. She wore designer yoga gear and he generally looked homeless. She read novels as if they were her lifeblood and the only thing Billy had ever read was a menu. They had no common interests. No shared friends. And after forty-five years of marriage, they were still hopelessly in love.

I replied, a mouth full of cheese. 'I know all this, but I don't see how it's relevant to Leo.'

May walked towards me and gave me a kiss on the forehead. 'If I'd never got to know him, I never would have known how happy he could make me. And vice versa. The ways we are different are the parts about us that I love the most.'

I was starting to understand what May was trying to say.

'Right. Well . . . in London I did kinda get to see a side of him that was . . . nice. But things got weird.'

Billy stood in silence, simultaneously munching away at his toastie and nodding at May with encouragement.

'Well, don't let it stay weird for too long. Life is too short, my dear,' May chirped.

'Thanks, Aunty.' I shoved a piece of melted cheese into my mouth, licked my fingers and gave Billy a wink and high five before wrapping my arms around May in a giant bear hug. 'Bedtime for me. I'm off at four tomorrow morning, so wish me luck now.'

'You don't need luck, kid,' Billy declared confidently. 'We'll be listening!'

I blew him a kiss as I sauntered back towards my room with a tummy full of cheese, closing the door behind me and collapsing onto my bed. Underneath the covers I felt my phone buzz.

A text.

You're going to be great. Brilliant, even. Leo.

What was it with the men with whom I had complicated relationships popping up tonight? What next? Was my dad about to knock on my window, apologise for the twenty-five-year absence and tell me to 'break a leg'?

The text was sweet. Obviously. But the little hamster in my brain was back on the wheel, and it was about to start spinning. And it wasn't going to stop spinning. And tonight, of all nights, I really needed a good night's sleep. Why was life so cruel? And why were men so infuriating?

I was hit by the urge to indulge in a cheeky little Selfridges perusal, but as I reached down to the ground to grab my laptop I spotted my yoga mat rolled up in the corner. And then, it was as if I was possessed by some other responsible, mature version of myself. I got up, unrolled my mat and slowly collapsed into child's pose. Maybe, just maybe, there was a way for me to deal with moments of anxiety or stress that didn't involve spending money.

〜〜〜

I'm not sure what time I eventually dozed off, but by the time I walked into the studio the next morning at 5 am, carrying a bag of McDonald's hash browns, the adrenaline had well and truly kicked in and I felt as invincible as Adele that time she won four hundred GRAMMYs.

Tom was putting the final touches on the planning whiteboard when I arrived. Essentially a visual grid outlining the three-hour show, from 6 to 9 am, he'd meticulously drawn every line with a ruler and colour-coded each section within an inch of its life. Hooks in red (the way we tell people what's coming up in the show to keep them tuned in), competition spots in blue, pre-recorded interviews in green and content breaks in pink. Today we were playing the Tilly Roy interview in three parts, which took up most of the 8 o'clock hour, and then giving away tickets to her newly announced Australian tour—news of which had been embargoed until today and was sure to jam the phone lines. Once we'd all signed off on the show plan, Georgia transcribed it into a document and printed a copy for each of us. After a quick coffee run it was 5:50 am and we had ten minutes till showtime. I wondered if I should call everyone in for some sort of pre-show huddle. Or a Beyoncé prayer circle. Then I had a better idea.

An in-studio dance party. Courtesy of One Direction.

I'm not sure I'll ever forget the image of Ferg the audio producer attempting a cartwheel when the chorus of 'What Makes You Beautiful' hit, but it instantly dissipated the last of my nerves as we all broke out in raucous laughter. There was fist-pumping, hip-thrusting and lots of pointing and clapping. Three minutes and nineteen seconds later, we all breathlessly high-fived, and with happy tears in my eyes I took a seat in my chair opposite Tom, just as I'd done hundreds of times before. He looked straight back at me and motioned surreptitiously over my shoulder. I swivelled my chair around to see Leo in his work uniform, standing on the other side of the glass. I gave him a thumbs up, which he returned somewhat awkwardly, then turned my chair back around and glanced at the clock.

Tom fiddled with the desk, pulling faders and adjusting microphones. 'Live in two minutes, doll. You ready to do this?'

'Sure am. Sorry again that I ditched you and disappeared to a desert island that one time.'

'I'd say it all worked out pretty well.'

'Me too, babe.'

'One minute.'

I winked back at him, and before I knew it the show opener was playing out and I was seconds away from introducing the Alex York Breakfast Show for the very first time.

'What a day to be alive, Sydney! My name is Alex York and we're gonna have some fun today!'

We were off and away.

‖‖‖‖‖

It was as if I blinked and the three-hour show was done, and I felt as though I had been carried on a wave of adrenaline, excitement and sheer disbelief that it was all actually happening every second of the way. As far as first shows go, it sounded pretty bloody good. The Tilly Roy interview was punchy, funny and super entertaining, and the first tickets to her show were awarded to a mum of two girls who sobbed so much she could hardly speak.

A 'mystery caller' phoned in at 8 am and was patched through by Georgia, and, while I was dubious at first, I was absolutely delighted to hear the loud, joyful tones of one Finley Stark down the line.

'I'm just calling through to wish my favourite radio host in the world good luck on her first day at her big-girl job!'

'Finley Stark, where are you in the world and are you in any state to be on live radio?'

'Saint-Tropez. Surrounded by hot babes, free-flowing champagne and pure and utter debauchery! So, probably not, to be honest.'

Tom rolled his eyes across the studio as I chuckled. 'I don't want to know.'

'No, you don't, Ms York,' Finley gleefully retorted. 'You're far too wholesome. But perhaps your audience would like to hear about what you got up to recently when you came to visit little old me in London town?'

Tom winced. 'I don't think anyone needs to hear about that . . . Let's keep it PG, please!'

Hearing Tom's voice down the line only spurred Finley on more. 'Here he is! The king of Soho himself . . . Mr Winter!

You didn't keep it very PG either. Where did you say those dancers were from? Essex?'

I laughed and a snort came out into the microphone, which made me laugh more. Finley was well and truly going rogue and I was loving every second of it, safe in the knowledge that we were on a seven-second delay and if he went too far Tom could very easily cut to a commercial break before anything too incriminating was broadcast.

'Now, if memory serves me correctly, we did some sort of an interview while driving through the streets of Knightsbridge and I shared some very salacious details of my life as one of the biggest pop stars on the planet. When are the people of Sydney going to hear it?'

Tom interjected. 'That would be this time tomorrow.'

'Well, I'll be listening! Actually, that's a lie, I won't be listening, I'll be on stage in Milan. But I'll be there in spirit!'

I cheered and clapped before wrapping it up. 'Thanks, Finners. Now go get back to whatever pop-star insanity you're up to your neck in. Thanks for calling in.'

'Alex York forever!' he yelled before hanging up.

I took a deep breath, shook my head in Tom's direction then pulled my mic closer to me and wrapped things up.

'Well, Sydney, never a dull moment here on the Alex York Breakfast Show. And while I can't guarantee surprises like that every morning, it's a great reminder that anything is possible on live radio!'

╫┉╫╫┉

The first week was like a fever dream. The shows went by so quickly that I hardly had time to take stock. When I got home every afternoon I fell straight into bed, completely exhausted, often not waking until my alarm rang out the next day at 3:30 am. Billy got into the habit of prepping extravagant takeaway breakfast packs for me, and every day I'd get to work and open my little bento box to find stewed fruits, pancakes, chia seed puddings, homemade granola and corn fritters. Nobody at work could quite fathom the fact that I brought in home-cooked meals for breakfast, let alone the fact that they were prepared for me by my uncle, with whom I was living rent-free.

On the Friday morning, my first official payslip appeared in my inbox and I sat in stunned silence at my desk, staring at the zeros that had been deposited into my bank account. Unsurprisingly, my first instinct was to go out and buy something ridiculous. But a minute or so later I had another thought. Maybe Leo was right. Maybe May and Billy were right. Maybe I should actually . . . talk to a professional to figure out what to do with my new-found wealth.

Then I thought about my maxed-out credit card and the sheer mortification that would come from someone knowing how much I'd spent.

I decided that there was only one thing for me to do, and that was something I'd never actually done before. I would pay off the entirety of my bill in one go. I would square it off. Get it back to zero. And once that was done, I would see whether the thought of meeting a financial planner still made me want to puke.

I sat at my desk, paralysed for another moment or so, scared to even log in to my banking app. I'd purposely hidden my credit card account from my home screen so that I'd never actually have to come face-to-face with the amount owing. I wondered if I should call Tom over and get him to do it for me. No. I would simply rip it off like a bandaid.

With trembling fingers, I clicked on my credit card account, closing my eyes while the screen loaded, and then ever so slowly opening my right eye to squint at the number in front of me. I felt like one of those kids on TikTok who films themselves opening their college acceptance offer.

And there it was.

Thirty two thousand, six hundred and fifty-two dollars. Almost my entire monthly pay.

My financial recklessness had always been a bit of a joke, but for the first time in my life it felt like the recklessness wasn't so fun anymore.

I took a deep breath and, in a few short clicks, without thinking, transferred the exact amount back into the account, watching as the total owing updated to zero.

A heaviness I didn't even know was there immediately lifted from my shoulders.

'Oh fuck. That actually felt pretty good,' I said, much louder than I had planned.

It did feel good. It felt *really* good.

I looked up to see that Mark Holdsworth had appeared beside Leo in the corridor and was whispering something in his ear. Leo was nodding seriously as they disappeared into the conference room. I opened Instagram for a quick scroll and, as if on autopilot, found myself clicking through a sponsored ad and adding a couple of pieces from the new SKIMS collection to my cart. Obviously I deserved a treat after paying off my credit card bill.

'Alex!' Tom's voice boomed across the office. 'I need you to head home and have a nap. We're all going out tonight to celebrate our first week.'

'Who's we?'

'Literally the whole floor. My social connections know no ends. I also told them the tequila is on you, so . . .' He shrugged innocently.

'Tom, I legit JUST paid my credit card off!'

'Great, you've made space! Off you go! Rest that pretty face up and I'll swing past yours in an Uber at seven.'

Tom quickly packed my things into my handbag, took me by the arm and dragged me towards the exit. As we passed the conference room, I glanced through the glass at Leo and Mark engaged in a very animated conversation. It almost looked like they were fighting. I craned my neck back as Tom dragged me past, desperate to get a sense of what was going down. Before I knew it, however, I was in the office lift, Tom had pressed the button for Basement 5 and I was on my way down to my car.

'I'll call you at six to wake you up, just in case!' I heard his shrill voice call out after me as the doors closed.

10

I did not feel human at 6 pm when Tom called to wake me up. It could have been January 2045 for all I knew, and after sleeping for six straight hours it took me five or six seconds to remember who I was and what was going on. With an hour up my sleeve to get ready, I stumbled to the bathroom and thanked baby Jesus that I'd had the wherewithal to get a mid-week blow dry, and the self-respect to cleanse and moisturise my face before I fell asleep at midday. Walking into the kitchen, I sang out to see if May or Billy were home but heard no reply. It was still light and balmy outside and I stared out the kitchen windows at the afternoon sun bouncing off the swimming pool. I loaded a coffee pod into the espresso machine, pressed the button and waited for the glorious shot of caffeine that would soon shock me back to life.

It felt important for me to attend tonight, and not just because Tom had told everybody the tequila was on me. We'd all worked hard to get the show live, and the past week had been a huge slog. It was important to celebrate. I suppose part of me also wanted people to know that, although I was now hosting the breakfast show, I hadn't changed. I was still Alex. I was still going to come out and party and end up smashing a 7-Eleven sausage roll in a gutter at 2 am just like old times.

On second thoughts, I could probably do without the gutter sausage roll.

I put my favourite 'get ready' playlist on my Bluetooth speaker, and the opening bars of Lizzo's 'Soulmate' came blasting out at me. Every killer night out starts with a killer outfit. And I knew exactly what the outfit was going to be.

The minute I'd laid eyes on the mini dress at Harrods I knew it had to be mine. I didn't even need to try it on to know that it was going to look incredible. It was a shade of fuchsia that looked almost edible. I wanted to pour it on vanilla ice-cream and eat it for breakfast. I teamed it with a pair of Prada creeper brogues that gave me some much-needed height but kept it comfortable in case Missy Elliott played and I needed to really move. I put some light waves through my hair with my ghd, a bit of smoke on the eyelids, and after a nice thorough brush of the teeth I was ready to go with five minutes to spare.

Tom wolf-whistled as I made my way down the front path and through the gate, illuminated by the lights of the Uber. He was dressed head to toe in black, with a fresh fade that he hadn't had when I saw him seven hours earlier.

'I have two questions,' I said as I slid myself onto the leather seat next to him.

'Hit me.'

'Are those pants Issey Miyake? And since when do you order Uber Blacks?'

'Yes, they are, and your credit card is still connected to my Uber account from London. I figured we'd treat ourselves.'

At that point he reached down into a plastic bag at his feet and pulled out two mini bottles of Moët of Chandon, which he proceeded to pop in quick succession. He placed a bright straw in each, passed one to me and held his in the air for a toast.

'To us! The hottest bitches on breakfast radio!'

I whooped heartily as I toasted him and took a generous sip from my champagne. Tom really did have the ability to turn any moment into something worth remembering. It was a gift that I would always be grateful for.

He pulled out his phone and began texting, the screen obscured from my view, a cheeky smirk on his face.

'Who are you text flirting with?'

He glared at me sarcastically. 'As if.'

His coyness when it came to his love life would forever drive me mad, but it was a hill I'd given up dying on long ago.

The mini bottle had me mildly buzzed pretty quickly, and by the time the BMW pulled up outside the bar, I had a lovely warm feeling in my tummy. I made a mental note to myself to have a glass of water as soon as we got inside.

A group of girls from the marketing team arrived at the same time and, judging by the volume of their hollering, they'd started drinking a lot earlier in the afternoon and were ready to keep the party going. One of them spied Tom and me, and within seconds there were squeals, shouts and chants—the likes of which you'd expect from a hen's party. Every single one of them told us how hot we looked, some of them even told us twice. One girl made me spin and then asked me how much my dress cost. Tom jumped in and answered on my behalf.

'More than any of us could afford, babe, but I can swipe it from her closet any time you wanna wear it, just ask.'

The girls all responded in unison with a chorus of 'yaaas queens' as we walked through the doors and headed downstairs to the bar, where a sea of familiar faces milled about happily under a moody glow. I spotted Georgia across the room, holding an orange juice and chatting with a couple of girls from the sales team whose faces I knew and names I didn't. I blew her a kiss, and she responded by raising her glass in my direction.

Ferg was huddled in a booth with the other audio producers, deep in conversation about something I no doubt wouldn't understand. I gave him a quick squeeze on the shoulder as I walked past and waved to the group before heading to the bar and ordering a tall glass of water. The bartender looked like the kind of guy I would have spent the night lusting over in my early twenties. He wore a loose tee with a scoop neck, subtly showing off his chest tatts, and a backward cap that somehow looked hot in an un-ironic way.

Seconds later Tom appeared by my side, clocking the obvious hotness of backward-cap-bartender guy as he leaned across the bar, raising his voice above the music.

'We're gonna need all the tequila in all the shot glasses you've got please! Like, at least forty!'

The bartender looked at Tom, not quite sure if he was taking the piss or not. Tom continued, 'Oh, and moneybags over here is paying!'

Tom held his open palm out towards me, switching his gaze between me and the silver Miu Miu clutch of dreams. I rolled my eyes, reached into my handbag and pulled my credit card out. He snatched it from my hands, blew me a kiss and handed it across the bar.

The bartender began lining up the shot glasses and I leaned across the bar and raised my voice loud enough so that he'd hear me, but quiet enough so that nobody else would.

'Let's cap that at five hundred bucks please!'

He pulled back and grinned. 'Am I pouring one for you?'

'The last time I started the night with tequila shots it ended very badly. I'll stick to the water for now!'

'Too easy. I'm Matt, by the way.'

'Hi Matt! I'm Alex!'

'I know,' he responded with a wink. An icky wink.

I worked the room with the tray of shots as happy friends and colleagues clambered over to get around the tequila. The gaggle of marketing girls I'd entered with had already created a makeshift dance floor near the speakers and told me all over again how hot I looked when I appeared.

The shots disappeared as fast as lightning in a haze of happy cheers and clinking glasses, until there were just two left. I looked around to check if anyone had missed out, and as I did so I spotted a familiar figure walking down the stairs.

I knew those boots. I knew those jeans. And that shirt. And I sure as hell knew those eyes. Eyes that darted around the room before settling on me.

Leo Billings had entered the building.

I lost him in the crowd as quickly as I'd spotted him. I tried my best to subtly scan the room, but it was too dark and I was too short. Instead, I stood in the crowd with two shots of tequila on my tray like an awkward waitress at a wedding, desperate to offload the last hors d'oeuvre. Why did Leo make me so nervous? I stared at the tequila. A shot would certainly help me relax a little.

I spotted Leo again a moment later. I stood up a little taller and smiled self-consciously, watching as he walked towards me, carefully and politely weaving his way through the crowd that was growing rowdier by the second.

'This is a surprise!' I called out as he approached.

He leaned in closer so that I could hear him, and as he did his stubble brushed across my cheek. For a second I let myself breathe him in as he spoke.

'Tom did invite me. Via email *and* text. I was alone in the hotel having dinner and thought I'd . . . pop in.'

'Oh, right.' I pulled back, raising my voice above the crowd. 'I was just handing out the tequila shots.'

'Yes, I figured. You're like the pied piper. In fuchsia.'

His eyes darted down to my dress. I sucked in my stomach and fiddled with the hem.

'A London purchase. Of course.' I grinned.

His eyes fixed on mine again. 'Of course.'

I regretted bringing up London, and immediately felt the urge to change the subject. The tray suddenly weighed ten kilos. I held it up towards him. 'Don't suppose you'll take the last one off my hands?'

He looked at the tray, no doubt puzzled that there were actually two shots on the tray, and then watched as I knocked one back.

Leo Billings was most certainly not a shots guy, and I immediately felt silly for offering. But then I watched as, almost in slow motion, he picked up the tequila and threw it back, holding my gaze as he did.

Shocked, I blinked a couple of times. 'Well, I didn't see that coming.'

'To be honest, neither did I. In fact, I'm not sure why I did it.' He winced.

We both laughed nervously. It was the first time I'd stood this close to him since London. It was the first time we'd really even had a proper conversation since London. My mind raced back to dinner at Marco's. How we'd been so relaxed, so free. It felt like a distant memory. Like maybe it had never happened at all.

The music got louder all of a sudden, and cheers rang out from the corner where the marketing girls had recruited a larger posse to their dance floor. Tom's head popped up among the gaggle of people. He looked at Leo, then at me, holding up a glass and toasting the air in our direction. I wondered how many of the tequila shots I'd passed around had ended up in his stomach. Bodies around us moved faster as the energy in the room intensified. But Leo and I stood still. Not speaking. My heart was pounding and I was sure that if the music hadn't been so loud he would have heard it *thump thump thump* all the way through my chest.

A group of people nearby all stood up and headed towards the dance floor, leaving a table in the corner free. I looked at the table and then back at Leo, who had the same idea. Moments later we were huddled in a corner with a perfect view of the unfolding madness around us, and I was painfully and bliss-fully aware of the fact that my knee was touching Leo's.

With his eyes still on the crowd in front of us, Leo spoke first. 'You did an amazing job this week. You should be proud.'

I replied without making eye contact. 'Thank you. Honestly, it still doesn't feel real. None of this does.' I hesitated. 'So does the tequila shot have anything to do with the tense conversation you were having earlier today with the big dog?'

I heard Leo inhale sharply. 'No, but the whisky doubles I had before I came did.'

I gave him a worried look.

'I'm kidding. Nothing you need to worry about.'

It occurred to me that Leo might actually be a little buzzed, which would certainly explain his decision to come. 'You know that day I met with Mark, it was clear he absolutely does not take me very seriously.'

'Yeah, look. He's old school. Amazing with numbers and structures; not so good with the human stuff.'

'So that's where you come in?' I asked.

'Precisely.'

'Speaking of men who don't take me seriously . . .' I groaned, my smile flattening.

Leo looked up to follow my gaze. Never one to miss a party, Darren Chase had appeared. His eyes scanned the room before settling on me and Leo. I looked back to Leo, pretending not to have clocked Darren at all.

'Is he still looking?' I asked.

'He sure is,' Leo replied, raising a friendly hand in Darren's direction. 'Although I'd say it's more of a death stare than a look.'

And then a sound rang out from the speakers that meant only one thing. It took a couple of seconds for Tom to find me, and from that moment on all attempts to fight the urge to dance were futile. Because when Missy Elliott plays, it doesn't matter where you are, or what you're doing, or who you're doing it with. You stop. And you dance. And you don't give a fuck about anything else.

I shot up, spun around and bent down so that my mouth gently brushed against Leo's ear. 'I apologise in advance for what you're about to see,' I said in a low voice, handing him my clutch as Tom held two arms out. In one hand was a tequila shot, which he passed to Leo; the other hand extended to grab mine and drag me away. I looked behind me where Leo, very bemused, was left alone in the corner, with no other option than to sink the shot.

I'm not sure how I ended up on the bar, but there we were one chorus later, doing the old 'dance like no one's watching' motivational quote justice. I was ecstatic. The whole room was electric. I opened an eye to look around me at the sea of wonderful, familiar faces all dancing and cheering below us and I felt like my heart might actually burst open as I danced and writhed and mouthed along with Missy as she ever so delicately dropped verses about her pussy. The song ended and a huge, raucous cheer broke out across the room. I spotted Darren in the crowd, arms folded across his chest, his eyebrows raised in a look so judgemental one could have assumed I'd just slaughtered a baby goat right there on the bar. I smiled at him sarcastically and took an exaggerated bow. As I did so, I saw that Matt the bartender had positioned himself to help me off the bar. I grabbed his left hand, hopped down carefully, and as I landed, his right hand firmly and very intentionally reached under my dress and grabbed my arse. It all happened so quickly that I did a double take, then firmly but subtly swatted his hand away, avoiding eye contact completely and darting away from him. The backward cap should have been a dead giveaway that he was a creep.

I made my way quickly through the crowd, my stomach churning as I climbed the dark stairs, forcing a big fake smile and nodding at people as they passed. Seconds later I pushed open the heavy door and the cool evening air hit my face. I was relieved to be able to breathe again. I found a nook in the wall of the alleyway a couple of paces away from the entrance, hiding myself away against the cold bricks. Eyes closed, I took some deep centring breaths until my heart slowed down. I heard the door open, followed by quick, heavy footsteps. I prayed that Matt hadn't followed me out to grovel.

'Alex? Are you out here?' Leo's calm, deep voice rang out into the alleyway.

I took another deep breath and stepped forwards into the light. 'I'm here. Just getting some air.'

Leo strode towards me, my silver clutch under his arm. He looked angry. 'Are you okay?'

His face told me that he'd seen everything.

I swallowed. 'I'm fine. I promise. I mean, it's bullshit, but I'm fine.' I replied with as much nonchalance as I could muster.

Leo was now pacing. 'Yeah, bullshit is right.' He stopped in front of me and seemed stuck as to what to do next. His hand moved towards me, and then he pulled it back. 'Are you sure you're okay?'

I grabbed his hand reassuringly. 'I promise.'

He stared down at our hands as I let go. I was taken aback by how worked up he'd become. 'Do you want to leave?' he asked.

I paused, weighing up my options. I absolutely wanted to leave, but I didn't want to be alone. I looked around the empty alleyway and then back at Leo, who had calmed down and was standing next to me protectively. 'I think so, yeah.'

'Wanna take a walk? Or do you want me to call you an Uber?'

'A walk sounds perfect. But my credit card is behind the bar.'

'Well, that I can handle.' He handed me my clutch. 'Wait here, I'll be two minutes.'

Leo disappeared back inside. I looked down at the silver clutch, thankful that Leo had grabbed it on his way out.

A couple of minutes later, the heavy door opened again, and Leo appeared, holding my credit card and looking smug. 'Backward-cap guy has gladly, and without any threats or coercion from me, comped the tequila shots.'

I smiled as I popped the card safely back inside my purse. 'Thank you for taking care of that.'

'Taking care of it would have meant punching him in the face, but I figured you'd prefer the $500.'

'I would. I mean, you know how much financial responsibility means to me.'

Leo laughed heartily. 'Yeah, I mean $500 is what, half a shoe?'

'Hmm, closer to three-quarters,' I teased. 'Oh, and you'll be pleased to know that I actually paid off my credit card today. In one go. It was terrifying. And amazing.'

Leo stopped in his tracks, turned to look at me with wide eyes, before slowly reaching his right hand up for a high five. It would have been patronising from anyone else, but he seemed genuinely happy for me.

'I know. It's the new me.' I reached my palm up to meet his. 'Speaking of expensive stuff—' I started walking again '—the watch. You said it was a gift. I've gotta know—who spends fifteen grand on a gift, and how do I become friends with them?'

'It's a pretty cool story, actually.' Leo pulled his sleeve up and beamed at his wrist. 'I saw it in a shop window a couple of years after Laney and I got together. We had no money back then, so we could never have afforded it, and years later when we could afford it, well, you know me—a Swatch suited me just fine. But she remembered I'd always loved it.'

We walked another couple of paces in silence, then Leo began to speak again.

'It was my birthday a couple of weeks before she passed. We both knew it was going to be the last one together. She organised someone to go pick it up, and she gave it to me in the hospital knowing that I would never actually buy it for myself. She also knew that I couldn't be angry with her, not even if I tried. So it was all kind of perfect.'

'Oh man. I gotta get me a Laney.'

Leo grinned. I grinned back.

We walked in comfortable silence for the next five or so minutes, the busy city hustling and bustling around us. I couldn't help but revel in the feeling of safety that came with walking beside Leo. Not just because he'd helped at the bar, but more in that general sense I'd felt before—that if he was around, nothing bad would happen to me. Like he would take care of things.

Before long, we were on George Street, where the bright lights of his hotel greeted us.

'Don't suppose you feel like a martini?' he asked.

'Consider my arm twisted,' I replied, trying to swallow my grin.

It didn't take Malik long to spot us in the corner, and as he walked towards me I gave him a pleading look as if to say 'please be cool'. He understood straight away, approaching our table with a calm, friendly smile.

'My old favourite and my new favourite. Happy Friday!' he said to us both, before focusing his attention on me. 'I saw the dress before I saw you. My God, babe, you look un-fucking-believable. Love to see it!'

'Harrods. After half a bottle of Veuve.'

'No regrets! Now. Your usuals?'

'Yes, thanks, Malik,' Leo replied warmly. We watched as he sauntered back towards the bar.

'So, be honest. How do you think the show sounded this week? Do you think it's going to work?'

'Do you want my honest answer?' he asked.

My stomach tightened. 'Of course.'

He leaned back in his seat. 'I knew the show was going to work fifteen seconds into that Tilly Roy interview in London. Watching you . . . do your thing. It was like watching Goldie all those years ago.'

I exhaled, trying with all my might to conceal a smile. 'Oh wow. Not the answer I expected.'

'Why is that?' He cocked his head to the side, intrigued.

I didn't know how to respond. 'Well . . . since London . . . you've . . .' I didn't finish the sentence. I just let myself trail off and bit my lip, hoping he understood what I was alluding to.

He took a deep breath, pulling both hands under the table and onto his lap. 'Right. Since London . . .'

'I mean, it's fine. I just thought you'd been angry with me or . . . I just feel like things have been weird.'

My heart was racing. He pulled his hands out again and placed them on the table between us. 'I suppose I owe you an apology, don't I?'

I immediately stiffened up. 'No, oh God no. It's fine—'

'No, Alex,' he cut me off. 'It's not fine at all. I was rude to you on that last morning in London. And I've been rude to you ever since.'

I didn't know what to say. I tried to keep my face as soft and calm as I could.

'You weren't rude, Leo. You just left me . . . feeling a bit silly.'

He winced. 'I'm sorry. I really am. You did nothing wrong, and it shouldn't have taken me a couple of shots to be man enough to tell you that.'

In my peripheral vision I could see Malik watching us from the bar, holding our drinks hesitantly. I beckoned him over. He silently placed what looked like whisky in front of Leo before passing my martini over and slipping away without a word.

I took a big sip straight away. Leo knocked his drink back in one go.

'I want to explain,' he said softly, without looking up.

I took another sip, settling my gaze on his glass.

'Alex. When I first met you, I was pissed off and confused and thought I'd made a huge mistake moving home. I was a real mess. And then, once I started coming to terms with the reality of what was happening, I suppose I let myself see you for what you are.'

My throat was dry but my eyes were irresistibly drawn back to his. 'And what am I?'

He didn't look up, his eyes still fixed firmly on the whisky glass. 'This explosion of colour and light and . . . life. It's like you're just totally in. Totally immersed in it all. I used to be like that.' He paused.

'I get it,' I whispered gently.

'That night, back at the hotel in London—'

I felt my face flush. 'You don't have to, Leo.'

'No, I want to. I need to.' He looked up at me, and then back at the whisky glass. 'When you looked at me the way you did, I felt . . .' He took a deep breath. 'Well, I can't even really describe what I felt. But I felt something. And it really fucking scared me.'

His eyes slowly rose to meet mine, and it was as though the air was being sucked out of my lungs.

'I felt it too.' It took all of my strength to hold his gaze as I uttered the words.

Leo exhaled, a relieved half-smile peeking through his solemn face. He placed one hand ever so gently over mine, where it rested on the table as we sat staring at each other. I watched his eyes flicker over to Malik at the bar and felt his hand subtly pull away as he did so. 'Could we have this chat somewhere a little more private?'

My heart was in my throat. 'Of course,' I whispered, as I gathered my purse, ready to take his lead.

Without another word, Leo stood up and made his way out of the bar.

I waited a moment, gathering myself. My hands were trembling. I looked up to where Malik was staring at me from behind the bar as he dried glasses. Wide-eyed. He raised his eyebrows, questioning. I slowly shrugged.

Leo was waiting for me at the lift, silent. I stood beside him as he reached out and pressed the button. I watched as the numbers on the lift counted down.

The doors opened. He stepped in first, his eyes ushering me to follow. The doors closed after us. His arm stretched out behind me to swipe his card and press number fourteen, and as he pulled it back I felt his hand brush ever so slightly across the small of my back, touching my bare skin softly with his fingertips.

The doors finally opened and we stepped out. The corridor was dark. He kept his fingertips on the small of my back as we walked, until he came to a halt outside his room. We faced each other at the door, his eyes seeing through me once more.

He reached out to swipe his card with his left hand, pushed the door open and watched me walk inside before following me through and letting the door close quietly behind us.

The room was immaculate, the king-size bed perfectly made up, two Moleskine journals stacked neatly on the bedside table alongside a phone charger and a pen. It smelled like him. I looked past the bedroom to a small sitting room by the window, a single lamp on the table exuding a beautiful warm glow. The two of us stood in the entry, the room dark apart

173

from the soft light of the lamp. I stared back at him, our faces centimetres apart.

His voice was soft. Earnest. 'I'm sorry I upset you, Alex. I hope you believe me when I say that's the last thing I wanted to do. Losing Laney, it just . . . I never expected . . .'

The room felt cold all of a sudden, or maybe I was just nervous. I hugged my arms around myself and waited for him to go on. When he didn't, I murmured, 'It's okay, Leo. It's complicated.' I shrugged. 'Life is complicated.'

His eyes were wet. I reached out and tenderly wiped a tear from his cheek with my thumb. He closed his eyes, and I gently pulled him closer towards me, wrapping my arms around his waist, my head on his chest. A moment later, his arms slid across my back. We stood for a moment in silence, suspended in time as I breathed him in, his strong body softening in my embrace. I wanted so much to say something to make everything better. Easier. But the words didn't come.

A loud noise startled us both. A phone. He gently pulled away from me, reaching into his back pocket with one hand, and wiping his eyes with the other.

'Right. Shit. I have to take this.' He stared at the phone, the name 'Jack' flashing up on the screen. 'If it was anyone else in the world I'd silence it, but I'm sorry . . . Stay here. I'll explain after.'

Before I had a chance to respond, Leo disappeared into the bathroom, closing the door behind him. I backed up to the edge of the bed and slowly lowered myself, a million conversations running loudly through my mind. I tried to make sense of what was happening, relieved that whatever I'd felt that night in London hadn't been in my imagination, but also terrified that I was stepping into something fraught with danger. The undeniable truth was that Leo did something to my insides that felt exhilarating and terrifying in equal parts. Terrifying because he was still *technically* my boss. My widowed boss. And I'd pretty much sworn off any sort of romance for the foreseeable future, let alone one that involved him.

Through a crack in the wardrobe doors, I could see a fluffy white hotel robe. I removed it carefully from the rack, and slipped it on, the softness against my bare legs and back warming me up as I sat back down on the bed.

I stared at the nondescript wall in front of me, wondering what would have happened if we hadn't been interrupted. How long would we have stood there, holding each other? Were we about to kiss? Were we about to get naked? I supposed I'd never know. Maybe I didn't want to know.

The bathroom door opened and Leo slowly emerged, phone in one hand, the other rubbing his eyes. He sat down a couple of centimetres away on the edge of the bed. 'Well, that couldn't have happened at a worse time. Sorry.'

'It's fine.' I smiled. 'Who's Jack?'

'Jack is my nephew.' He sighed. 'In London. He's eight. His mum is Laney's sister.'

Things were making a little more sense now. 'Gotcha,' I replied, pulling the robe tighter around me.

'His dad has never been on the scene, and we've always been close. Laney and I were at his birth. Me leaving London was hard on him; really, really hard. I promised that if he ever called me, no matter where I was or what I was doing, I would answer. Obviously when I made that promise I never expected to be . . . here—' he smiled a little awkwardly '—with you.'

'But a promise is a promise. I understand.' I paused. Leo didn't seem to know where to look. I gently touched his chin, slowly swivelling his face so that it was facing mine. 'It's fine, Leo. I don't feel awkward. It's all good. We're all good.'

'Thank you for saying that. Tonight took me by surprise. All of it.'

'You're telling me!' I grinned. 'I thought you were off me forever!'

He raised his eyebrows, a serious look on his face. 'No, Alex. Of course I wasn't. I was just . . . confused.'

'I understand that now, I promise,' I replied sincerely.

'Do you think things happen for a reason?' Leo asked.

The question was jarring. I pulled back a little, instantly wondering whether he was already regretting what had almost just maybe-but-maybe-not happened. 'You mean, did the universe just interrupt us to save us from doing something stupid?' I asked coolly, hoping he would enthusiastically reply that I'd misunderstood the question entirely and that he'd like very much to pick up where we left off, such was my delightful magnetism and charm.

Instead, Leo seemed lost in his own thoughts.

I stared at the ceiling for a moment, wondering whether the atmosphere had got tense or whether I was just being paranoid. 'We don't have to say any more if you don't want to,' I said. 'We can just leave it for now. I think that's okay, right?'

He stood up slowly and pulled a second robe from the cupboard, then let out a long breath as he shrugged into it and sat back down. 'That works for me.' He looked at me with eyes that said 'sorry' and 'thank you' all at once.

I relaxed a little. 'So. What are the chances that this joint has club sandwiches on the menu?'

Leo smiled as he reached over me to the hotel phone beside the bed and dialled to order. 'Consider it done.'

As I watched him on the phone, his question replayed over and over in my mind. Did Leo really think I was so dangerous that the universe would spend its energy stopping us from making out? I mean, surely there were more important things for the universe to spend its time working out. Like world peace. Or even just a *Gilmore Girls* feature film that was worth watching and lived up to the pure, bingeable perfection that was the television series.

Eventually he hung up and I was able to snap myself out of my existential spiral long enough to change the subject. 'Are you ever going to move out of this place?' I asked.

He laughed. 'Why would I, when I can have club sandwiches delivered *to my bed*?'

I was sure he didn't mean to make the words 'to my bed' sound as suggestive as he had, especially since he was so convinced being in it with me was a bad idea. 'I'm sure most Uber Eats drivers would do that too for an extra tip,' I quipped.

'Well, to answer your question, yes. Eventually. I wanted to settle in at work before finding somewhere permanent.'

'And have you? Settled in?' I asked.

He took a thoughtful moment before replying. 'Getting there,' he said with a slow smile.

He had a beautiful smile. The kind that catches you by surprise and forces you to smile along with it. 'Jack is lucky to have you. I know what it's like to have a father who doesn't want to be your father. It's cost me a lot of money in therapy. So really, if nothing else, you're saving him cash,' I mused.

'Daddy issues, eh?' he asked, shifting his body around to face me. 'On a scale of one to ten, how bad are we talking?'

'Oh, ten. He left when I was five and never came back.'

'Phone call on your birthday? Christmas?'

'Nope. Nothing.'

'And do you ever think about tracking him down?'

I screwed up my face. 'Absolutely not. If he wanted to contact me, he could. And he hasn't in twenty-five years, so . . . his loss.'

Leo shook his head. 'I'll never understand it. Never. Jack's dad didn't even show up to his birth. Didn't call to ask if it was a boy or a girl. Didn't call to see if Tessa was okay. Just completely checked out.'

'It sounds like he would have been a pretty shitty dad if he had stuck around. So maybe it's a good thing Jack got you instead.'

'Does it still hurt? That he left?'

'Sometimes. Kinda reinforced the idea that something was wrong with me. That men only existed in my life to leave me. I think that made my last break-up a little tougher. But I think I've done pretty well for myself, considering.'

'I'd agree with that.' He grinned at me, and a tiny surge of adrenaline coursed through me. My God, he was handsome, with his dark hair and his stubble and his honey-coloured eyes glistening. I couldn't help but stare back at him, and before

178

I knew it, I was once again wondering what would have happened if we hadn't been interrupted. Wondering how his body would have felt under me. Strong and tender.

I shook my head, refocusing my attention.

'Anyway. Back to you. How's Jack's mum going now?'

'Good and bad. She and Laney were incredibly close. She took her sister's death pretty hard, and there have been some pretty dark moments. I worry about her and Jack a lot. Worry that I've done the wrong thing by coming out here. Worry she won't cope. Worry that Jack will feel alone. I'm still figuring it all out, but I'm doing my best to be as present in his life as possible. Even from over here.'

'Can I see a photo of Laney? Is that a weird thing to ask?'

Leo reached over to his phone. 'Of course you can.' After twenty seconds or so of tapping and scrolling, he showed me the screen. There she was. Strawberry blonde hair and huge blue eyes. She was holding an enormous bunch of flowers and laughing.

'This was her twenty-ninth birthday. We had a glorious year of good health in between her two bouts of cancer. She loved peonies.'

'She's beautiful,' I said. And I meant it. She was stunning. The kind of stunning that you can't create. You just are. 'Tell me about the first time you saw her.'

I lay back on the bed, staring at the ceiling as Leo regaled me with stories of falling in love with Laney. What should have felt morbid instead felt entirely sacred. Almost magical. Listening to this wonderful man retell the story of his great love affair. He let me ask all the questions, and he answered

179

each with love, care, tears and laughter. Leo wasn't scared of my questions, and I wasn't scared of his tears.

I wondered if she was watching over us. And if she was, what she thought of me, lying there after what had just happened, asking about her.

The doorbell rang and soon enough we were sitting on the bed in our robes eating club sandwiches and fries. I dipped mine in ketchup, he dipped his in aioli. I was perfectly content.

We kept talking well into the night. I remembered the evening in London, and how I'd so desperately wanted this moment with him. To see him. To be seen by him. I wanted to tell him everything.

I texted May at about midnight to let her know I wouldn't be home that night, and without really even discussing it we switched off the lights and fell asleep next to each other, still in our robes. At one point in the night I woke to the weight of his hand resting on my shoulder. I rolled over to face him and it fell gently onto the pillow next to my head. The city lights peeking through the window illuminated the wedding band on his finger. I watched as it shone in the dark, centimetres from my face. I was grateful that nothing had happened that night. Grateful that, instead, I was finally getting the chance to really know him. Tears welled up in my eyes. Leo Billings was more than an office fling, and more than a one-night stand. Leo Billings might just be the best man I'd ever know.

11

Leo was already awake when I opened my eyes the next morning. He was freshly showered and quietly sipping on a coffee in the corner, looking out over the sun-soaked city below. I took him in for a moment, so well put together as always. A huge, loud yawn escaped my mouth, and he quickly put his coffee down and pivoted to observe me lying there staring at him, wrapped in the hotel duvet, which I had pulled up under my chin.

'Please don't tell me you've already been to the gym,' I groaned playfully.

He rolled his eyes and gave me a half-smile. 'I'm not *that* much of a nerd, just a shower and a coffee.'

We looked at each other in comfortable silence for another second or two. It occurred to me that this moment really should have been awkward. But it wasn't. Not one bit.

'Well, good morning,' I said eventually.

He grinned. 'Did you sleep okay?'

'Surprisingly, yes. You?'

'Well, once I found the hotel earplugs to drown out your snoring, the night improved.'

I shot up defensively. 'Take that back! I am not a snorer! I sleep silently and beautifully like a Disney princess and you know it!'

'I admit it. You're a regular sleeping beauty,' he replied, as he walked towards the Nespresso machine and popped a pod in. 'Black coffee okay?'

'Perfect,' I replied.

My eyes fell on my fuchsia mini dress, which at some point in the night I'd removed from under my robe. It was now folded on a bench with the Prada brogues placed neatly on the floor below. Definitely not how I had left them. Did this man have an irresponsible bone in his body?

Leo appeared at the edge of the bed, coffee in hand. He took a deep breath in, releasing it with a happy sigh as he handed me the mug. A smile broke out across my face and overflowed into a laugh.

'So, what do we do now, Alex York?'

'I suppose we need to talk marriage,' I mused.

His expression froze and he fell back onto the bed with a laugh. I propped myself up next to him, coffee in hand.

'Well, fuck. This whole thing is a plot twist I never, ever saw coming.' I paused. 'Did you?' I added seriously.

'Did I think I'd end up pouring my heart out to you over room service and then having a sleepover? Absolutely not!

I blame the whisky. And the tequila! I haven't let myself relax like that in—' he sighed '—years.'

I took a long sip of my coffee, holding his gaze. 'Usually I'd make fun of you for calling it a sleepover, but we did have a midnight feast and talk about our crushes, so I suppose it *was* a sleepover, in the traditional sense.' He smirked when I said the word 'crushes'. My God, I wanted to kiss him. But every fibre of my being was telling me it would be a bad idea. I certainly wasn't going to let my feelings for a man derail my career *twice* in one year.

'Better to dip out now while we're ahead, yeah?' I murmured.

He exhaled loudly. 'You're on the precipice of something huge. Just focus on that.'

I took another sip of coffee. 'Okay. Friends. No more weirdness. No avoiding each other. Let's just knuckle down and get this show pumping, yeah?'

'That sounds great.' I searched his face, hoping to catch a glimpse of hidden disappointment, but all I saw was relief.

'Now all that's left for me to do is rock a solo walk of shame through the hotel lobby wearing the world's least subtle dress,' I groaned playfully as I ordered an Uber.

He chuckled. 'I have a hoodie you can wear, if you like?'

'That would be perfect, thank you.'

The hoodie was buttery soft, and unbeknownst to Leo I had decided never to return it before I'd even put my arms in. He stared out the window to give me some privacy as I got changed, slipped my shoes on, grabbed my purse and walked towards the door. 'Bye, friend.' I called out to him across the room. 'Promise you won't go cold on me again?'

Leo crossed his arms and cocked his head as he looked back at me. 'Bye, friend. I promise.'

᎐᪲᎐᪲᎐᪲᎐᪲

Alex York, 9:30 am: I'm in an Uber. I may have woken up next to Leo this morning. No P in V.

Vanessa Blake, 10:00 am: HUH? I thought you guys weren't talking????

Alex York, 10:01 am: We weren't. Till we were. Last night was a whole thing. He admitted that he 'felt something' that night in London.

Vanessa Blake, 10:01 am: And what did you say?

Alex York, 10:02 am: That I felt it too.

Vanessa Blake, 10:02 am: And then?????

Alex York, 10:03 am: Well, we hugged. And then maybe almost kissed. And then his phone rang. And then we ended up just hanging out all night and talking. And then we fell asleep.

Vanessa Blake, 10:04 am: So what. What's going on? Do you like him or not?

Alex York, 10:05 am: How I feel is irrelevant. We work together. He's got a super complicated past. We both decided to just focus on the show. I'm not throwing away my career again over my feelings.

Vanessa Blake, 10:06 am: So you're just going to pretend last night didn't happen?

Alex York, 10:06 am: Yep.

Vanessa Blake, 10:07 am: Good plan (not!). You're surrounded by hot single pop stars all day and you choose to fall in love with your boss. Classic.

Alex York, 10:07 am: I haven't fallen for him!

Vanessa Blake, 10:08 am: . . .

Alex York, 10:08 am: ANYWAY! You seeing anyone?

Vanessa Blake, 10:09 am: I'm seeing everyone, baby! I will not be held back!

Alex York, 10:10 am: Why is it always so easy for you?

Vanessa Blake, 10:10 am: Because I'm not a romantic like you. And I never want to get married. Or have kids. Or do any of that boring shit.

Alex York, 10:11 am: And I do?

Vanessa Blake, 10:11 am: Yeah, babe. You do.

Alex York, 10:12 am: You're right. I totally do. Love you xxoxoxo

Vanessa Blake, 10:14 am: Ditto xoxooxo

᠁ᦙ᧞ᦙᦙᦙᦙᦙ

There's no guidebook on managing a professional working relationship with someone you keep having random moments of deep and slightly horny emotional connection with in hotel rooms. I would know, because I googled it.

While I knew that our decision to focus on the show was the safe, mature and ultimately correct one, it didn't stop me from zoning out every now and then and spending a couple of glorious minutes reliving our hotel encounter. I sometimes even found myself doing this while he was in the room, and a couple of times I got the distinct feeling that he was remembering exactly the same thing.

On the Monday after 'nothing happened', I gathered the team in a meeting room for our regular post-show debrief. This was usually the time we discussed what worked, what didn't, and started to get ahead on tomorrow's show. These meetings traditionally happened slowly while everyone flipped between sharing ideas and sharing funny memes. Occasionally we'd give up and all walk to Starbucks.

Leo and I were the first to arrive, and we watched as one by one the team appeared, clocked Leo's presence, looked at me with confusion, and hesitantly sat down. Tom walked in last, holding a coffee the size of his head in one hand and a croissant in the other. He held Leo's gaze, with a look I can only describe as dubious, and slowly sat down, still staring.

He dramatically cleared his throat, ensuring all eyes were on him as he slowly sat down.

I stood up. 'Well, my loves, we have a new addition to the show meeting today as you can see. Leo and I actually thought from here on out he would run these,' I announced confidently, mustering every bit of believability I could. 'I think it'll be great to have another set of ears and eyes on the show, especially someone with a bit of distance from it.'

Hushed silence fell across the room. This was going to be a hard sell. I looked at Leo nervously. He stood up to speak with an air of confidence that seemed as natural to him as breathing.

'I know what you're all thinking, and you're absolutely right. The show sounds great and no one needs the lame boss around—'

A couple of smiles broke out across the room. Leo continued.

'—and while I may be the lame boss, I've been doing this a long time, and in my experience the best teams aren't the ones that spend their whole lives at work in long meetings. They're the ones that have full, exciting lives to draw from when they walk into work every day before the sun comes up. So, from now on these meetings will be limited to thirty minutes, but they will be thirty glorious minutes where everyone brings their A-game. I then want to see every one of you out the door by 12:30 pm. Earlier, if possible. That's what you're paid for and you all have the ability to get everything you need done in that time frame. If you can't get it done, then we need to expand the team, not your hours. Does that make sense?'

Tom slurped loudly on his iced coffee, nodding. Everyone else nodded too.

As it turned out, I didn't love having Leo around just because he smelled good and gave me butterflies occasionally. I loved having him around because he was really fucking good at his job.

As he became more involved in the show day to day, it very soon became clear that within a work setting, he was the ultimate yin to my yang. He had the ability to put legs on my wild ideas, keeping things manageable without losing the magic. The thing that I'd feared most (him getting too involved) had actually turned out to be a godsend.

Leo put Georgia on a leadership fast-track program, teaming her up with a mentor—one of the veteran senior producers upstairs. Her confidence flourished, and her work went from excellent to extraordinary.

Ferg almost instantly started to look younger and healthier as a result of no longer sitting in his dark audio production suite until 3 pm every day, sustained by an apparently limitless supply of Maltesers and energy drinks.

It took me a full week to convince Tom I'd had neither a lobotomy nor sex with Leo, such was his shock and confusion at our new-found chumminess. But he soon believed that we'd simply 'buried the hatchet' and began to get on board with Leo's involvement. It helped that Leo made an extra effort to butter him up with a weekly Starbucks budget and a new part-time junior producer to go and fetch it. His name was Raj, and he was fresh out of radio school and eager to please. He worshipped the ground Tom walked on, which certainly didn't hurt.

The show sounded better than ever. Tom was happy, I was happy and we were having fun, which shone through on air. Every day it felt like we were making people's dreams come true. We sent a group of mums who'd been friends since high school to New York to see the Backstreet Boys, revelling in their joy as they called in to the show buzzed on Aperol from the back of a limousine en route to the concert. We broadcast from primary-school talent shows and made a local celebrity out of the school's maintenance guy, who pulled off an incredible rendition of 'Halo' by Beyoncé. Footage of his performance appeared on the news that night, much to his and his family's delight. It was those kinds of moments that filled me with the sort of satisfaction I'd never experienced at work before.

As per my initial pitch to Leo about the kind of show I wanted to make, every morning at 6 am we got on air with one job and one job only—to bring the joy. We broke the best new music and transported people back in time with the kinds of songs we'd all heard at the clubs back when we used fake IDs. Our DMs were flooded every day with fans of the show, thanking us for helping them transform their stressful mornings into something more manageable. It really felt like we were doing more than just entertaining people; we were reminding them of the joy that still existed in the world, even when bills were due, kids had colds and traffic was a killer.

After our hotel room encounter, Leo and I had a good two weeks of workplace bliss before trouble reared its ugly head in our perfect little radio paradise, and this particular brand of trouble had a name. Darren Chase.

Tom had been a little touchy all week. My sixth sense told me he was having some sort of boy issues, but as usual he was reluctant to share, so I stopped asking and decided just to ride the emotional wave until it was over. There was furious texting, random groaning and a package that arrived on his desk but remained unopened. I spent two days staring at it, desperate to pick away at the wrapping to see what was inside. Death glares ensued. He seemed resolved to let it sit there, like some sort of protest. Whatever this person had done had obviously pissed him off on a monumental level, as his packages were usually opened with much fanfare and sometimes even an Instagram live unboxing.

It was around midday on a Tuesday when Tom came screeching over to my desk, filled with the kind of rage that was generally saved for when somebody had opened a can of tuna or fried an egg on the sandwich press in the staff kitchen. He breathlessly sat down next to me, pulled out his phone and placed it down on the table facing me.

'Look what I just got sent!' he cried.

'Is this the reason you've been pissy all week?' I asked without looking up from my computer.

'Oh, I've put that on pause for now to focus on THIS. LOOK!' he shrieked.

There on his phone was a photo that had obviously been taken from very far away and possibly from behind a pot plant. It was grainy, but I could just about recognise Darren Chase's big fat head in the picture deep in conversation with two men. One I didn't recognise, and one whose face I knew straight away. It was none other than our *darling* CEO, Mark Holdsworth.

'What the hell is that peasant doing in a hotel lobby three blocks away, outside of work hours with the CEO?' Tom hissed. 'He's up to something, I just *know* he is.'

'When did this happen? Who took this?'

'Tristan, that hot tech who I'm convinced wants to marry me, was there last night on a date and snapped it for me. Oh and the other guy with them? It's Darren's manager.'

'You really do have spies in every corner of this joint.'

'Babe, I've even got one in the loading dock. Her name is Patty and she smells like Winnie Blues and Red Bull. I slipped her a double pass to P!nk and ever since then she's been my eyes in the basement. You can never know too much. Anyway, back to more pressing matters. Like what the hell the scumbag that is Darren Chase is cooking up.'

I squinted at the photo, pinching the screen to zoom in.

'What are they holding in their hands?'

'I'm pretty sure they're smoking cigars. Cigars! Old white men smoke cigars when they have something to celebrate!'

My stomach dropped. 'I'm sure there's an explanation for him being there that has nothing to do with us. Don't have a menty b just yet. AirDrop that photo to me and I'll chat to Leo to see what's going on.'

I pulled out my phone and shot off a text.

Where are you? Have you got a second?

Darren catching up with Mark wouldn't be completely out of the ordinary, but the fact that this meeting happened offsite, in the presence of Darren's manager, told me that Tom may be on to something. Managers only ever came when there was business to discuss.

My phone buzzed.

Just wrapping up with some clients upstairs. Back in ten. All good?

If anything was going on, Leo would know about it. And if I had reason to worry, then I knew he would fix it.

Yep! I'm at my desk. Come find me when you're back.

He hit me with the classic Leo thumbs-up emoji. I remembered how safe I'd felt that night in his hotel, waking in the dark to his hand resting on my shoulder, his gentle breath on my neck.

My moment of indulgence was interrupted by Tom's voice a couple of metres away, gossiping with a group of girls, no doubt gathering more intel.

I spent the next ten minutes obsessively clocking the elevator door, waiting for Leo. I wasn't sure whether I was checking it because I wanted to clear up the whole photo thing or because I just wanted to see him. When he did appear, he quickly scanned the room and rested his gaze on me just long enough to tilt his head slightly towards his office. I promptly stood up from my desk and followed him, mobile phone in hand.

'Everything okay?' he asked, closing his office door before dumping his briefcase, notebook and mobile phone on the desk and taking a seat. I passed my phone over, with the picture on full display.

'This is doing the rounds . . .'

Leo squinted his eyes, moving the phone closer to his face. 'When was this taken?'

'Last night at some hotel across town. The third guy is Darren's manager. Please tell me I'm crazy to be worried,' I pleaded.

He closed his eyes for a moment, rubbing the bridge of his nose with his index finger and thumb. 'I don't know what is happening in that photo, but I'm willing to bet it's nothing. Probably. I don't know.'

'That doesn't exactly fill me with confidence. Darren Chase is an absolute arsehole and I don't want him anywhere near me or my show.'

Leo looked puzzled. 'What do *you* think is going on?'

'I don't know. But we both know that Mark doesn't take me very seriously,' I said, collapsing into the seat across from him.

'Wait.' He sat up. 'You think he's coming after your job?'

'Yes! I absolutely do!'

'Right. Well, if it will make you feel better, I'll chat to Mark.'

I relaxed a little. 'Thanks. I appreciate it.'

He leaned back in his chair again, focusing his gaze on me once more. 'How are you going, anyway?'

'What do you mean?' I asked.

'You getting enough sleep? Not too stressed?'

'Do I sound like I'm tired and stressed on air?'

'No! You sound like you're finding your stride, enjoying yourself and making great radio. I'm just doing my due diligence here and making sure you're okay.'

'Due diligence as my boss? Or . . .?'

He narrowed his eyes cheekily at me. 'Or what?'

I pursed my lips and shrugged. A loaded silence hung in the air. His mouth twitched. Obviously flirting with him was a bad idea and outside the realms of our agreed working relationship, but sometimes I deserved a free pass to indulge in a little playfulness. Perhaps as a way of keeping some sort of a spark alive, just in case we ever wanted to reignite things later. Or maybe I was just a masochist who only ever wanted what I couldn't (or shouldn't) have.

Leo's phone rang (it rang every five minutes, so this was not entirely unexpected), which I took as my cue to go. 'You take it. I'm gonna head home.'

I swore I noticed a flicker of disappointment in his eyes as I got up to leave, before he snapped back into work mode and checked his phone. 'Thanks. I'll chat to Mark. I promise.'

His promise brought some relief. Because that was the thing about Leo. He always made everything okay.

Tom was waiting for me, impatiently tapping his fingers on my desk as though I were a schoolkid late for detention. 'Well?' he cried, exasperated.

'Leo doesn't think there's anything in it. He's going to investigate. He says not to worry.'

Tom made a 'hmmph' sound. I wondered if this was going to snap him out of his funk, or if we still had another week of huffing and puffing to endure.

'Well, that's good news, I suppose. Doesn't mean I'm not going to be giving Darren death stares at the Ivy Penthouse tomorrow night.'

'Ahh, fuck. I completely forgot about that.'

Every now and then, the record labels would organise intimate dinners where some of their up-and-coming artists would perform, usually alongside one of their big internationals, who'd be flown in for the event so everyone could get a good pic for their Instagram (and also to ensure that people would actually come). Tomorrow's big guest was a 'surprise', which could mean one of two things. The first? That it was going to be a letdown. The second? That the artist was so big they didn't want gatecrashers and therefore needed to keep it under wraps. I was hoping for the second.

There was always amazing food, too much booze and a healthy amount of disdain in the air between competing radio talent. Darren would no doubt appear with some Only Fans model on his arm, and I would spend the whole night avoiding him like the plague.

Tom put his hands on his hips. 'Well, you'd better unforget about it right now, Alex York, because I sure as hell am not going alone. And if you do go, you need to look amazing. Like, "don't fuck with me" amazing. Have you got something fierce to wear?'

I stared back at him with disgust.

'What am I talking about? Of course you have something fierce to wear. I'm sorry. I deserved that.'

I quickly texted my make-up artist lifeline, Carla, hoping she was somehow free at late notice.

What are the chances that you're free tomorrow to get me ready for 7 pm? I'll pay you double! Triple! Must look hot! Love you miss you love you!

Three dots appeared straight away.

Needed an excuse to avoid dinner with Nico's parents. It's a win-win. See you at six, amiga!

12

I resurrected the Versace heels I'd worn to the Tilly Roy interview in London, this time around pairing them with a black SKIMS short-sleeved bodysuit and high-waisted silver pants. Love her or hate her, Kimmy K knows how to snatch a waist and this baby was delivering tonight. Taking inspiration from the seventies heels, Carla gave me big hair that was somewhere between Tina Turner and Farrah Fawcett.

I texted a selfie to Tom. He 'liked' the pic and shot one back of his get-up seconds later. A classic all-black look with new Yeezy sneakers that would have set him back a week's wage. His dedication to monotone chic would one day bankrupt him, but he looked so good that I agreed it was worth possible homelessness.

Me in SKIMS and you in Yeezys. Love that for us. ETA 7:15 x

Me too. Slay, bitch x

I shared the lift up to the penthouse with Cameron Black, a music journalist who had been in the business for what felt like longer than I'd been alive. She wore black jeans and sneakers to every event, no matter the dress code, and no one ever batted an eyelid. The only thing she loved more than music was white wine, and she always had one happily cradled in her hand as she chatted away. If Cameron liked you, you were in. If she didn't like you, there was no way of coming in from the cold. Nobody knew more about the industry than her, and absolutely nothing went on that she didn't know about. She was cool as shit and had always been mates with Goldie Miller. While Goldie was older, they'd come up through the ranks at the same time and were the most high-profile females to ever do their jobs. It had bred a real toughness that was completely necessary and a huge part of the reason they'd both been so damn successful.

Legend had it that in the early nineties, when Cameron was starting out in print media and Instagram didn't exist, everyone assumed she was a man thanks to her androgynous name. This made for some amazing, now infamous stories from junkets where ageing rockers were somewhat flabbergasted when a twenty-year-old raven-haired Cameron walked in, notepad in hand, ready to get down to business. Legend also had it that she'd capitalised on this surprise more than once, although she never commented on the rumours of whirlwind romances over the years with lothario rock stars.

Cameron had always been indifferent to me, which I counted as a good thing. Then she'd sent me a note when I was announced as Goldie's replacement. It simply read 'Let it rip, Alex'. It had made me smile, and served as a timely reminder that my show's success was important not just for me and my team but also for all women who wanted to do what I do. It also gave me hope that her indifference had morphed into acceptance.

'Goldie would be very proud of those pants, Missy.' Cameron said as I stepped into the lift.

'I can think of no greater compliment!' I laughed. 'Don't suppose you've heard from her lately?'

Cameron shook her head. 'Not a peep. When she said she was going off-grid, I thought she meant for a week. But nothing. Radio silence. Pun intended.'

I frowned, puzzled. 'Well, I suppose it's her prerogative. But I could certainly do with a little Goldie wisdom.'

Cameron crossed her arms and faced me. 'Let me guess, not everyone is as delighted as we are about another solo female taking jobs away from the boys?'

I laughed, then half-groaned. 'That's kinda the vibe I'm getting. We'll see. I'm still trying to get to the bottom of it.'

Cameron reached out and put a hand on my shoulder. Her face was serious. 'Don't bother trying to get to the bottom of it, Alex. Because whatever is at the bottom of it will only disappoint you deeply. You gotta block it out. And do what you do best. Make fucking good radio and keep your self-respect intact. Nobody can argue with that. No journalist, no listener, no boss and certainly no pathetic, jealous radio host whose ego is so big he can't stand the idea that you earn more money than him in a better timeslot.' She paused. 'Got it?'

'Wow. You really do know everything that goes on,' I replied, both buoyed by her pep talk and dejected that she'd seemingly confirmed my suspicion.

'Chin up. Self-respect.' The elevator door opened. 'And now it's time for a wine. Enjoy yourself tonight, Alex. It's the best job in the world.'

And with that, Cameron disappeared into the dark, busy room.

I always expected that Darren would be pissed off about me getting the gig, I just didn't think he'd actually do something about it—especially so quickly—before I'd even had the chance to fail or succeed. I scanned the room for Tom, who I spotted texting furiously on his phone in the corner.

'You okay?' I asked as I approached.

He snapped his head up and put his phone in his pocket. 'Yep! Let's grab a drink. You look hot.'

We walked towards the bar, wading through the small crowd of industry figures, most of whom I knew by face only but waved at and greeted with much warmth and enthusiasm. There were two cocktails on offer, and I ordered the one with gin in it, not worrying about the rest of the ingredients. I'd never met a gin I didn't like.

The penthouse was filled with furniture covered in peach-coloured velvet, which actually looked less Playboy Mansion than you'd imagine, and it opened out into a courtyard outlined by palm trees and featuring a luxurious swimming pool. Knowing how rowdy these parties usually got, someone might or might not end up in the pool fully clothed, which was why a lifeguard sat in a chair by the pool—although, by the looks of him, he could very well be a male model hired for the evening to sit there, look buff and jump in after anyone who happened to fall in. I hoped he could actually swim.

We walked outside into the warm, balmy air and found two lounge chairs. I put my cocktail on the ground and cleared my throat, my eyes fixed on the moonlit pool.

'Anything you wanna talk about?'

Tom slowly sipped on his drink. 'Nope.'

I groaned internally. 'Okay. I'll ask again on Monday.'

'Answer will be the same.'

'I know.' I paused. 'You psycho—'

Our giggles were interrupted by some microphone feedback inside. I looked over to see Miles from the record label fiddling with something on a small stage in the corner. We quickly got up and made our way in, where a crowd was gathering.

'Thank you all for coming tonight to celebrate some of the talent that we're so excited about this year.'

I could tell straight away that he was hiding something, such was the barely suppressed energy pouring out of him. In the years I'd known him, I'd never seen him this buzzed.

'I know you're going to love the entertainment we've got in store for you. We've got three artists to introduce you to tonight—some of you may have heard of them and many of you won't have. But we thought we'd kick things off with a very last-minute surprise. In fact, I only knew this was happening this morning. Now, we usually wait till the end of the showcase to bring out our guest of honour, but tonight's guest is always the life of every party, so we figured we'd bring him out nice and early.' At this point I felt as though he was about to have an aneurysm from excitement.

I looked at Tom, confused. He was staring intently at the stage. I could see the cogs in his brain ticking.

'Our only request is that you don't put anything on social media for the next hour or so. As a favour to security, yeah?'

The mood of the crowd grew excited. Tom looked sideways at me, eyebrows raised. I narrowed my eyes, thinking.

It couldn't be. Surely he would have told us.

Miles looked over at me knowingly, as if I was in on the surprise. 'Please welcome to the stage the one and only . . . Finley! Fucking! *Stark*!'

The crowd around us erupted in shock, disbelief and euphoria.

'What the actual fuck?' Tom hissed at me as the entire room shook. 'Did you know about this?'

A loud cackle escaped my lungs. This was classic Finley 'fucking' Stark.

'I had no idea. I would have told you. But you know Finley . . . he gets off on surprises,' I replied, giggling as I finished off my drink.

Moments later Finley appeared on the stage, looking as beautiful and electric as ever. His auburn hair was pulled back off his face with a jade-coloured scarf (it looked like Hermès, but I couldn't be sure), and he wore a black button-up shirt that was more unbuttoned than buttoned. His arm tatts peeked out from beneath rolled up sleeves. I watched his eyes scan the room until they found us. He grinned at me, and then settled his eyes on Tom. I felt Tom tense up immediately.

'Well, don't you all look fucking fabulous tonight, my friends?'

The crowd cheered. Even the waitstaff had their phones out.

'I was in the studio in Madrid yesterday and I thought to myself . . . fuck it! And here I am. In my favourite city. With my favourite people.'

The room erupted again. Out of the corner of my eye I spotted Darren pushing his way to the front of the crowd. Once he got there, he started taking selfies.

'What a loser,' Tom spat. 'I hope Finley trips, falls on top of him and breaks his nose. But then again he's such a starfucker that he'd probably get off on it.'

'Whoa. That was bitchy, even for you, doll.' I laughed. 'Are you okay?'

Tom ran his hands down his shirt as if he was ironing out imaginary creases. 'Yep. Fine. Sorry, Darren just really irks me.'

Back on the stage, Finley continued to chat to the crowd of guests and staff, most of whom were staring at him the way you stare at someone while you imagine having sex with them. A look I may have been guilty of once or twice when Leo took the floor in work meetings. I glanced around before I could drift into another hotel daydream. I had wondered if Leo would make an appearance tonight. He was, of course, invited but these sorts of events weren't really up his alley. Schmoozing was not his style; his Instagram was non-existent and therefore he didn't need the penthouse pics. Plus, he'd been doing this long enough not to be lured by the promise of free alcohol. I imagined he was at his hotel reading a book and sipping on whisky. An oddly alluring image.

I shook the thoughts out of my head, refocusing my attention on the stage, where Miles was speaking again.

'Finley will perform a little later in the evening, but in the meantime, please find your seats. First course will be served in five minutes, and we'll kick off the first of our showcase artists.'

As the low buzz of excited conversation replaced Finley's vocals, I looked at Tom, bemused. He still seemed a little pissed off.

'I just don't know why he didn't tell us he was coming,' he said, almost under his breath.

I shrugged. It was clear that for whatever reason, he didn't find the 'surprise' as amusing as I did. But I'd given up trying to understand Tom's thought processes years ago and knew that after a couple of drinks he would find some other drama to focus his attention on.

'I'm just gonna go to the bathroom,' Tom said. 'I've already checked and we're sitting together. You go ahead.' He pointed towards a table at the front of the room. I headed to the bar for another cocktail en route. Once I got to my seat, I was surprised to see a place card for Tom to my right and one for Leo to my left. I didn't think this event was really his thing, and he hadn't mentioned that he'd be attending. I was beginning to scan the room to my right for Tom's return when I heard the chair next to me move. I swung around as Leo pulled it out. A tiny bolt of lightning shot through my chest. He was wearing a shirt almost identical to Finley's, albeit with all the buttons done up—and no silk headscarf, unsurprisingly.

'I didn't think I'd see you here!' I said, trying to conceal the slight buzz that his unexpected appearance had elicited inside me.

'Well, I wasn't going to come, but then they told me about the guest of honour so I thought I should make an appearance.'

'You knew?' I asked, wide-eyed and shocked.

'Perks of being the boss. I was sworn to secrecy.' He pretended to zip up his lips. 'I didn't mean to be so late though. Reckon I can steal you for five minutes? We need to chat.'

I raised my eyebrows. Before I knew it, he'd beckoned for me to follow him and led me to a private room off the main hallway towards the kitchen. He closed the door behind him.

'So, I got to the bottom of the Darren thing.'

My stomach dropped. Despite Cameron confirming my suspicions, I had still fully expected him to tell me that it wasn't even Darren in that photo, just some doppelganger who was meeting Mark to discuss new hand dryers in the bathrooms. I took a deep breath. 'Right. Continue.'

'It was Darren in the photo. With his manager. And Mark.'

I stiffened. 'Mm-hmm.'

'Mark said it was just a chat about Darren's future. Wouldn't go into details.'

'Right. Okay, well I suppose that could mean anything. It could have nothing to do with me, right?' I pleaded hopefully.

'Well, I don't know. But . . .' his voice trailed off.

'But what?'

'Mark *has* mentioned lately that he . . . wants to put some drama into the show. Some tension.'

I stiffened. 'Right.'

'That's what we were having a heated discussion over that day you saw us in the boardroom. He's never *loved* the idea of the show being too positive. Too . . .' He paused, hesitant. 'I'm trying to figure out a way to say this that doesn't make him sound like an arsehole. He doesn't want the show to be too . . .'

I had an inkling where this was going. 'Feminine?'

Leo exhaled and winced in the affirmative.

'That son of a bitch. He knows it's not 1955, right?'

'I know, Alex. But drama and tension are what get clicks, it's what gets attention. He can't seem to get past that.'

'So, what? He wants to bring Darren Chase into the show to just . . . disagree with everything I say and cause drama? As some sort of cheap entertainment?'

'It would appear so. Look, it was just something he mentioned. I'd know if he planned on making any decisions. But if Darren smells even a hint of a possibility that Mark will give him the gig, then we both know he's going to do everything he can to make it happen. Even if that means playing dirty, which is why I'm telling you this now. I just want you to be . . . prepared.'

'How could Mark do this? What about Goldie? What about what *she* wanted?'

'Well, nobody has heard from Goldie in weeks. We don't even know where she is. She's gone completely MIA. Maybe Mark sees this as his chance to pounce.'

I closed my eyes and took a couple of deep breaths, trying my best to stop the rage from taking over before I said something I regretted. I wanted to cry. And scream. And march into Mark's office and tell him to his face how entirely mediocre I found him. Of course, men in this industry were allowed to be mediocre. They could survive decades of mediocrity, collecting pay rises and respect along the way. Women, however? No, we had to be excellent. And if we weren't excellent immediately? See ya later.

I didn't want to cry in front of Leo. And I was scared that if I opened my eyes I wouldn't be able to stop myself. So instead, I kept them shut and asked to be left alone.

'How about I just sit here with you in silence for a minute or two?'

I took some slow, deep breaths. As I sat there, I imagined how many women in this company, this industry, this bloody universe, had sat down, closed their eyes and tried not to cry. How many had felt diminished and disrespected in their workplace, unable to let their anger out for fear of being labelled 'emotional' or 'dramatic'.

'Fuck this shit,' I said out loud, before clearing my throat and deciding that sadness was going to help nobody. After all, I wasn't sad. I was livid. I opened my eyes.

Leo stood and held out a hand to help me up. 'You look amazing, by the way.'

Another little jolt of excitement. I really wished my body didn't do that every time he paid me a compliment. I centred myself and looked at him squarely. 'I know. Now, let's not let Darren and Mark ruin a fun night of small talk with industry people whose names we don't remember.'

Leo threw his head back and laughed. 'Well, at least I have the excuse of not living here for the past decade.'

A minute later we were getting comfortable at our table. I poured myself and Leo a glass of pinot noir, but before I had the chance to put the bottle down I was interrupted by a familiar voice behind me.

'I'll have one of those too, thanks, Ms York.'

I swung around. Finley was beaming at me, Tom at his side. He enveloped me in a huge hug, kissing my hair before proceeding to pinch my cheeks as if I was a baby. 'Scooch over and make some room, will ya?'

Leo had already commandeered a chair that he wedged between Tom and my place settings at the table.

'Finley, this is Leo. He works with us.'

Finley looked at me like I was crazy. 'Mate, I'm a pop artist who lives in London. I know who fucking Leo Billings is. The King of Pulse! All right, mate? Good to see you again.'

Leo reached out across me and shook his hand. He was full of surprises.

'I actually met Leo in the bathroom at the BRITs a couple of years ago. I was about to walk out with my fly wide open. God knows the *Daily Mail* would have had some fun with that picture.'

Raucous laughter erupted around us. Unsurprisingly, the entire table was now listening to our conversation. I suppose that happens when you're one of the most famous people on Earth.

I rocked my chair back to make eye contact with Tom behind Finley, giving him a questioning look.

'He wanted to surprise us,' Tom whispered. 'Rock stars, am I right?'

He rolled his eyes, but I wasn't convinced. Ever since he'd first seen Finley, something had been off. What was going on? He motioned to Leo. 'I'm almost more surprised to see him here. Lucky I made you wear something fierce.'

I reached over and smacked him playfully. 'Shut up!' I whispered. 'He had intel on Darren. I'll fill you in later.'

Tom scrunched up his face in disgust.

We returned to the conversation to find Leo and Finley chatting away about streaming royalties.

'Trust Leo to somehow get you talking about business in three seconds flat,' I said cheekily.

Tom cleared his throat and mumbled something under his breath. While I didn't understand what he'd said, I knew it was offensive. Everything made sense moments later with the appearance of Darren Chase, who had slithered over from whatever rock he'd been hiding under.

'So, this is where all the cool kids are sitting, is it?' Darren said. I'd never noticed how shiny his face was up close. I wondered if it was Botox or sweat or both. 'Great to see you again, Finley! I haven't seen you since LA last year.'

Finley's face was completely blank. Silence hung in the air. It was clear Finley had no idea who Darren was. I hated Darren Chase but I hated awkward silences even more. I fiddled with my earrings, willing the moment to end. I was on the verge of saying something when Leo piped up.

'Great to see you, Darren!'

Finley hopped back into action. 'Yes, Darren—of course. How are ya, mate?'

The damage had already been done. It had been far too obvious to everyone at the table that Finley had no idea who Darren was. I wondered whether the whole situation had legitimately given Tom a hard-on. I subtly looked across to him, and he blew a chef's kiss into the air.

Once Darren had scurried away, Tom and I burst out into giggles.

'Leo, you are too nice for your own good,' Tom said.

'I have a feeling our friend here knows exactly who he was talking to,' Leo whispered loudly, raising his eyebrows towards Finley.

Finley grinned. 'Of course I know who Darren Chase is. I just think he's an absolute cockhead. And while I can't insult someone to their face, I can pretend I don't know who they are. When it comes to people like him, that's the worst insult of all.'

I wanted to lean over and kiss him on the mouth.

'He once said in a magazine article that he "discovered me". Sorry, what? Plus, a little birdie told me he disrespected you, York. So he can get in the bin.' He raised an eyebrow at Tom, who gave a triumphant look.

I remembered what Cameron had told me in the lift. To keep my eyes on the prize and block out the noise. To do what I do best. To maintain my self-respect. I wouldn't have to play dirty to defeat the Marks and Darrens of the world. Especially when I had backup like this.

Finley was soon whisked away, leaving me to fill in Tom on what Leo had told me. If he'd hated Darren before our conversation, then he hated him even more now.

'Can't you do something, Leo? Say something?' Tom pleaded.

'Believe me, I've made it more than clear to Mark that I think it's a bad idea. The best thing we can do now is to make sure the show rates. If there's one thing he can't argue with, it's numbers.'

Tom made a disgusted face. 'Ugh, boring.'

'The show will rate,' I declared. 'I know it will.'

'I agree,' said Leo, holding up his glass of pinot towards me. We clinked glasses and both took a sip, holding eye contact. Tom cleared his throat next to me, which was his way of saying he'd clocked the prolonged stare and he would be interrogating me about it later. But this time, I was resolute on being the one keeping a secret *from him* for a change.

As mains were served, Miles bounded up onto the stage and once again introduced the guest of honour. Finley rarely did acoustic sets anymore, so I was surprised when the lights dimmed and he reappeared with a guitar in hand and settled himself on a simple stool, looking out at the crowd as if he were at some sort of regional open mic night.

'Is that lobster I see?' He strained his eyes under the stage lights, trying to get a better look at the food. A couple of cheers rang out, confirming his suspicion. 'You know,' he continued, his eyes twinkling with laughter even as he adopted a soulful expression, 'there's a place in New York that serves up the best lobster mac 'n' cheese on the planet.' He was strumming the guitar as he mused aloud. 'I once ate nothing but their lobster mac 'n' cheese and drank nothing but French champagne for a whole weekend. I suppose I don't need to clarify that it was a hotel . . . and we didn't leave the bedroom.'

Cheers and whoops rang out from every direction. The crowd was loving it.

But for me it felt like time had slowed. All of a sudden it seemed blindingly obvious. Lobster mac 'n' cheese. French champagne. New York. Hotel. I peeked across to look at Tom, who was white as a ghost. He stared at the table in front of him, obviously aware that the penny had dropped. I had never felt so stupid in my life.

'Oh. My. Fucking. God,' I whispered slowly. 'You!'

Finley was playing by now, and under the cover of darkness Tom stood up and headed towards the lifts.

I sat there, frozen. Finley and Tom. Tom and Finley. They'd always been friends, but friends didn't spend the weekend holed up in an expensive hotel eating lobster mac 'n' cheese and drinking champagne. On my credit card. Also, that was eighteen months ago. How long had they been hiding this from me? And . . . why? My head was spinning. Finley continued to play, the blinding lights obscuring Tom's quick departure.

I got up to leave and felt a hand grab my arm, pulling me back to my seat.

Leo leaned in to whisper in my ear. 'Let him go. Just give him space.'

I stared back at him, confused.

'He obviously has his reasons for not telling you,' Leo said in a hushed voice.

What the hell was Leo talking about? Why was he acting like he knew what was going on? I stared back at him for a moment. His eyes were full of kindness. Compassion. Calm.

'You knew?' I asked.

He leaned in again. 'I saw them in the hotel corridor the night you all went out in London. I was on my way to your room to see if you'd come home.'

Oh my God. I couldn't believe the words that were coming out of his mouth.

'Do they know that you know?' I asked frantically.

Leo shook his head. 'Nope. I never mentioned it. Not my secret to tell, I suppose. I thought you might know. That's why I asked whether you and Finley were together. When you said you were all like family, I realised you didn't know.'

I couldn't believe Tom had never mentioned it. He'd carried on acting like the three of us were mates. The three musketeers. And then what? They were sneaking off behind my back and hooking up? I mean, I understood why they would want to keep it a secret from the world. But me? *That* I couldn't understand. Under the table, Leo reached across and softly placed a hand on my knee. I instantly felt steadied. I took some deep breaths and looked up at Finley, still there wooing the crowd, unaware that he'd inadvertently revealed to me whatever secret he and Tom had been keeping. I wondered if they were in love. If they were exclusive. I always knew Finley's sexuality was firmly in the 'ambiguous' column but, as far as I was aware, he'd hardly been celibate. My phone vibrated. It was Tom.

Come downstairs. I can explain.

I showed Leo.

'Just listen to what he has to say. And remember, Alex, it's not about you,' he said gently.

While it hurt to hear the truth spoken so bluntly, it was a truth that I needed to hear. I took a couple of calming breaths and made my way towards the lifts.

Tom was waiting for me on the street below. He was pacing up and down across the entrance, wringing his hands.

213

I quickened my step, opened my arms and enveloped him in the biggest hug I could muster. After a moment I pulled back and looked him in the eye. 'I love you, and you don't have to tell me anything you don't want to. But also—what the actual fuck?'

He took a step back, wrapping his arms around himself. 'I know. I'm sorry. I should have told you.'

'Are you guys like, together? Do you just have sex every now and then? What's going on? And why didn't you tell me? Don't you think you can trust me?' The questions were tumbling out of my mouth, but then I remembered Leo's advice. 'Sorry. This isn't about me. What I mean is . . . would you like to explain to me what's happening? If not, I understand. I'm just shocked. That's all.'

Tom took a deep breath. 'Well, obviously I fell in love with him the moment he walked into our studio for the first time. But who didn't, right?'

'This is true.' I nodded my head in serious agreement.

'But nothing happened until New York. He messaged me after the junket and suggested we have a drink at our hotel. One thing led to another. "Another" being . . . the greatest weekend of my life. At first I thought it was just a fling, but a month later we were still texting and calling. Remember that time I went to Bali to stay in that bougie villa my dad rented?'

My eyes lit up. 'With the infinity pool that overlooked the ocean? Yes, how could I forget.'

'Yeah, well, I wasn't there with my dad. In fact, pretty much every holiday I've taken since New York has been with Finley. I once flew to Japan on a long weekend to hang out with him

214

in Tokyo. I told you I was in the Blue Mountains with no phone reception.'

I was amazed. I shook my head in slow, giddy disbelief. 'You're like an international spy!'

'Pretty much.'

'So, are you together?'

'It's complicated. Finley *wants* us to be together. In fact, he *wants* to go public.'

'And you don't even want your best friend to know about your love life . . . let alone the entire world.'

He finally made eye contact, and there was a desperate fear in his eyes. 'Exactly. And what if his career tanks? I mean I know we all like to believe a gay man can still be a hetero sex symbol but . . . I don't want to be the reason people stop buying his records. Alex, I'm fucking petrified. I have no idea what to do! I cut things off between us for good last week and told him not to contact me anymore. What does he do? Hops on a fucking plane. He's insane!'

I stepped back towards him, took him into my arms and spoke softly into his ear. 'My darling. It doesn't sound like he's insane. It sounds to me like he's in love.'

I felt Tom nod. I rubbed his back and held him until I felt him relax. Behind him, I saw Leo walk tentatively towards us from the lifts.

I cleared my throat and stepped back, looking meaning-fully over Tom's shoulder at Leo as I said quietly, 'Leo knows, by the way. He saw you two in the hotel in London.'

Tom stiffened and his mouth dropped open. 'He did? And he didn't tell you?'

I shook my head.

'Wow. He really isn't the arsehole we thought he was, hey?'

I shook my head again.

Tom called out over his shoulder, 'The coast is clear, Leo, you can join the huddle! We're just discussing the fact that the hottest man on the planet is, for some bizarre reason, completely obsessed with me and how I'm so freaked out about the situation that I dumped him. Three times.'

I burst into laughter. Tom followed suit.

Leo looked relieved and amused as he reached us. 'Finley is looking for you both. I told him something work-related had come up and you had to take a call. I was very convincing.'

Tom put his hands together in the prayer position and bowed dramatically towards Leo like a very camp yogi. The three of us walked back towards the elevators, Tom and I holding hands and Leo following close behind.

'So what do I do now?' Tom asked as we waited for the doors to open.

I glanced back at Leo, hoping he had some wisdom to impart.

'Well, that depends, mate. Do you love him?'

Tears welled up in Tom's eyes. He looked at me, and then at Leo, and whispered, 'Yep.'

'But you're scared?'

'Terrified.'

'Well then, you have to choose. Love or fear.'

The elevator door opened, and for a moment or two none of us moved.

Love or fear. The question swirled around in my head.

And then, with a loud sigh, Tom took a step forwards. Leo and I followed his lead, and we headed back into the party.

After dessert, Finley and Tom slipped out separately, and the next musical act took to the stage: an artist called Stella I'd seen once before. She was still a teenager, with a Stevie Nicks-esque voice and the long blonde hair to match. She held a guitar that looked huge in her arms, and next to her on stage were a double bass and violin. She finished her first song to rapturous applause as I slipped away, still overwhelmed from the evening's revelations.

'Are you all right?' I heard Leo's voice behind me as I stepped out onto the deserted pool deck, the breeze cool on my face. Inside, Stella started singing another ballad.

I looked back. 'I just felt like some air, that's all. Care to join me?'

'I would, yes,' he replied, as he stepped towards me, his face softening into a smile. *That* smile.

I was sure nobody else had even noticed me slink out of the room, and yet here Leo was, appearing before me in the moonlight, making sure I was okay. I stared back at him, the darkness giving me silent permission to take him in a little more.

He reached a hand towards me. 'Care to dance?' he asked, his head slightly tilted to the side.

The invitation surprised me. If he was so sure that the universe had already intervened once to stop anything from happening between us, surely asking me to dance on a deserted pool deck underneath the stars was playing with fire.

And yet, I watched my hand reach out to grab his almost automatically, as he pulled me ever so gently towards him, his other hand on the small of my back. Exactly where it had been in the elevator in his hotel, the same jolt of energy running up my spine as had happened that night when his fingertips brushed against my skin.

'Thank you for your help tonight,' I said quietly, looking over his shoulder back towards the party.

'I'm always happy to help you, Alex. You know that,' he replied in a whisper, moving his head closer to mine, my chin tucking closer into his neck.

And that's the thing. I did know that he would always help. It was just how he was. I sighed in quiet agreement, unable to find the right words to say back. Instead, I did my best to breathe steadily as we swayed to the music. Once again, it seemed that Leo's guard was down and he was letting me in to some quiet moment of intimacy. I savoured every second, not wanting to speak for fear of ruining it.

'This is nice. It's been a long time since I've danced. With anybody,' Leo murmured wistfully.

I wondered if he was thinking about Laney, about the last time they danced together. Whether him pulling me close was his way of pretending she was still here.

'Do you miss her . . . all the time?' I asked tentatively.

He squeezed my hand. 'I do, yes. But that doesn't mean I'm sad or angry all the time. I was at first, but . . . she never would have wanted that.'

I gently squeezed his hand back, and a moment later he continued. 'I'm trying. To be happy again.'

Was he trying to tell me something? Or was he just answering my question honestly? I couldn't tell. 'You deserve to be happy again,' I replied.

He pulled his head back a little, his eyes searching my face for a moment before staring straight into my eyes.

'Alex . . .' His voice trembled.

'Yes?'

And then a loaded pause. I could tell he was holding his breath. Nervous. The music inside swelled, the sounds of violin filling the air. I closed my eyes, too unsure of where to look or what to do. When I opened them again, the look on his face was different. He was somewhere else. The moment had escaped us. He shrugged, almost apologetically.

Maybe I shouldn't have brought up Laney. Maybe I shouldn't have danced with him in the first place. We swayed in silence for another couple of minutes, and when the music stopped Leo gently led me back inside, where not a single soul had even noticed we'd been gone.

I stared out the window of the taxi home that night, replaying our conversation over and over, wondering what had happened, where things had gone wrong. Feeling silly for imagining that something was about to happen, that perhaps he was about to kiss me. Feeling even sillier for maybe really wanting him to.

13

I'd never seen Billy flustered in my life, but the bombshell I'd just dropped had certainly hit him for six.

'Let me get this straight. Finley Stark. Is coming here. For lunch. In five hours.'

I'd caught him halfway down the stairs at 7:30 am, before he'd even made his morning coffee.

'Yes. But you don't have to cook if it's too much pressure! We can totally order takeaway. It's just that restaurants are a little hard with him. We never end up lasting too long before things get hectic and we have to go, so we figured this way we could relax. Plus, he flies out first thing tomorrow morning so that really only leaves lunch.'

Eyes closed, Billy stroked his chin slowly. 'He's not vegan, is he?'

I shook my head. 'Nope. Eats all the animals.'

He paused another moment, before opening his eyes and resolutely checking the time on his wrist.

'Okay. The butcher opens in twenty-three minutes. Go and wake up your aunt. I'm gonna need my sous-chef.'

I fist pumped the air. 'You're the best! But please don't go to too much trouble.'

He had already disappeared into the kitchen. I headed upstairs to tell May, my head still spinning from last night's revelations. Finley was ecstatic that I finally knew, and while it was still all a bit too unbelievable to imagine, I was glad it was all out in the open. Tom and Finley. Finley and Tom. I wondered what other insane surprises the year had in store.

By the time 12.30 pm rolled around, the house was full of the kind of incredible smells that made my stomach do little flips with anticipation. Uncle Billy had most definitely gone to too much trouble, but watching him and May swan about the kitchen stealing cheeky kisses and giggling like teenagers made everything feel happy and right. It was a sunny day so May had set up the table in the backyard, surrounded by her gorgeous native bushes and with the calming sounds of her koi pond supplying a sublime soundtrack. It had to be perfect given that Tom would be incredibly self-conscious about rocking up with his 'boyfriend'. He'd be self-conscious even if his boyfriend wasn't Finley Stark. So this was pretty huge. There weren't many people on Earth I trusted more than May and Billy, but that didn't stop me from giving them both a ten-minute lecture about privacy and the importance of not mentioning our lunch guests, or their relationship, to a single soul outside of the house. May couldn't have given two shits about the fact that Finley was famous, she was just 'delighted that Tom had found a man'.

I peeked through the front window when I heard the car's engine come to a halt outside. Finley's security hopped out first and gave the street a cursory glance before he appeared from the back seat, skipping down the garden path to the front door carrying a case of Veuve. A single bottle would have been a nice touch, but hey—Finley was doing Finley. Tom followed close behind, and I watched as they reached the front door. Finley kissed him on the forehead. My heart skipped a beat, for no other reason than I truly wanted Tom to feel safe and loved. I hoped to God this would have a happy ending. For his sake.

By the time I made it to the front door, May was already embracing both boys, despite having never met Finley before, and despite him being one of the most famous humans on the planet. After kissing both of them on the cheek and giving Tom an extra squeeze and a wink, they came inside where Billy was putting the finishing touches on the ceviche. I pulled Finley in for a big hug, making eye contact with Tom over his shoulder. I mouthed the words 'this is crazy' to him with a huge grin. 'I know,' he mouthed back, with a grin just as big.

We feasted on stuffed peppers, cheesy potatoes, smoky barbecued pork and a whole roasted barramundi. Billy had lived in Peru in his younger years and had a soft spot for this kind of food, much to our delight. Finley had been there a handful of times on his travels, and the two swapped stories of their favourite adventures. I'd never seen Finley so relaxed, so off guard. He was like an entirely different person.

It occurred to me that he might actually be stoned.

'So, what's the plan, my darlings? How are you going to make this work?' May asked.

Oh God. She couldn't be stopped.

'Whoa, whoa, whoa, May. Let's not ruin a lovely lunch with details,' I quipped, with a faux joviality that sounded as forced as it felt. I mouthed the words 'sorry' to Tom, who shrugged, unbothered.

'That's a great question, May,' Finley said, wrapping one arm around Tom and popping a small piece of potato in his mouth. 'One that currently has no answers. But for now, I would love to just have a nice lunch with the people I love and pretend that life is easy.'

And with that, Billy popped another bottle of champagne and refilled our glasses.

'To pretending life is easy!' Billy sang out, glass in the air. And to that, we toasted, and laughed and cheered as he announced that it was time for dessert.

May followed him back into the kitchen and left the three of us sitting at the table, glasses in hand.

'You'll work it out, guys. I know you will,' I said with as much hope as I could muster.

Tom pulled out his phone, swivelled it around and showed me his calendar app, scrolling through the next six months, which had been colour-coded in the most Tom way possible. 'This morning we went through Finley's tour schedule from now till the end of the year and it looks like we can see each other once a month at a minimum. It means I can focus on the show, he can focus on the tour, and we'll always have the next visit locked in. So, for now, we're good.'

'And you're going to keep it under wraps?' I asked.

Finley cleared his throat. 'For now, yeah.' He looked at Tom, his eyes glistening, before fixing his gaze back on me. 'It means a lot that you know though, and I'm going to introduce him to Mum and Dad over FaceTime.'

I couldn't help but grin like a kid with an Xbox on Christmas morning. Tom was meeting the parents. It all still felt too unreal to be true.

'Will they be surprised?' I asked.

'What, that Tom is a guy?' Finley threw his head back and laughed. 'My mum asked me if I liked boys or girls before I turned thirteen.'

'And what did you tell her?'

'That I wasn't picky.'

We were all laughing now. Moments later I felt a tap on my shoulder. It was May, who whispered in my ear that I had a visitor. 'This time, I feel like I should be clear with you that it's Leo. And he said it's urgent.'

I felt a pang in my stomach straight away. I found Leo waiting for me at the front door, looking panicked.

'Leo. Is everything okay?'

'This morning I got a video call from Jack, he was in tears. I'm worried about Tessa. She's not getting out of bed. He had to miss school yesterday because there was nobody to take him. The poor kid looked terrified.'

I reached out and took his hand in mine gently. 'Oh, Leo, that's horrible.'

He squeezed my hand.

'You should go and be with them as soon as you can,' I said, trying to sound calm.

He sighed. 'I am. I'm on my way to the airport.'

I swallowed my disappointment. 'We'll all still be here when you get back. Please just do what you need to do.' I hesitated, and the silence felt heavy between us. 'I mean, obviously I'll miss you.'

A car horn rang out and I jumped with fright.

'Sorry, that's my taxi,' Leo said, looking towards the road and then back at me. 'I didn't want to just leave without a proper goodbye.'

My heart sank. I didn't know what a proper goodbye looked like between us. I didn't know whether to hug him. I didn't know what to do. So instead I just stood there, wanting desperately to slow the moment down. Wanting desperately for him to stay.

He leaned in and kissed me, ever so gently, on the left cheek. I breathed him in. He pulled his head back slightly so that it was just centimetres from my face, our lips so close they were almost touching.

'Safe travels, Leo. I hope everything is okay at home. I really do,' I whispered, unable to look him in the eyes.

He slowly pulled away. 'Thanks, Alex. We'll speak soon.'

I watched him walk down the garden path towards the taxi. I hated watching him leave, but he had to go. Because whatever magnetic pull seemed to be drawing me to him wasn't stronger than the pull of the promise he'd made to his family. And I could never expect it to be.

I had no claim on Leo. And he had no claim on me. We were colleagues, and nothing more. And although this was the way we had agreed it needed to be, I suddenly felt stupid for ever thinking it would be enough.

He gave me a quick nod as he hopped into the taxi, and a moment later he was gone. I wondered how long it would be until I saw him again.

I wondered if he'd ever come back.

Alone again, I looked across at the empty, quiet street before wiping the tears from my eyes.

'See, Alex? They always leave you,' I whispered as I gave myself a quick shake and headed back inside.

I sent Goldie a text before bed that night and watched as the message bubble turned from blue to green. I wondered if she'd thrown her mobile phone into the Mediterranean and decided that I wouldn't blame her if she had. I thought that with the time difference I might get a reply by the morning, but nothing came.

I couldn't sleep that night. My brain was in rumination overdrive, and no matter what I did I couldn't seem to make the thinking stop. I imagined Leo asleep on an aeroplane somewhere between Sydney and London in a dark cabin. Or maybe he was wide awake just like me? A month ago, I didn't want him anywhere near me or my radio show, and now I wondered how on earth we would cope without him.

At midnight, with no hint of sleep in sight, I rolled out my yoga mat in the dark and let my weary body make its way through the familiar poses. Before long, I felt my anxiety settle and my eyes grew heavy. I crawled back into bed, pulled the covers tight and drifted off into a peaceful sleep.

⸺ ıılııılı ⸺

'What do you *mean* he's gone to London?' Georgia demanded, her big brown eyes staring back at me, confused.

Ferg cracked his knuckles. 'When will he be back?'

I took a deep breath and tried to look as calm as possible. 'I don't know guys, sorry. We're still working out the logistics—he literally hasn't even landed yet. But he isn't ditching us. He'll just be helping from . . . afar.'

Georgia took a sharp breath. 'Right. Okay. Sorry. I didn't mean to freak out, he's just—'

'I know. He's amazing,' I replied warmly. Tom looked at me with one eyebrow raised. 'In the meantime, we just have to do our best to press on without him physically here. We can't drop the ball now.'

'Especially if our ratings suck tomorrow,' Tom quipped, snapping his head up to beckon Raj, his coffee gofer. 'We're gonna need double shots today, and maybe a couple of croissants.'

Raj jotted down the command on his phone.

I glared at Tom with as much effort as I could muster at 5:30 am. 'Our ratings will *not* suck.'

Our ratings better not suck. If I was going to have any chance with Mark Holdsworth, we'd need to have the numbers to back up my show. A drop would be catastrophic. It would give him the arsenal he needed to bring in Floggy McFloggerson, aka Darren Chase. But in all honesty, who didn't expect us to drop after Goldie's departure?

Radio shows rarely, if ever, hit double digits, and Goldie had left on an eleven. Talk about big shoes to fill (or, in her case, big diamanté-encrusted Roger Vivier loafers). Her listeners had tuned in for decades and I was the new kid on the block. Shit. I really wished Leo were here to say something smart and comforting.

I clapped my hands together. 'All right, kids, let's press on. Tom, what have you got for us?'

Tom stood up and found his usual spot in front of the whiteboard, snapping back into action. 'Okay, this week we're sponsored by McDonald's, so please avoid any mentions of Zinger burgers, Alex. I know this will be a challenge, but we all believe in you.'

Georgia stifled a giggle as I pretended to lick my lips.

'The new Sam Smith single dropped at midnight, it's a fucken banger. We've got it scheduled for 6:30 and 8. Gentle reminder of Sam's pronouns. We should have a chat with them early next week, so let's all have a think about some interesting angles. Next on the agenda . . . We had a complaint yesterday. Somebody actually called reception bitching about the *Game of Thrones* spoiler that you dropped last week—'

'The finale aired years ago! Surely there's some statute of limitations when it comes to show spoilers,' I retorted.

'Yeah, well, she also referred to you as Ashley York so I don't think she's a baked-on fan. And finally, we've got a couple of briefs that the sales team wanna go through after the show. Leo usually does these for us, but he's not here, so . . .'

I groaned. Figuring out ways to shoehorn brands into the show in a natural way was my least favourite part of making radio, but thankfully something Leo excelled in.

'I'll cop those meetings while he's away.' I looked over at Georgia. 'You can come too. It'll be like a bonding exercise!'

Georgia gave me a sarcastic thumbs up. As would anybody who'd ever spent an hour in a meeting with a group of money-hungry sales reps trying to convince you that having the show sponsored by a brand that sold incontinence products would be totally natural and not weird at all.

Ferg raised his hand. 'I have a question!'

'Babe, you can just yell over us, no need to raise your hand,' Tom said.

'Right. Uh, Leo usually goes through all the audio promos and podcast edits with me every afternoon. Who should I run them by now?'

Oh God. The first show without Leo hadn't even aired yet and I could already feel the wheels falling off in his absence. 'Tom, you can handle that. Unless you wanna do the sales meeting instead?'

Tom pretended to dry-retch. 'Just tell me when you need me, Ferg. I'll be there.'

With five minutes to go until we were live, Tom and I headed into the studio and settled into our spots. He began to fiddle with the desk.

'What the fuck?' he muttered to himself.

My head shot up like a meerkat. 'What's wrong?'

'The desk is dead . . .'

'What do you mean dead?'

Tom was furiously pressing buttons, pulling faders up and down. 'Like, there's no power. Nothing. Look!'

I glanced up at the clock. 'We're live in three minutes! Fuck.'

Tom shot out of his seat and opened the studio door. 'Georgia, can you see if any of the techs are in yet? Quickly!' he called, before frantically racing back inside. I'd never seen Tom so flustered, not even when Timothée Chalamet told him he had nice hair on a red carpet in Berlin.

Ferg appeared at the door. 'What's happening? Can I help?'

'The desk is dead. It can't be a power outage because the screens are working. I . . . I've got nothing,' Tom replied, as he indiscriminately banged on random buttons.

In a flash, Ferg was on his hands and knees, burrowing his way under the desk. Ten seconds later, we heard his voice calling out. 'Well there's the problem!'

'What? What's wrong?' Tom replied, bending down to see.

'The main power cord is gone. As in, someone's removed it.'

Tom looked at me, eyes wide. My jaw dropped.

'That fucking weasel!' Tom roared. 'I'm gonna murder him!'

'Calm down, doll, it could have been anyone. It could just be a harmless mistake. Take a breath. Accusations can wait,' I said hastily, feeling as murderous as he looked but doing my best to stay calm. Ferg raced into the other studio to procure a replacement cable. I looked at the clock. We had ninety seconds.

Ferg reappeared, cable in hand, and disappeared under the desk again. Tom motioned towards my chair, I hopped in, adjusted my microphone and stared at the clock: forty seconds; thirty seconds. The light on my microphone flicked on.

'Thank fuck!' Tom yelled as he madly adjusted levels on the desk. 'We're good.'

'Amazing work under there, Ferg,' I called out. He lifted his arm out to give me a thumbs up as the show intro began to play. If Tom was right about Darren attempting some sort of sabotage, he'd have to try a whole lot harder than that.

⠀⠀⠀⠀⠀⠀⠀⠀⠀⠀⠀⠀⠀⠀⣿⣿⠀

We had no way to prove that Darren was responsible for what had happened that morning. The CCTV was being upgraded, and with the office empty in the eight hours before our show, there weren't exactly any eyewitnesses. The perfect set-up for a crime, some might say. Confronting him about it would only give him immense satisfaction, so instead we all took an oath of silence and pretended nothing had happened.

By the time I left the office that day I was positively exhausted. I was starting to understand just how many annoying show-related decisions, meetings and queries Leo had been filtering on my behalf. The exhaustion, however, did nothing to help the insomnia that crept in the second I put my head down on the pillow that night.

I never sleep the night before ratings come out. Nobody does. Ordinarily, I'd buy shit online as a means of self-soothing, but May and Billy had taken it upon themselves to book me in to see their financial planner, so it felt like the wrong time for any big purchases. I wanted to walk in there and give off 'independent, financially secure businesswoman' vibes, not 'compulsive shopper who buys shoes and bags in lieu of therapy' vibes. I looked at my phone. It was 11 pm. My alarm was going to go off in five hours.

My groan was interrupted by vibration. I picked the phone back up to see a text from Leo.

Landed safe in London. Hope you're fast asleep and the pre-ratings insomnia hasn't got the best of you.

I sat up in the dark to type my reply.

Wide awake. How did you know?

Three dots appeared straight away.

I just do. Off to sleep. You'll be right.

I put my phone away and lay in the dark, willing myself to sleep.

The sleep only came after one tiny purchase. A pair of Tom Ford sunglasses I'd had my eye on that had finally gone on sale. It would have been rude not to buy them.

⸱⸱⸱⸱⸱⸱

Two days later, I sat outside Mark Holdsworth's office wishing I was dead. Or at least in a coma. Anything that involved lying down with my eyes closed. My underarms were wet, furiously trying to rid my body of the copious amounts of chablis I'd consumed twenty-four hours ago, and no matter how much I loosened my collar, I couldn't seem to get enough air in my lungs.

Having to get through a live radio show at 6 am with a white-wine hangover was bad. Having to then meet with the CEO of my company who was already trying to boot me off my own show seemed particularly cruel. I heard the sound of a glass clinking and opened my eyes as Victoria placed a glass of water and two paracetamol tablets on the coffee table next to me. I blinked at her in mute adoration and then swigged them both back, hoping to God it would be enough to get me through whatever awaited me on the other side of the mahogany door.

Unfortunately, the hangover wasn't born from celebration, but rather commiseration and perhaps lurking despair. This was an 'ahh, fuck, our ratings went down a point and the CEO will probably use this to bring my nemesis onto the show so we may as well eat lobster and drink white wine and pretend everything is fine' hangover. We had rated a ten, which was an impressive result, but it was still a point down from where Goldie had left off. If I'd been in my right mind, I would have abstained from the alcohol and spent the afternoon preparing my case ahead of my inevitable chat with Mark.

I was not in my right mind.

Leo had taken one week's personal leave, which made me think the situation in London was worse than he'd hoped. I'd texted him to see if he was okay and he hadn't replied, which filled me with an all-too-familiar panic. I hated feeling desperate, and yet once again it seemed that an important man in my life was destined to leave me. I wondered how long Tom would stick around before he too joined the club and scurried off to be with his famous boyfriend, leaving me alone with my shoes and my handbags in the spare room at Aunty May's house.

My sweaty distress was interrupted by Mark Holdsworth's voice booming out from his office, summoning me inside. I mouthed the words 'kill me now' as I peeled myself off the chair, catching Victoria's eyes as I did. She chuckled knowingly.

'Sit down, Alex,' Mark said, without taking his eyes off the computer screen.

Head held high, I placed my handbag on one of the chairs opposite him and took a seat in the other. After the rucksack debacle, this time around I'd opted for something a little more 'boss bitch'. A black leather Saint Laurent tote that was a little bit Parisian chic and a little bit dominatrix.

He continued to type for a moment or two. I stared at him, examining him as he worked. If his coldness was meant as some sort of tactic to put me in my place, it was not working. It made me want to reach over and punch him in the face. Not that I'd ever actually done that before, nor did I even know how to hold my fist to try. A moment or so later, he took off his glasses and swivelled his chair around to face me directly.

'So, Alex.'

'So, Mark.'

We stared at each other for a moment more. I wasn't sure whether he was expecting me to speak, and, if so, what he was expecting me to say. He was the one who had asked to see me, so as far as I was concerned I didn't have to say a thing. I let the silence hang in the air awkwardly, doggedly rapping Jay-Z lyrics to myself as a distraction until he cleared his throat.

'I suppose we should begin with yesterday's results. Not exactly what we'd hoped for, are they?' he said, finally.

I wondered who he meant by 'we'. Was he referring to the two of us? Or him and the other crusty old men on the board? I stared at him, confused, narrowing my eyes and crossing my legs to the other side.

'Well, I think everyone was bracing for worse, to be honest. A dip can only be expected in the circumstances, so I'm not taking it to heart. I *know* the show is great.'

'A show doesn't just need to be great,' he snapped. 'It needs to get people *talking*. Generate headlines. Weasel its way into the zeitgeist.' He paused. 'Do you think your particular brand of sunshine and flowers is going to do that, Alex?'

'Well, Goldie seems to think so. As does Leo.'

'Leo. Right.' He gave a loaded pause. 'Which brings me to the next point I'd like to discuss. I didn't just bring you in here to talk ratings.'

I ran my fingers through my hair, rubbing my temples. Mark swivelled his computer around. My stomach dropped as two photographs flashed up on his screen.

'Where did you get those?' I demanded, my voice panicked.

'Through a press contact,' he replied, not making eye contact. 'Luckily for you, they're not going to run them. But I think we can all agree it's not a good look.'

I stared at the images. The first, Leo and I walking into his hotel. The second, taken the next morning when I emerged wearing his hoodie. Mark was right. It wasn't a good look. I could feel the threat of tears stinging the corners of my eyes, a rising fury in my gut. I cleared my throat and gave my head a quick shake. I had to do everything in my power to remain calm in front of Mark.

'I'm not sure what you think is happening in those pictures, but you're mistaken. Leo and I have never been anything more than friends. Not that it's any of your business.'

Mark pushed his glasses further up his nose, and clasped his hands together in front of him. 'I assure you, Alex, it is absolutely my business. You know there are some people in this building who don't think you're up to the job. I'm not saying I'm one of them, I'm just saying that this sort of behaviour doesn't help when it comes to optics.'

I knew exactly who he meant by *some people.*

'Darren Chase has hated me since way before I got his dream gig. I wouldn't take much of what he says very seriously.'

'Well, Darren Chase isn't the one being photographed entering a hotel late at night with the head of the station!' he spat.

'No. He's too busy buttering *you* up over cigars and whisky!' I retorted, louder than I meant to.

Mark snorted. 'Well that's hardly illegal is it? Darren and I are friends; he's worked here for years.'

I couldn't believe the words that were coming out of his mouth. The blatant double standard.

'So, I've got nothing to worry about then? You won't be shoehorning Darren into my show?'

'Respectfully, Alex, I decide what's best for the show and the station, and if that means putting Darren in with you, then that's exactly what I'll do.' He raised a stern eyebrow, as if I were his teenage daughter and he was about to ground me for sneaking out and smoking ciggies in the park. 'Nothing is decided, but I suggest you take some time to get used to the idea.'

I stared back at him in disgust. It was official. Mark Holdsworth was a pig. Now that I knew this deep in my bones, I felt somewhat better about the fact that he had no faith in me to do this job. What do pigs know about good radio? Nothing. They spend all day prancing about in their own shit.

Unfortunately, this particular pig was still the CEO and therefore wielded total control over my career, which was not ideal, to say the least. Without saying a word, I collected my Saint Laurent tote and walked unhurriedly but purposefully towards the door. I wasn't scared of an old man who didn't know the difference between Travis Scott and Travis Barker.

Horrid CEO aside, everything about this felt off. I was hardly famous enough to be stalked by paparazzi. In any case, I certainly wasn't going to be bullied into submission over a couple of pictures. I had to prove Mark and Darren wrong. But first, I had to get in touch with Leo.

᎐ᥱ᎐᎐

Eight hours and four frantic texts later, my phone rang. I leaped at it when Leo's name appeared on the screen.

'Leo!'

'Hi. Sorry it's taken me so long to be in touch.' He sounded tired. Very tired.

'My God, don't apologise. Is . . . everything okay over there? How's Tessa?'

'She's better now than she was when I arrived. She misses her sister.'

'Of course she does. And how are you?'

There was a pause on the line. I could hear him breathing so I knew the line hadn't gone dead.

'I miss her sister too. But is everything okay there? What's going on?'

I hated the thought of adding to his misery. But I had to tell him about the meeting. He had to know about the photos.

'I had a meeting with Mark Holdsworth today.'

He didn't reply. I felt the knot in my stomach grow. 'Leo, someone took photos of us. Press, I think.'

He cleared his throat. 'Photos? Photos of what?'

I swallowed. 'Photos of us going into your hotel that night. Photos of me coming out the next morning. It looks bad.'

I heard a long sigh down the line. 'Right. Are you okay?'

My shoulders softened a little. 'I'm okay. It's all just a bit of a shock. Like, in what universe am I famous enough to be trailed by paparazzi? And Mark was a real pig about it. I think he wants to bring Darren in as co-host. He pretty much told me I don't deserve the job and this only proves it.'

'Hey, that's not true, Alex. You know you deserve it,' Leo said matter-of-factly.

Tears welled in my eyes. 'Thanks, Leo.' I inhaled and exhaled slowly, trying to steady myself. 'Oh, and the photos won't go public, in case you're worried about that.'

'I don't care about a couple of stupid photos, Alex. Not for my sake, anyway.'

'How long have you known Mark is the worst?' I asked.

'Honestly? From the moment I met him. I've tried my best to shield you from it. You need to just . . . try to put him out of your mind. Focus on the show. Keep doing what you do best. Make great radio. I'll clear things up with Mark.'

I exhaled, my breath catching.

'I'm sorry I can't be there, Alex,' he said, his voice soft.

'Please don't apologise. You're where you need to be,' I replied, willing myself to believe it.

'Have you told Tom?' Leo asked after a beat.

'No.' I sighed. 'He still doesn't even know we left the work party together that night. Let alone . . .' My voice trailed off as a flashback of Leo's face sleeping peacefully beside me took centre stage in my mind.

'Well, if you need to tell him, I'll understand. How is he, anyway?'

'Oh, counting down the seconds until his next jaunt. We've got that week of leave coming up in April, so he's off to see Finley in Singapore, I think. I still can't believe you knew all this time.'

'Well, if you ever need someone to keep a secret, you know who to call.'

The mere suggestion of a shared secret made my heart skip a tiny beat. I knew I should let him go, but I didn't want to say goodbye. After feeling so scared, so untethered, a two-minute phone call with Leo had brought me back down to earth and I wanted to hold on as long as I could.

'It's good to hear your voice, Leo.'

I could somehow hear him smile as he replied, 'It's good to hear yours too. I'm so sorry you've had a terrible week. But this will all blow over in time. I promise.'

I knew he was lying, but chose to believe him anyway. 'I hope so. Seeya, Leo.'

'Bye Alex.'

As soon as I hung up, I realised that there was one thing I'd forgotten to mention.

PS I'm seeing a financial planner tomorrow. Proud?

His reply came in the form of a single thumbs-up emoji.

14

As it so happened, May and Billy's financial planner was not the balding man in his sixties that I'd expected. Henry Tan had the skin of an eight-year-old child who'd never seen the sun, perfect teeth and the kind of black shiny hair for which I would gladly trade every pair of Gucci loafers I owned. Just before midday on Thursday, I found myself standing outside his office staring at him in his perfectly tailored suit, leather shoes that looked like they'd been polished thirteen seconds ago and bright smile. His put-togetherness was almost off-putting.

'I'm Henry, take a seat!' he said cheerfully as he held the door open and ushered me inside.

He was like a model. Not a hair out of place, not a scratch. Not a pimple or a blemish or even a hint of pigmentation. It was like he had a real-life Instagram filter on his skin.

The thought of somebody peeking into the state of my finances was as terrifying now as it was a month ago when May and Billy had first suggested it. I took a swig from my giant green water bottle, hoping that it would calm my nerves, spilling half of it down my front in the process.

'Shit,' I spluttered as I wiped down my chest. 'I'm not gonna lie, Henry, I'm a little nervous being here. I've had the worst week known to man, and drafted multiple emails this morning in an attempt to cancel this appointment, which I obviously never sent.'

He calmly undid the single button on his jacket as he sat down. 'You'd be surprised at how often I hear that.'

'Can I just ask . . . how does one even become a financial adviser?'

'Well, if I'm honest, I've always loved money. I had an investment portfolio by the time I was twelve, which I tracked hourly, to the point of obsession. Sounds pretty nerdy when I say it out loud, to be honest.' He chuckled. 'Anyway, my parents always pushed us towards law, which is what my very-smart and very-terrifying sister Miriam ended up doing. But finance turned out to be a better fit for me. I wish I'd figured it out before I'd finished my law degree, but hey.'

'Eek,' I mumbled through half-gritted teeth. 'Bet your mum was stoked!'

'She was delighted!' he said with a laugh. 'Oh, and—before I forget—I believe we have a mutual friend.'

'Do tell,' I said, my interest piqued.

'Georgia Jones. I'm pretty sure she works on your show?'

I smiled, relieved to have found some common ground with the man who was about to take a magnifying glass to my bank account. 'Yes, she does. I adore her! How do you know each other?'

'Her big brother is one of my best mates—in fact I think I had more family dinners with the Jones family than I did with my own family in high school.' Henry smiled and cleared his throat. 'But, I digress. We're here to talk about you, Alex. How can I help?'

I straightened in my chair and took another swig from my drink bottle, this time managing to get all of it in my mouth. 'Well. I'm horrendous with money. Which has been fine because I've always earned good money. But now I'm earning, well, really good money. And I want to know what to do with it. I need some semblance of control over what's coming in and going out. Does that make sense?'

Henry's expression was warm. 'It sure does. Have you ever seen a financial planner before?'

'Oh God, no. Nobody has ever really been across my finances. Not even me.'

'No worries. A couple of quick questions so I get an idea of what we're working with here. Do you currently have any investments?'

I squirmed in my chair. 'Define investments.'

'Something you've invested money into with the intention of making a profit.'

Had this been anyone else, I would have tried to argue that some of my better handbag purchases would surely appreciate over time, but I was too nervous to even try to plead my case. I shook my head.

'That's fine. And do you have any debts? Car loans? Credit card debt? Personal loans?'

I shook my head again. 'Nope, I'm a clean slate!'

'Savings?'

I spoke through gritted teeth. 'Ish?'

'Got it,' he replied without a hint of judgement as he typed notes into his computer.

'And how much rent do you pay?'

'None.' I sighed. At this point I figured that I might as well just lay it all out on the table. 'I live with my aunty and uncle. For free. But they've alluded to maybe wanting to downsize, aka kicking me out. Anyway, my only real expense is the stuff that I eat and wear. Unfortunately, I have very expensive taste. I know that my financial situation is out of the ordinary and that's why I'm here. So I don't completely fuck up my incredible luck. Also, my credit card recently declined. In front of people. All because I didn't even know what my limit was or how much I had spent. It was mortifying.'

Henry sat back in his chair and cocked his head as he looked back at me. 'I would argue that you're probably more than just lucky to be in the situation you're in, Alex. It's clear to me you've worked very hard and have a unique skill that, yes, luckily for you, pays well. So, let's call it a mixture of talent, hard work and luck. But all that is beside the point. I understand where you're coming from, and I'm happy you're here.'

I took another nervous swig of water.

He continued, 'I think we can put together a plan for you that allows you to do the things you love and buy the things that make you happy . . . within reason. But we can also plan for your future and use your money wisely. How does that sound?'

I could have cried with relief. 'Show me where to sign, Henry Tan.'

He laughed. 'If I give you some forms to fill out, what are the chances that you'll get them back to me within the week?'

'Slim to none, if I'm honest.'

'Okay. Well, I've got you here for another—' he checked his watch '—twenty-five minutes, so if you can handle the interrogation then I think together we can gather all the information I'll need to put together a little plan for you, which we can go over tomorrow, if you're free? Better to strike while the iron's hot.'

'You mean, strike before I lose interest, block your number and hit up Balenciaga instead?'

He smiled knowingly. 'Bingo.'

My shoulders relaxed a little. 'That sounds . . . great,' I replied. 'But I do have one request.'

He gave me a curious look. 'Shoot.'

'All this grown-up money stuff freaks me out enough without the fancy office and the formal vibe. The next time we catch up, can we do it somewhere casual? Somewhere I can have a drink, or at least some comfort fries?' I paused. 'Wait, that definitely sounded like I was asking you out on a date. Shit. See? I told you this stuff makes me nervous. I didn't mean—'

He smiled knowingly, raising a friendly hand to show me he understood. 'I get it, don't stress. We can absolutely catch up somewhere over greasy carbs if you'd prefer.'

'I'd definitely prefer.' I replied, relieved. 'Now, let's get stuck into this interrogation.'

Henry jumped into action, firing off questions and typing things into a giant and very scary-looking spreadsheet. It felt like one of those movie montages where the main character makes incredible progress and gives the audience a definitive sense that everything is going to be okay after all.

At 12:30 pm I walked out of his office with the kind of pure relief you feel after finally getting an overdue pap smear. I felt invincible.

To celebrate, I went straight to David Jones and bought myself a new pair of sneakers.

ılı·ıl|||ılı·

The sneakers, together with my new-found sense of financial liberation, certainly helped my mood the next day, but I still found myself slipping into moments of quiet panic as I relived my meeting with Mark. Tom, on the other hand, looked like he'd just had the best sex of his life (which admittedly would have had to have happened over FaceTime), such was the general aura of joy that surrounded him.

At approximately 6:35 am, while we were halfway through an in-depth discussion of Selena Gomez's most underrated bangers, I realised that the glow had nothing to do with sex. And everything to do with some brand-new bling. I quickly cut the chat short, threw to a song and practically climbed over the desk to examine it further.

'How long has that Cartier bracelet been on your wrist?' I squealed, holding his wrist up to the light.

Tom beamed. 'An hour and thirty-five minutes. It's about fucking time you noticed!'

We'd seen the bracelet at Harrod's during our London trip, but the £3000 price tag was far too prohibitive, no matter how much champagne we'd consumed on that fateful morning.

The white gold glistened under the studio lights. I was deeply jealous and utterly thrilled for him.

'It arrived via courier yesterday afternoon. I'm dead.'

'So far it would appear that boyfriends with infinite access to disposable cash are the best kind of boyfriends,' I mused wistfully.

Tom kept staring at the bracelet as he replied, 'Obviously this is the bit where I say something about how I'd love him even if he was poor. Blah blah blah.'

The last chorus of 'Hands to Myself' hit and I scampered back to my side of the studio, quickly plonked my headphones on and readjusted my microphone. Tom beamed back at me from across the desk as we both moved our heads rhythmically to the beat of the song.

I looked outside where Georgia, headset on, was cheerfully chatting away to one of the hundreds of callers who'd phoned in to request a song or beg for a prize. I leaned back and peeked through the glass to Ferg's studio as he tapped away at his giant computer screen, small figurines adorning every centimetre of his desk.

One thing was clear. Darren Chase didn't belong here, in our happy little studio.

I just had to think of a way to make Mark see that once and for all.

I remembered his words: 'It needs to get people talking.' But how could I 'get people talking' about my show without selling my soul completely?

After our last break that morning, Georgia knocked on the studio with a worried look on her face.

'Alex, can I grab you for five?' she asked, after I beckoned her inside.

Tom, visibly upset about being excluded, leaned in towards her. 'Is this about borrowing a tampon or are you two forming some sort of a secret alliance without me?'

'It's . . . about Darren. I think he's up to something.'

Tom turned off the desk, giving me a nod of assurance that the studio was now a cone of silence.

'Well, you'll never get him out of the studio now, so go for it,' I said. 'What's happened?'

Georgia pulled up a chair and sat between us at the desk. 'I just spoke to Sarah, the other senior producer on Darren's show. We're still mates, and she's a bit of a legend. Anyway, she overheard him on the phone to someone. He was whispering. Your name came up, which rang alarm bells.'

'Ugh.' Tom rolled his eyes. 'We all know he's been telling anyone who'll listen that he deserves to have Alex's job. It was probably just another one of his hangers-on having to listen to him bitch about our girl for the twentieth time that day.'

'Well, that's what Sarah thought at first too,' Georgia said. 'But then the next day, she was sitting with him at his desk working on the runsheet when his phone rang again. He shot up to take the call in a private room and . . . left his emails open.'

Tom gasped. 'Go on.'

'An email popped up from Mark Holdsworth. It was a reply. The subject line was "private".'

Tom was literally on the edge of his seat. 'For the love of God, please tell me she opened the fucking email.'

'She opened the fucking email,' Georgia confirmed, looking towards me sheepishly. 'And when she scrolled down she saw some images. Images that it would appear Darren had sent to him.'

I swallowed hard. 'Right.' I stared back at Georgia, the lack of surprise on my face signalling to her that I knew exactly which photos she was referring to.

'What photos? Alex, what's going on?' Tom spluttered, aware that I'd cottoned on to something he didn't know.

Heat rising in my chest, I sipped my coffee and did my best to relax. Then I took a deep breath and told Georgia and Tom the whole story.

'I *knew* something had gone down between you two the second you both waltzed into the show meeting that day like besties,' Tom announced as I brought them up to speed.

Georgia readjusted her ponytail. 'Yeah, and if I'm honest I think I always kinda assumed you two had at least pashed once or twice. I mean, I wasn't *that* surprised when Sarah told me about the photos.'

'Well, to clarify, nothing is going on and we haven't pashed,' I replied sternly. 'This show is my priority. Our priority. It's what we both agreed.' The last line slipped out a little less convincingly.

Georgia looked sideways at Tom, who rolled his eyes as if I'd just promised I was never going to buy another handbag.

'Anyway, none of that is even important right now. What's important is making sure Darren Chase doesn't succeed in his ridiculous quest to ruin my life.'

'Hear, hear,' Georgia agreed.

'You can bring Darren down *and* have sex with Leo you know. The two aren't, like, mutually exclusive,' Tom said under his breath. I shot him a death stare as Georgia sucked her lips in to stifle a laugh.

'Georgia, you know this guy better than we do. What's the game plan here? Do I confront him?'

She shook her head emphatically. 'No way, he thrives on confrontation. It's like oxygen to him.'

'Okay, yeah that makes sense. I guess for now we all just have to keep one eye open until we figure out what to do.'

'Does Leo know about the photos?' Tom asked.

'Uh-huh. Although he didn't seem too upset about them. He was more concerned about me,' I replied.

'Such a good quasi-boyfriend,' he said, sighing cheekily. I shot him another death stare.

⸻

The drama only continued later that day with Kai Scott, an Australian singer-songwriter who had won one of those reality singing contests and, unlike most winners, gone on to achieve moderate success. He had a particular brand of non-offensive acoustic suave, and while his music wasn't exactly lighting the world on fire, the songs sounded good on the radio and served as the perfect filler between Gaga bangers and nineties dance reboots.

Kai Scott was also incredibly good-looking, which probably helped.

He was scheduled to come on for a pre-recorded acoustic performance followed by a short interview, which was the kind of thing that happened at least twice a week on the show. This time, however, when Tom let the team know in our WIP later that morning that Kai had been locked in for the following week, it was hard to ignore the look on Georgia's face.

'All good, Georgia?' I asked casually.

'Yeah fine. But Kai Scott is a creep and, if it's fine with you, I'd rather not have anything to do with him.'

Not wanting to press her any further in front of the team, I made a mental note to chat to her later. 'Of course, doll. Tom, can you get us an extra set of hands?'

'Yep. I'll get that sorted,' he replied without a fuss.

When the meeting was over, I caught Georgia's eye and motioned towards the lift.

'Wanna go grab a coffee?' I asked.

Five minutes later we were sitting in a corner booth downstairs, me sipping on a piccolo while she nursed a soy chai.

'So. Kai. Wanna talk about it? Totally fine if not . . .'

She slurped her drink. 'Sure, I mean it wasn't some big traumatic event, but once someone shows you who they really are, you gotta believe them, right? He came in for an interview while I was working on the drive show. Commented on my tits in the elevator. I looked at Darren, expecting him to say something, and he just laughed.' Her tone was casual. I felt my skin begin to prickle.

'Georgia that . . . that's disgusting. I'm sorry.'

'Yeah. Kai Scott sucks. And so does Darren. In fact, that was the final straw. After months of dealing with his bullshit, it finally got personal. I realised that nobody was going to look out for me, so I had to look out for myself. Hence my decision to email you about a job. If you'd said no, I would have just quit. So I kinda felt like I had nothing to lose.'

'I understand, and I'm so glad you emailed me. Obviously Kai is now banned from the show for life. I'll make sure the label knows. And if you want to go to HR about this, I'll come with you. You deserve to feel safe at work.' I reached over and placed a hand on her forearm, giving a gentle squeeze.

'Honestly, I haven't got the energy. The last six months have been exhausting, and it finally feels like I'm settling into a job I love with a team I love.'

'Well, if you change your mind . . . please let me know. We've all got your back,' I replied, my heart racing with anger. 'How is simply existing as a woman still so fucking hard?' I exhaled slowly, willing myself to relax. 'You know that night we all went out and got smashed on tequila? The bartender shoved his hand up my skirt.'

Georgia sat forwards. 'The backward-cap guy? Are you kidding me?'

'No joke. Nobody saw except Leo, who was far more shocked that it had happened than I was.'

'That's the shitty thing,' Georgia cried out, exasperated. 'It's not that we're used to it. We just . . . aren't that shocked when it happens.'

'Bang on, babe. Bang on,' I replied.

We both stared off into the distance for a moment, interrupted only when a waitress appeared to check in on us. I ordered the bill, paid and walked back towards the office lift with one arm slung over Georgia's shoulder.

'Oh, I forgot to tell you. I met a friend of yours recently.'

'Oh yeah?'

'My new financial adviser.'

Georgia rolled her eyes as she turned her face towards me. 'Let me guess. Henry bloody Tan.'

'The one and only!' I replied dramatically.

'I knew him when he went through puberty. He didn't even have pimples back then. Infuriating!' she said with a mock scowl.

'If he wasn't so nice, I suppose I'd have to loathe him,' I replied.

⑈⑈⑈⑈⑈

'I'm beginning to understand why so many women hate men,' Tom mused as we took a walk in the sunshine after work that day.

'You're only just getting it? Now? Lucky you . . .'

'I can't believe I used to think Kai Scott was hot. What an absolute mole,' he hissed. Georgia had filled him in and Tom had promised to procure the relevant voodoo doll to truly channel his hatred.

'I know. Poor Georgia. I'm glad she felt comfortable enough to tell us.'

'What did the label say when you cancelled the Kai chat?'

'It was fine until I told them I wouldn't reschedule. I think that may have got some alarm bells ringing. I suppose we'll find out soon enough.'

It was Friday by now. I'd given Georgia the rest of the day off and organised a massage and facial at Venustus, an exorbitantly priced but worth every penny day spa in Paddington. The kind of place where Sydney's rich go for some pampering and a cheeky aura cleanse. After her horrid experience with Kai and Darren it was my way of letting her know we were looking out for her.

Tom and I continued walking in the afternoon sun, but I wasn't really listening to a word he was saying. I couldn't stop thinking about both my and Georgia's recent experiences with creepy men. How at the very least I'd had Leo there, but she'd felt as though she had nobody. That her best option was to find another job.

Our meandering had led us to the Botanic Gardens, and we chose a sunny spot on the perfectly manicured lawns to lie down and catch some rays. Men in suits had taken their shoes off and were lounging about eating sandwiches on the grass, while groups of old tourists took photos of each other posing next to flowers. I watched one of the gardeners slowly and carefully prune a rosebush and I thought that seemed like a relatively lovely way to spend a day at work.

My phone buzzed in my handbag, and I took it out to see an unknown number calling. I watched my screen until it had rung out, but then a second later the same number called again.

'Hello, this is Alex,' I answered, with a professional tone of voice that made Tom scrunch up his face.

'Alex. Mark Holdsworth. Got a second?'

I quickly sat up, mouthing the word 'Mark' to Tom, who flinched. He sat up and tapped his ear desperately. I put the phone on loudspeaker and held my hand out between us.

'Hi, Mark. What can I do for you?'

'This won't take long. You'll have Kai Scott on the show and that will be the end of things. You're getting involved in something you have no right to. Your opinion of someone has nothing to do with anything. I don't pay you to get on soapboxes and cause tensions with major record labels, compromising working relationships that have been in place for decades. Understand?'

Tom's eyes were open so wide they looked like they were about to burst out of his head. He mouthed a very long 'fuuuuuuuuuuuuuuck' in my direction.

'Right,' I responded, shock catching up with me.

'Don't bite the hand that feeds you, Alex. Trust me. Especially after the last conversation we had. Now, I've told Kai's management and label that you've had a change of heart, so I'll leave it up to you to reschedule on Monday. Air the interview. And move on. Got it?'

I swallowed my anger and shock and let out a quiet, obedient 'yep' before he hung up without saying goodbye.

'What the actual fuck just happened?' Tom gasped as I slowly put my phone down on the grass. 'He's, like, a total psycho! What's his problem? Did you poison his dog or something?'

I sat in silence for a moment, letting the conversation play out again in my mind. Things were becoming clearer and clearer with every second.

'You know what, darl?' I replied calmly. 'I'm beginning to think that he never believed I could do this at all.' I thought for a moment, and then continued, my voice more resolute. 'No, it's worse than that. I don't actually think he *planned* on letting me succeed.'

Moments ago I'd been thinking that Georgia was the powerless one, and now my own powerlessness was staring back at me.

'So . . . what are you going to do about it? Should we call Leo?' Tom asked.

'Leo's got his own shit to deal with. I think we're gonna have to figure this one out on our own,' I replied, in a tone that sounded as unconvincing as it felt.

⫻·⫻⫻⫻·

That night, I nursed a gin and tonic as I waited alone at Muggsy's, a Bondi burger joint that offered a menu of fried delicacies and free-poured cocktails. I had chosen a quiet, private booth at the rear of the restaurant and was feeling decidedly less nervous about seeing my financial planner than I had been the first time around. I shouldn't have been surprised that Henry lived locally—everyone here was either an influencer or worked in finance. May and Billy belonged to a revered group of locals who'd purchased fifty years ago when Sydney real estate was affordable and who were now sitting on properties worth upwards of five million dollars. Either way, I was glad to be close to home to ensure an early-ish night.

Henry waltzed in bang on 6 pm, wearing a light grey suit, white open-collar shirt and shoes that once again looked like they'd never been worn. This man was pristine.

'How many of those tailored suits do you own?' I teased as he got closer.

'What can I say?' he retorted happily as he sat down. 'Clothes maketh the man!'

He placed his phone and keys on the table and poured himself a glass of water.

'I feel the same way, obviously,' I said. 'You've seen my credit card bill.'

'I have indeed. Two big-ticket purchases at Miu Miu and $4000 in one year at MECCA.'

'Ah-haaaaah,' I exclaimed. 'No wonder they're so nice to me when I go in.'

'Also, I'm pretty sure you paid for Kim Kardashian's latest Bentley with the amount of SKIMS you've ordered online.'

'They're quality basics. I will not be judged,' I declared.

We both laughed, and a waitress approached. Henry politely asked for a Coke, quickly clocking my surprise and explaining that weeknights were for gymming, not drinking. He really did belong in Bondi.

There was a lightness and an ease about 'after hours Henry' that I hadn't expected. He'd been friendly at his office, but focused on the task at hand. This Henry was somebody I could easily see myself being mates with, even if he didn't drink on weeknights.

He took a quick sip of his Coke once it arrived, placed it on the table, sat back in his chair and rubbed his hands together. 'So has your terrible week improved?'

'I think it's somehow gotten worse,' I said. 'Long story short, the CEO of my company has it in for me, there's a truly horrible dude at work who's after my job, and I just found out one of the biggest pop stars in the country is a pig.'

'Oh God, I'm sorry to hear. That sounds horrible. Almost like working in law, which is, funnily enough, why I quit. It can be cut-throat like that. You should hear some of the stories my sister Miriam tells me about the corporate drama and back-stabbing. No thanks. I'm much happier with my spread-sheets. Hey, speaking of which—' He pulled his laptop out of his briefcase, opened the lid and began tapping away. 'Are you ready to hear how I plan on putting those dollars of yours to use?' Henry's eyes sparkled as he spoke.

I chuckled. 'Oh my God, you're almost drooling!'

'Well, I love money. And I love helping people make more of it! All I'll say is that, with a multi-year contract, this kind of income and no debt, you could pretty much be living wherever you want in this town. In a place you own.'

I scrunched up my nose. He stared back at me, and then shook his head in confusion. 'Why does that not *excite* you?'

'I don't know, Henry. I just like living with May and Billy. It feels safe. I'm happy there. I hate that I might have to leave.'

'Yeah, but what about when you, you know?' His face looked suggestive, cheeky.

'When I what?'

'When you want to bring someone home? Do you, like, leave a sock on the door or something?'

I scoffed. 'I don't plan on bringing anyone home ever again. I've decided that I'm married to my work. It makes me far happier and more satisfied than any man I've ever had in my bed.'

'Sounds to me like you haven't had the right man in your bed.'

I shook my head at him incredulously. 'Are you flirting with me, or are you like this with everyone?'

'I'm like this with everyone,' he said. 'But if you'd like me to flirt with you, then I can definitely switch lanes.'

Henry had taken me completely by surprise. I'd gone from thinking he was an old man, to a young and hot but potentially boring man, to a full-blown probable playboy. Today could not get any weirder.

I reeled in my hanging jaw and raised an amused eyebrow. 'Well, Henry, your confidence is impressive.'

He leaned forwards and placed his laptop on the table between us before relaxing back in his chair with his Coke and crossing his legs. 'It's not confidence, Alex. I just don't play games. I'm too old for that shit. I work in finance—I like black and white. I don't do grey areas. I reject the idea that we have to speak in some kind of code when it comes to sex and dating. I think we complicate things that don't necessarily have to be complicated.'

'Well, it always seems to be complicated for me.'

'Maybe that's *your* fault.'

'Impossible. I'm perfect. Anyway, I came to chat about my finances, not about my sex life.'

'Yeah, well, money is the only thing I love more than sex, so I'm happy to return to the spreadsheet,' he said as he leaned forwards and swivelled his laptop around to face me. 'I've done you up a very loose budget, all working towards this number.'

I stared at the large bold figure at the bottom of the page, confused. 'What's that number?'

'That's your house deposit.'

I continued to stare blankly at the number, and then at him. Then back at the screen. 'Is that *five* zeroes?'

'You've got it.'

If Tom had been here, he would have done a fake pass out at this point. I took a deep breath, shook my arms loose and let the number wash over me. Henry sensed my overwhelm.

'I knew that number might be a little daunting for you, so, check this out.' He drew my attention back to his laptop, where a new document was showing. It kinda looked like a collage. 'I made a visual representation of what three hundred grand looks like, based on designer bags, shoes and holidays that you've paid for in the last couple of years. I thought this might help contextualise it a little more.'

At this point, there was nothing left for me to do except laugh. I laughed so hard that I choked on my own saliva, which made me laugh more. Henry, delighted that his collage had worked, was beaming with pride.

Half an hour later I bade Henry farewell and took the scenic route home, walking along the water with Tilly Roy in my ears. Some people called her songs a 'guilty pleasure', but I've never believed in feeling guilty when it comes to music.

My mind settled on Leo, as it so often did lately when I was alone with my thoughts. I wondered if he was sad, and if being back in London with Jack and Tessa was making him have second thoughts about moving back to Australia. If he was more upset than he let on about those stupid photos. But most of all, perhaps selfishly, I wondered whether he missed me at all. Because, as I watched the waves crash lazily onto the shore, the sun setting over Bondi Beach, I couldn't escape the feeling that, however complicated things were between us, I was happier when he was close by. And right now, he couldn't be further away if he tried. I wondered if deep down this was more than just 'absence makes the heart grow fonder'.

I stopped walking and stared at the horizon. Did I just miss Leo? Or . . . did I love him?

Definitely not neither.

Possibly both.

I closed my eyes and let my mind run through a sort of picture show, like the kind of memory montage your iPhone creates for you for no reason. His bemusement as my credit card was declined at the bar, the way he fiddled with his ring the next day in Goldie's office. Him sipping whisky on the plane to London, his exasperation at my hungover state on that first morning. The way his eyes glistened with joy when he tasted Marco's tiramisu. The fire in his gaze as he stared through me that night. The night that changed everything. His tears as he stood in front of me weeks later, admitting that something had changed. His face when he slept peacefully beside me. Our tearful goodbye as he drove away in the taxi.

'Oh, shit,' I whispered to myself, finally. 'I think it's both.'

⊪⊪⊪⊪

Alex York, 8:34 pm: Van. I think I love him.

Vanessa Blake, 8:36 pm: Fuuuuuuuuuuuuuuuuuuuuck

15

May and Billy were away for the weekend on a winery trip in the Barossa Valley with Mum and some of their friends, which gave me the perfect opportunity for some much-needed thinking time. The invitation had been extended to me, and, while the thought of getting sloshed on white wine with a bunch of seventy-year-olds was surprisingly tempting, I needed to figure out what to do about the Mark Holdsworth/ Darren Chase/Kai Scott triangle of stress. There was only so long I could avoid the record label before Mark would be on my back again with more threats, and I knew this would only give Darren more ammunition to weasel his way in.

By Sunday afternoon, I still didn't have much of a plan. I was in the backyard hammock with my eyes closed and Leon Bridges in my ears, the volume down low enough for me to hear the back door open and slam shut. I quickly shot upright, took off my sunglasses and squinted across the yard, trying to make out the figure standing on the deck. At first

I thought I was imagining things. Maybe I'd been in the sun too long. Maybe all the SPF had leaked through to my brain. Or maybe it was real—maybe a bleary-eyed Leo Billings was standing in my backyard wearing boots, Levi's, a navy-blue tee and a half-smile.

I yanked out my AirPods, rolled from the hammock and walked towards him in a daze of shock and relief.

'The front door was unlocked. I tried ringing the doorbell,' he called out.

'Is it really you? Or is this some sort of mirage?' I exclaimed as I got closer.

'It's really me,' he said quietly as I hugged him. 'Hello again.'

I pulled back, taking him in. 'Honestly, I think I'd convinced myself I'd never see you again!'

I laughed, still shocked that he was physically in front of me again. His stubble had become more of a beard and, despite his obvious exhaustion, he looked as gorgeous as I remembered him. My mind was racing. Why was he here? And why hadn't he told me he was coming? I could barely wipe the excitement off my face. 'The beard suits you.' I chuckled and then noticed a hesitancy in his eyes that made me uneasy. 'Is something wrong?'

He led me to the outdoor lounge and sat down, gently encouraging me to do the same. My heart dropped. Leo had come home for a reason, and it wasn't for the happy reunion I had stupidly imagined.

'Leo, I'm scared. What's happened? Is everything in London okay? Are Jack and Tessa okay?'

'They're fine, Alex. They're doing great.' He closed his eyes for a moment. When he opened them again, he stared straight into mine and squeezed my hand. 'It's Goldie. She died.'

⑊⑊⑊

There was, of course, a reason Goldie Miller left when she did. And it was all part of her resolute decision to not let disease get the better of her. She would go on her own terms, while her mind was still her own. But first she would secure her successor and then gallivant through Europe with her lover one last time.

She took her final breath at a clinic in Switzerland with Joanie by her side as 'Bridge Over Troubled Water' serenaded her to sleep, just as she'd always planned. Everything had been part of her plan.

That afternoon, Leo and I sat for hours on the back porch, watching the sun slowly disappear into the horizon. There was nothing to say. So we simply sat, our silence sometimes punctuated by tears. I'd never known a world without Goldie Miller in it, and I had no desire to. She was the guiding light, the one who showed us all what was possible. Unbreakable. Unstoppable.

I couldn't let her down now.

'Have you got somewhere to stay tonight?' I asked Leo, finally breaking the contemplative silence.

He shook his head. 'No, actually. I came straight from the airport. I'll head to the hotel though. I'm practically family there.'

'Don't be silly,' I scoffed. 'May and Billy are away. There are five bedrooms in this house and the one next to mine is always made up for guests. Plus, you must be absolutely exhausted. Come on.' I stood up, beckoning him to follow, and he did so, grabbing his suitcase on the way back down the hallway. 'I'll get you a towel so you can have a nice hot shower.'

Leo rubbed his swollen eyes. 'Thanks, Alex. I'm sorry.'

I stopped and swung back to face him. 'For what?' I asked, confused.

'I'm sorry I haven't been here. And I'm sorry that I've come back with such shitty news. It's not exactly how I imagined our reunion would be.'

I wondered what he meant by 'our reunion', and what he'd imagined might have happened instead. Or if he was just so tired that the words weren't coming out properly. 'You don't have anything to apologise for, Leo. It means a lot that you came all this way to tell me.'

'So far only a handful of us know. Joanie is going to release a statement tomorrow morning.'

'Okay. Well, we can figure out a plan tomorrow. But first you need to get some sleep.'

It felt nice to take care of Leo. To be the one handling the situation for once. I stood at his door, towel in hand as he took off his boots, neatly placing them against the wall. 'I'll shower upstairs. Your bathroom is the last door on the left as you walk down the hall. All my toiletries are in the top drawer— help yourself.'

'Thanks,' Leo said as he sat, exhausted, on the edge of the bed.

'Let me just grab my toothbrush and then the bathroom's all yours,' I replied as I left.

My head spun as I hopped in the shower upstairs. Leo was back. Goldie was gone. Everything had changed. I leaned my head against the tiles and let the hot water run down my hair and onto my back. By the time I got out, my skin was warm and pink. I wrapped myself in a towel, tied up my wet hair, brushed my teeth and switched off the bathroom light. I heard footsteps in the hallway as I made my way downstairs and I froze, hoping to let Leo pass without seeing me. A moment later he appeared, catching me in his peripheral vision. He looked up, one hand holding the towel around his waist.

'Sorry,' I murmured quietly in the dark, trying desperately not to stare at his broad, wet chest.

He gazed back at me, silent. I wondered if he knew how good he looked half-naked.

'Did you find everything you need?' I asked.

Leo nodded, his eyes boring deep into mine, a drop of water falling from the tip of his nose. He wiped his free hand across his face and combed his hair back behind his ear. 'I did. Thank you,' he replied softly.

My heart was racing. Every part of me wanted to run down the stairs and throw myself into his arms, to have him carry me into the bedroom and finish what we'd started all those months ago. To give myself completely to him, in the desperate hope that maybe there was space enough in his heart for me too.

But he hadn't come back for me. He'd come back for Goldie, and I didn't even know if he planned to stay. In fact, when it came to Leo's feelings, everything was a mystery. All I knew for sure was that my heart wouldn't recover from any more rejection. I imagined his face responding to the news that I *might* be in love with him—the confusion, the awkwardness, the pity. Ew. No, thank you.

I carefully took a step down the staircase, tightening the towel around me. The silence was torturous.

'I'm glad you're home, Leo,' I said finally as I broke my gaze from his and slowly made my way down the hallway towards my room, part of me silently begging him to stop me.

'Me too, Alex. Goodnight,' I heard him reply.

I closed the door and lay on top of my bed in my towel. Outside, I heard his footsteps approach, and then stop. I sat up, straining my ears towards the hallway, frozen, knowing he was standing just outside my door. I stared at the door handle, willing it to turn. Willing this to not be the last time I'd see him tonight. And then, the sound of two more footsteps followed by his door gently closing.

'It'll pass,' I whispered to myself. 'It'll pass.'

࿊࿊࿊

My heart was in my chest the next morning as Leo and I made our way to my car in the dark. I dialled Tom's number before we got in. He answered straight away.

'Please tell me you're not calling in sick, I'm too hungover to cover for you today,' he groaned.

'No, don't worry, I'm on my way in. I just wanted to let you know that Leo is back and I'm grabbing him on the way.'

'What?'

'I know. I just need you to let the team know and not make a big deal of it when we walk in, okay?'

'Babe, you sound worried. Is everything all right?'

'Yes and no. I'll see you soon. Love you.' I hung up before he could reply. I didn't want to tell him about Goldie over the phone, and I would see him in a couple of minutes. It could wait.

'Oh, there's one more thing I forgot to tell you,' I said, my eyes on the road. 'I banned Kai Scott from the show for some problematic behaviour towards Georgia. Mark found out and hit the roof. Says I *compromised our relationship with the record label* or some shit.'

Leo quietly groaned. 'Yeah, him and the label CEO are mates. They go way back. Like, high-school days. I believe their families do an annual yacht trip to Turkey.'

'Of course they fucking do.' I rolled my eyes as I pulled into the carpark. 'That explains why he was so angry. Anyway, tomorrow's problem.'

Silence hung in the air as we gathered the team in Leo's office. Judging by the look of unease on everyone's faces, they could tell the news wasn't going to be good.

Leo switched into caring boss mode in an instant, announcing the news without beating around the bush. He was calm and direct. Goldie was gone. And now it was up to us to do her proud.

'When will it be announced?' Georgia asked, misty-eyed.

'Joanie will release a statement to the media at 9 am this morning; until then we'll have to carry on as usual. I know it'll be weird, but it's imperative that it stays under wraps until then, out of respect for Goldie's family. We'll announce it during our final break.' Leo replied calmly.

'Right. Got it.' Then she looked back up at him. 'Are you okay? I know you were close. I'm . . . I'm sorry for your loss.'

Leo swallowed. 'Thanks, Georgia. We were close. I was lucky in that respect.'

Georgia stood up and without another word wrapped her arms around Leo. Tom stood up and did the same. Before long, the whole team was wrapped up in one giant bear hug, with Leo at the centre.

I loved us. I loved us all so damn much. And it was all thanks to Goldie. She had brought us all together.

Leo was right, it was strange trying to get through three hours of breakfast radio with a knot in my stomach and a lump in my throat, constantly staring at the clock both wishing it was 9 am and yet also dreading it entirely.

At 9:03 am, Leo gave me the nod. The statement had been released. It was time to break the news. I watched as the team walked into the studio: Leo sitting on the chair next to me, Georgia leaning against the glass, Ferg's big brotherly arm around her as she nestled into his shoulder. I listened to the last ad play, making eye contact with everyone. I cleared my throat and gave my body a quick shake, my gaze finally resting across the desk on Tom, who counted me in and then gave me the signal. In front of me was a piece of paper with some words scribbled down. I picked it up with my left hand, which was trembling.

'Good morning, Sydney. It's 9:03 am and we have some news to share with you all. It's news I don't want to share because . . . it's news I wish wasn't true.'

I took a deep breath and looked down at the paper.

'A statement was released to the media just minutes ago announcing that Goldie Miller, my eternal hero, has left us forever—no doubt riding on a wave of gold and glitter to whatever world awaited her. As with everything in her life, Goldie faced death on her own terms. None of us even knew she was sick. For decades, she so generously shared her life with all of us, and I'm so glad that in the end she and Joanie were able to enjoy their own private world, one they'd built over a lifetime of loving each other. I'm not sure many of us will ever get to experience a love like theirs.'

The words were coming out slowly, punctuated with deep breaths and a voice that sometimes shook, but I was getting through it, looking to Tom for a reassuring nod as I continued.

'Goldie was completely fearless. She walked her own path, clearing the way for so many of us to follow. If I'm completely honest, I'm only just starting to understand how hard this road is to navigate, and I wish I had an ounce of her strength to help me.

'There will be plenty of time for us all to celebrate her incredible achievements. But for now, we just want to say that we will miss you, Goldie—' my voice cracked, hot tears escaping down my cheeks '—we will love you forever. And we will always, always try to make you proud.'

I stood back from the microphone as Tom pressed play on the track. The piano intro began. 'Bridge Over Troubled Water' filled the studio. Leo closed his eyes, wiping away a tear. Over his shoulder, through the glass I could see Darren Chase staring right at me. He was smiling. He looked . . . triumphant. I excused myself from the studio and marched straight over to him, hot angry adrenaline coursing through every part of my body.

'Such *tragic* news,' Darren cooed in a way that was so over-acted he could have been delivering a line on *The Bold and the Beautiful*.

'You're pathetic, Darren. Absolutely pathetic,' I spat.

'Oh spare me, Alex.' He rolled his eyes. 'You're just sad that your gravy train has come to an end.'

'My . . . gravy train?'

'Yes. Goldie is the only reason you got this job in the first place.' His voice was growing louder. 'The job everybody knows should have been mine. Too bad I'm not a *girl*. Let me guess, the two of you planned it over a mani-pedi? A champagne brunch?'

'Well,' I replied, almost in a whisper, 'I'm glad you finally had the guts to admit out loud that you're jealous.'

'I'm not jealous, Alex,' he scoffed. 'I'm fucking furious.'

'Furious enough to sabotage my studio? Furious enough to hire a photographer to follow me? And take private images of me? So you could pass them on to Mark in some sort of fucked up attempt to make me look bad?'

'You made yourself look bad, Alex. And Mark doesn't want you here either. He was delighted when I showed him the photos. Our plan was always to oust you—we just didn't think you'd make it so easy.'

Another kick in the gut. I never even stood a chance.

He said nothing now. He simply stared at me, his eyes full of fury. His face growing redder by the second. I relaxed my shoulders, took a deep breath in and out, and asked myself what Goldie would do. Goldie wouldn't yell or scream. She would simply speak the truth. Loud, clear and calm.

'Goldie was ten times the broadcaster you'll ever be, Darren. And yeah, she wanted me to have this job. Don't you ever wonder why? Because she knew that this business is full of men like you who will do everything they can to keep women like me in an airless box. You benefit from a boys' club that keeps you in power, somehow thinking that power is your God-given right. And the second the shoe is on the other foot, you lose your tiny mind over it and cry foul. Sure, Goldie gave me a leg-up, but she did it because she sure as hell knew nobody else was going to. She knew I'd have to prove myself to mediocre men a hundred times over in order to be taken seriously. Do you have any idea how exhausting that is? I know you don't think I deserve this job. But Goldie did. And her opinion means a whole lot more than yours. Because everybody loved her. Everybody respected her. Everybody knew she was the best to ever do it. And what do people think about you, Darren? They all think you're a sad, jealous little pest.'

'Yeah well. At least I'm not fucking my boss,' Darren spat back, every word laced with venom.

I gasped. He'd really said it. Out loud.

'Let me get one thing clear, Darren,' I said, pointing at him. 'Not that it's any of your business. I never, ever—'

Before I could finish my sentence, he was on the floor. I whipped my head around to see Leo standing beside me, his fist still clenched. Darren groaned.

'Leo, what the fuck did you just do?' I stuttered.

He shrugged. 'He deserved it.'

The room erupted in loud cheers. I'd been so wrapped up in the confrontation that I'd failed to notice the crowd of people gathering to see the action, and now every single person was clapping—some even had their phones out. I grabbed Leo's hand and led him back towards the safety of the studio.

'I'm pretty sure I'm gonna get fired for that,' he said under his breath as we walked.

I stifled a laugh. 'Was it worth it?'

'Abso-fucking-lutely,' he replied, squeezing my hand.

ılı₊ıl₊ılı₊

Vanessa Blake, 8:00 pm: I can't believe Leo punched him. What a legend. Also . . . if he gets fired he technically won't be your boss right? And the two of you can admit you love each other and have babies?

Alex York, 8:02 pm: He doesn't love me. If he loved me . . . he would have told me by now. Or at least . . . given me some sort of an indication. Which he hasn't.

Vanessa Blake, 8:03 pm: Why can't you just . . . put it out there? Ask him?

Alex York, 8:03 pm: There's only so much rejection a gal can take in one lifetime . . .

Vanessa Blake, 8:04 pm: You two will figure it out.

Alex York, 8:05 pm: Maybe. Or maybe he'll move back to London next week and I'll never hear from him ever again. Anyway. All good with you?

Vanessa Blake, 8:06 pm: Yep. Starting to get itchy feet. The next adventure might be calling . . .

Alex York, 8:07 pm: Please tell me the next adventure lies somewhere closer to me?

Vanessa Blake, 8:10 pm: Galapagos!

Alex York, 8:10 pm: Where the fuck is the Galapagos?

Alex York, 8:11 pm: I just googled it. Ecuador. Great. Thanks. Legend.

Vanessa Blake, 8:12 pm: Gotta run. Adios!

꜊꜊꜊꜊

With our April break only a week away, it was decided that we would all begin our holidays early, with a plan to reconvene once everything had calmed down and HR had decided where to start. Leo was put on leave in the meantime, although he didn't seem altogether that upset at the prospect of losing his job. I suppose it made sense. He'd never loved it like I had.

Henry put me in touch with his sister, Miriam, a contract lawyer who was as expensive as she was terrifying, but I would have paid any amount of money to be removed from the back and forth with Mark and his cronies, should it come to that. I forwarded both her and Henry a copy of my contract and they got to work.

On Tuesday evening, Billy made a lamb roast and Tom joined us for dinner. Leo was still in the spare room, which felt both completely normal and completely strange. I was glad the bathroom had a lock, as I wouldn't have put it past May to accidentally walk in on him in the shower just to cop a good look. She was positively giddy over his presence in the house, and she waited on him hand and foot, which he didn't seem to mind. More than anything, it hit home that Henry was right—I really needed to get my own place.

We were all on our second plate of lamb when Tom's phone buzzed, the word LISA popping up on his screen.

'Who's Lisa?' I asked, confused.

'It's Finley's code name. The perils of dating a celebrity! You won't find his name mentioned once on this entire iPhone. I even delete work emails that mention him. God knows where I'll accidentally leave this thing one day. Let's send him a pic; say cheese!' he cooed as he snapped one of the three of us at the table, my mouth full of lamb.

Tom took a moment to read Finley's reply, before slowly putting down his phone, clasping his hands in the prayer position, closing his eyes and grinning. When he opened them again, he looked as if he'd just had fourteen Red Bulls and a line of coke. 'Finley's promo tour in Singapore was cancelled this week. He wants to know if we want to meet him. He won't say where, but it's all booked. And none of us has work, so all you have to do is say yes. PLEASE say yes!'

'Oh, wow,' Leo said, shocked. 'You guys should definitely go,' he added, cutting another potato and popping into his mouth.

Tom gasped, offended. 'I said WE. As in YOU too! Come on, it will be so fun, we'll be like the awesome foursome! And I don't mean like the lame Australian rowers, I mean like the royals before Harry and Meghan ditched them for LA.'

Leo did a double take. 'You want . . . me? To come?'

Tom groaned, looked towards me and raised his eyebrows impatiently, willing me to interject.

I looked to Leo. 'Come on. You're homeless and we might not have jobs next week. Plus, we haven't seen you in forever. For once in your life, Leo Billings, I implore you—'

'—WE implore you,' Tom interrupted.

'Yes, *we* implore you to do something crazy and say yes.'

Leo still looked hesitant. Tom sat up straight, with a serious look on his face.

'Leo, Alex, I think at this point there's only one question we need to ask ourselves.' He cleared his throat. 'What would Goldie Miller do?'

And there it was. The clincher.

The hesitance on Leo's face gave way to joy. 'For Goldie? I'm in.'

Tom shrieked. Leo laughed. I poured us all another glass of wine.

⊪⊪⊪

Copies of our passports were soon scanned and sent to Finley's management team, who told us nothing about the destination other than it was a 'swimsuit and carry-on luggage only' situation. I wasn't sure whether the aloofness was for security reasons, or if Finley just really liked surprises. Either way, I was buzzing with anticipation when the three of us rocked up at the international terminal at 7:30 am the next morning as instructed. One by one, our phones vibrated as boarding passes appeared in our inboxes. I stared down at my phone at a first-class ticket to Singapore with my name on it. Seconds later, a second boarding pass arrived for our connecting flight.

'Holy shit—we're going to the Maldives!' I cried out. 'This week has gone from bad to un-fucking-believable!'

Ninety minutes later, we were seated up at the pointy end of the plane, toasting 2012 Taittinger and taking an obscene number of selfies.

Tom knocked his champagne back in one go. 'To Lisa!'

'To Lisa!' I echoed, holding my glass towards Leo. He clinked his glass on mine, holding my gaze with a quiet grin as we took a sip.

'Okay, now phones off, everybody. Time to leave the real world behind,' Tom called out, snapping his fingers in the air bossily.

Leo and I did as we were told, and I noticed the distinct way my shoulders relaxed as my screen powered down.

'Wow. That actually felt good.' I said, smiling. 'I should do it more often.'

Unsurprisingly, the sixteen-hour journey felt like thirty minutes. We snacked on Osetra caviar, warm spiced scallops and lobster thermidor. I had three desserts before we'd even landed in Singapore, one of which was an espresso parfait that I legitimately would have made love to had it been anatomically possible. Leo and I were seated next to each other, with Tom (who had chosen to get in as much sleep as possible in order to look 'fresh' for his arrival) directly behind us.

With our phones off and the stress of work a million miles away, and Aunty May's prying eyes nowhere to be seen, Leo and I finally found ourselves with an opportunity to catch up. Goldie's news had taken precedence since he had arrived home, and I was yet to properly hear about Jack and Tessa.

Leo thoughtfully savoured every sip of the $300-a-bottle whisky he'd been served as we spoke.

'Things were pretty dark when I arrived. Tessa just wasn't coping, and Jack was doing his best to take care of her but of course that's not his job. So, I got in touch with her GP, who set her up with a great therapist and a grief support group, which seems to really be helping. Hopefully she'll be back at work soon. She's a lot like Laney. So determined. The sadness just got the better of her, which happens to the best of us sometimes.'

'And how's Jack?'

Leo's eyes shone. 'He's just such an amazing kid. You should have seen him, bringing Tessa cups of tea, making breakfast, cleaning the house. All without complaining.'

'Was he okay when you left?'

'He understood. And he's excited about hopefully coming to stay for a while.'

'He's coming here?' I asked, surprised.

'Well, if his and Tessa's visas come through then they'll be here soon. They can stay for a year, see how they like it,' he replied with a glint of coy excitement in his eyes that he quickly shook the second I clocked it.

'What?' I leaned forwards, shocked, and grabbed his arm. 'Leo! That's huge!'

'We'll see. I don't want to get excited until the visas are approved.'

'They will be. I know they will be. I can't believe you're staying!'

'Of *course* I'm staying, Alex. When I commit to something, I commit to something,' he said decisively. 'And the change of scenery has been good for me.' There was a suggestive tone in his voice that made my insides flip. He was staring right at me now. Almost like he was taking in the scenery as he spoke. 'Plus, May and Billy still have two more empty bedrooms.'

I let out a loud cackle. 'Well, I think there might be three soon. I've got Henry looking for a place for me.'

Leo cleared his throat and sat forwards, eyebrows raised. 'Henry?'

'He's that financial planner I've been seeing. He's been amazing.'

'Ah, right. Henry.' Leo sounded odd, as if his mouth had temporarily forgotten how to say words. He sat back. 'That's great, Alex.' He pulled a book out of his bag and began flicking through the pages.

I kept talking, keen to pull him back into the conversation. 'Although I suppose I won't be buying a house if I lose my job. I'll have to just rent somewhere. Either way, I can't turn thirty at May and Billy's place, can I?'

Leo didn't answer for a second, clearly absorbed in whatever had taken his attention, and then he looked at me briefly. 'You're Alex York. You'll figure it out,' he replied, in the kind of matter-of-fact tone that made me believe I really would. He knocked back the last of his whisky, placed the book on his lap and fixed his gaze on the empty sky out the window beside him.

My excitement that Leo was staying in Sydney suddenly deflated like a released balloon, the shrunken remains landing limp and pathetic in the pit of my stomach. What was going on in that head of his? What had I said to suddenly lose him like that? One thought drilled through me and sat like lead in my chest as I watched him stare out the window, his mind far away in an inaccessible world. He may be back for good, but he certainly wasn't back for me.

16

'I've done some cool shit in my life, but I think this is the coolest!' I shouted over the whirr of the seaplane as we marvelled at the bright blue ocean below us.

Leo sat silently on the other side of the narrow aisle, hands on his knees. We were a long way from the quiet, safe luxury of Singapore Airlines First Class, and I supposed seaplanes in paradise weren't for everyone. 'You okay?' I mouthed at him.

'Yep,' he mouthed back, closing his eyes and taking a deep breath. He was still wearing jeans and boots, leaving me to wonder whether he even owned any beach-holiday–appropriate clothing. I, on the other hand, had gone full *Crazy Rich Asians* and opted for a floral blue Dolce cotton sundress, Chanel sandals and the biggest pair of sunglasses I owned. If I was going to spend a week in the Maldives, I was going to bloody well look the part.

The pilot soon announced our imminent landing, letting us know we were about to get a beautiful aerial shot of our island out the window.

'Our island?' I squeaked. I looked across to Tom, my eyes wide, but he simply shrugged.

And that's when we saw it.

'Well, fuck me, he's really done it this time,' Tom called out, deadpan, as our home for the next five days came into full view. Leo opened his eyes to take a peek, and I watched the colour flush back into his face. A tiny white island, floating like a grain of rice in the most brilliant sapphire sea. In its centre sat a sprawling white house in a grove of vivid green palm trees. A bright blue infinity pool shot out into the blindingly white sand. As we got closer, I spotted a figure on the jetty waving. The lime-green short-shorts were an instant giveaway. Even from the sky, Finley Stark, with his arms in the air and hopping about like an excited puppy, looked like the happiest human who had ever walked the face of the Earth.

'How do I look?' Tom called out to us.

'Perfect!' Leo and I shot back in unison.

'Welcome to paradise, you sexy animals!' Finley yelled out as he ran down the jetty towards us, bare feet sandy, his shaggy hair in a topknot and a thin string of white pearls hanging from his neck. Leo and I stood back, letting the two lovers have their reunion. I cheekily pulled out my phone and snapped a photo as Finley drew Tom into his arms, dipped him backwards and kissed him passionately, paying no mind to who was watching. I was so happy for Tom I could have burst into a million pieces. I had no option but to pull out my phone again a moment later when Finley proceeded to dip Leo back in exactly the same fashion, although this time without the passionate tongue kiss.

'Finley, this is insane! I don't have any words! I'll never have the words! Thank you fifty million billion!' I said as he pulled me in for a hug and nuzzled his damp hair into my neck.

'Hey—anything for family,' Finley whispered back in my ear. 'I'm so fucking proud of you, kid.' He kissed me on the forehead, returning his attention to the wider group. 'Now, shall we start with a quick tour? Actually, it won't take long. The sand is here. The ocean is there. And that's the house. We've got the master suite upstairs and you two can take downstairs.' He looked dubiously towards Leo and me. 'I'm not sure if you are schtuping or not but there are four other bedrooms to choose from so you can have your own rooms, share a room or christen every single one if you like!'

While I was 100 per cent certain that Finley knew we weren't sleeping together, Leo was less accustomed to his trickery. As was evident by the beetroot colour that had taken over his whole face.

'He's joking, breathe!' I teased, silently devastated over how embarrassed he seemed at the very prospect of sleeping with me.

Leo forced an awkward laugh as the flush on his face subsided. 'Thank you, Finley. This is unbelievable.'

'You're welcome, Mike Tyson. Now, that's the end of the thankyous, you lot. I understand, my benevolence and generosity knows no end, blah-blah-blah. Now!' He cleared his throat. 'The island has twenty-four–seven private security, and I've got my own here too, of course, but apart from the chefs and a couple of staff, we've got this place to ourselves. So nudity is encouraged, but not required.'

Leo's eyes grew wide as Tom's rolled.

'Oh, and we may be in the middle of nowhere but there's satellite internet, courtesy of Elon. I've made the password 'fuckdarrenchase'; one word no capitals, should be easy to remember, yeah?'

'Finley, how the hell did you pull this off in forty-eight hours?' I asked, my mind still spinning.

'Let me guess,' Tom mused as he took Finley's hand in his. 'Knowing this *psycho* as well as I do, there never even *was* a Singapore promo trip.'

A cheeky grin swept over Finley's face, dimples appearing on each rosy, sun-kissed cheek. He'd been found out. 'Yeah, I booked this months ago.'

'A-ha!' Tom dropped Finley's hand and crossed his arms. 'I knew it!'

Finley shook his head, still grinning. 'As a romantic getaway for me and my love over here, I'll have you know! But then you all went and blew up your careers, so I figured the more the merrier!'

Mesmerised, I grabbed my bag and walked towards the closest bedroom, positioned to the left of the infinity pool. A four-poster, king-sized bed sat proudly in the middle of the room, with a soft canopy above, sheer curtains tied to each post. Glass doors opened onto a private deck, with two deckchairs and a hammock, framed perfectly by two palm trees. Behind the bed was a hidden bathroom, with a deep soak tub and an outdoor shower. I looked through the glass to my right, across the pool deck to the other bedroom, where Leo was sitting on the edge of his bed, staring out at the ocean.

The last time I'd arrived at any sort of paradise, I was running away from my life. But this time it felt like I was running towards a more authentic version of it. I was proud that I had stood my ground with Darren, and proud that I had called Darren out on his bullshit, regardless of the outcome. For the first time in a long time, I was totally at peace. Doing what I'd done hadn't exactly been the smart option, but I knew it was the right one. And somewhere, somehow, it would lead me to where I was supposed to go. I just had to get through the next week, which, judging by my surroundings, was not going to be difficult.

I opened my small suitcase and had started unpacking when I heard a frantic knocking at the glass door. Tom was jumping up and down, holding his phone.

'Bitch, you're not going to BELIEVE what's happened—'

'Did Hilary Duff finally comment on your Lizzie McGuire lip-sync video?' I called out as I kept unpacking.

'EVEN BETTER!' he squealed as he pulled the glass door open, scurrying towards me. 'You've gone viral! Twenty-fucking-three million views! And counting!'

'What are you talking about?'

'Someone from the office put the footage of your fight with Darren online.'

I looked at him, an eyebrow raised. 'Someone?'

'It wasn't me, I swear!' He held a pinky finger out towards me. 'It's got over fifteen thousand comments! It obviously all happened while we were in transit. Tilly Roy shared it—look!'

There it was. Staring back at me from Tom's iPhone, shared with the caption 'Go, Alex! #bringdowntheboysclub'.

'Heaps of celebs have shared it since. The comments are insane. Obviously I just made Finley retweet it too. I hope Mark is shitting himself.'

I scrolled through the comments, tears forming in my eyes straight away. The support was immense. Thousands and thousands of women from all around the world had rallied, and they weren't just angry for me, they were angry for all of us.

'I'm gonna go tell Leo his right hook is famous, be right back,' Tom said, as I rummaged through my handbag for my own phone, which had been off since we'd boarded the flight for Singapore.

I switched it on and connected to the wi-fi, my hands trembling, adrenaline coursing through my veins. Notifications started relentlessly popping up from all my apps, as messages, emails and missed calls registered. My phone was dinging and vibrating as if it was having some sort of seizure. I tried desperately to keep up, squinting at the screen as more and more came through. The thirteen missed calls from my mother alone were enough to make me want to switch it back off again.

And then the phone began ringing. Henry Tan's name appeared on the screen.

'Henry! Hello!' I answered, breathlessly.

'She lives! We've been trying to get on to you forever. You cool? Where are you?'

'I'm cool, I'm cool. I'm actually on a private island in the Maldives, would you believe.'

'Oh, fuck, yes! Please tell me you didn't put that on the credit card?'

'Ah, no. I'm here as somebody's guest.'

He gasped. 'Sugar daddy?'

'Um, no. A friend's boyfriend.'

'Right. Well, are you aware of the fact that you're pretty much everywhere right now?'

'I literally found out minutes ago . . . It's insane.'

'It's brilliant. Firing you would be a PR nightmare. We might not be saying goodbye to that Bondi penthouse just yet.'

'Who said I wanted a Bondi penthouse?'

'Everybody wants a Bondi penthouse. Anyway, Miriam and I have gone through your contract and neither of us think they've got grounds to fire you. I mean all you did was have an argument with a co-worker. We've all been there. It's not your fault someone put it online. Leo might not be so lucky. Remind me to shake his hand if I ever meet him, by the way. What a punch. Hey, I thought you said you'd sworn off having anyone in your bed?' he teased.

'We're not . . . it was a . . . misunderstanding.'

'Disappointing. He's a good-looking man. Anyway, go enjoy your holiday, superstar!'

'Thanks, Henry.'

I hung up and saw seventy-two new emails, ninety texts and eighty-five missed calls waiting for me. The onslaught could wait. I switched my phone off, threw it back on the bed and walked out onto the pool deck where Tom was chatting animatedly to Leo, who'd miraculously changed into shorts.

'Who knew you had knees? And calves?' I called out as I walked towards them.

'Twenty-three million views and she wants to talk about your calves. She's *obsessed* with you, babe,' Tom stage whispered to Leo.

'Oh, shut up! I was just on the phone to Henry; he thinks because this has blown up so much the network would be insane to fire me, so, who knows? I may not be penniless after all.'

'This is Henry your . . . financial planner?' Leo asked.

'Yeah, but he *also* has a law degree,' Tom quipped.

'I see,' Leo replied flatly.

'Drinks are served, castaways!' Finley's voice boomed out from behind us as he appeared from inside the house with a tray of cocktails, each looking like its own work of art. I grabbed one that smelled like coconut and had a huge wedge of pineapple stuck to the rim.

'I propose a toast!' Finley announced. 'To Goldie, who even in death appears to be inspiring serious badassery in women, and men—' he looked towards Leo and winked '—around the world.'

'To Goldie.' We all cheered as we clinked our glasses and took a sip of the tropical deliciousness, everyone's eyes fixed on the bright blue sea. Everyone's but mine. Mine were set directly on Leo who, standing there barefoot in shorts, drink in hand, had never ever looked better.

᮰ɪᴧᴧᴧɪ᮰

I stood looking in the mirror four hours later. I was wearing a long lilac and gold Zimmerman dress, my curls crunchy and salty from an afternoon spent hopping between the hammock in front of my room and the warm ocean that lapped at the shore just metres away. I was already becoming myself again, finding space and time in my mind to come to terms with where my life was at and the array of possible outcomes that awaited me on my return home.

Finley and Tom had gone up to get ready for dinner after hours of frolicking about, drinking cocktails by the pool, and Leo had taken a nap. I couldn't shake the feeling that he had more on his mind than he was letting on. Perhaps he was worried about Tessa and Jack's visa situation? He'd seemed a little distant, a little distracted. Here, but not really here. I'd suggested he take a nap and he didn't fight me on it, instead retreating to his room and pulling the curtains closed. They'd been closed for four hours and no one had heard a peep out of him since.

'Should we wake sleeping beauty? There's lobster,' Tom said, leaning against my door. He was wearing a silk Versace shorts and T-shirt set and looked like a white Bruno Mars.

'Hmm, I don't know. I suppose I should check on him.'

'Any excuse to get into his bed.' He replied, eyebrows raised.

'Tom! I do not want to sleep with Leo!'

'Oh, shut the fuck up, Alex!' Tom snapped, stepping into my room and closing the sliding door behind him. 'It's me! You can lie to everyone else, but you can't to lie to me. I know things are complicated, but—fuck, it's pretty obvious that there's something there, Finley and I can both see it. If you *can't* be together, I totally get it. Of course I get it. But if you're just too proud to admit that you want him, or if you're just putting it all in the "too hard basket" or whatever, then that's just dumb.'

I stared back at him, shocked. I opened my mouth to reply, and then stopped myself, swallowing my words. In the distance, we heard Finley whistling. Tom peeked over his shoulder, before looking back at me. 'I'm not trying to be mean, Alex. I just don't want you to miss out on something that could be really wonderful. Love or fear. Those were *his* words.'

'I know, I know.' I sighed. 'But in this instance—maybe choosing "love" means choosing to walk away. There's just so much else at play. And I don't know if I'm enough to make him want to push through it all. And I can't rush it. I can't rush him. I don't even know if he ever *wants* to date again, let alone date me. The truth of the matter is—' I paused, looking out the window '—he's allowed to love Laney, and only Laney, for the rest of his life, and how can I even be mad about that?'

Tom took a step forwards, wide-eyed, and hugged me. 'Right. That makes sense. Sorry, I'll chill.'

'Thanks,' I whispered back. 'Now, I'm gonna go make sure he's alive in there.'

'Okay. I'll see you in a minute.'

Tom disappeared into the house as I crept over to Leo's room, gently knocking on the door and bringing my ear close to the glass to listen for a response. When I heard nothing, I hopped onto the sand and walked around to the other side where the screen door was wide open. The gap in the curtains was big enough for me to peer through: first spotting his luggage in the corner of the room, still packed, and then spotting Leo, fast asleep in the foetal position on the edge of the bed.

In a moment of what I can only describe as paradise-induced-madness, I knelt down beside him, and slowly, carefully stroked his head. He breathed out deeply, almost sighing, eyes still closed. And then, without even really thinking, I leaned in and kissed his forehead, ever so gently. He sighed again.

'My darling,' he whispered, eyes still closed. 'Hello, my darling.' A smile gently washed across his face as he nuzzled back into his pillow and fell back to sleep. My heart jumped into my throat, as if I'd just interrupted a private moment for which I had no right to be present. I felt guilty, and incredibly silly. I quickly pulled back and, as I did so, something caught my eye. Something shiny. There, just centimetres from his face, sitting alone in the middle of the bedside table was Leo's wedding ring.

I stared at it for a moment, confused. He began to stir again. I crept towards the sliding door, tripping on my hem as I reached for the handle.

'Hello?' I heard Leo call out sleepily.

I spun on the spot to see him rubbing his eyes and looking around, a little disorientated.

'It's Alex,' I whispered back. 'I was just making sure you're okay. We're about to have dinner.'

Leo switched on the bedside lamp. 'Far out, how long have I been asleep?'

'Uh . . . four hours or so. But you're welcome to stay in bed if you want. No rush.'

He sat up, still rubbing his eyes, and swivelled himself around so that his feet were resting on the floor. 'Was I talking in my sleep?'

My heart leaped into my throat again as I swallowed, trying to find some nonchalance in my reply. 'No, no. You were sleeping soundly.'

He raked a hand through his hair, perhaps not entirely believing me. 'Right. Well, I'm actually starving, so I'll have a quick shower and be right out.'

'Take your time,' I replied.

'Oh and . . . Alex,' he called out as I began to turn. I looked at him, eyebrows raised. He opened his mouth to speak, and then caught himself. Silence hung in the air.

'You okay?' I prompted, instantly desperate to know what was on his mind.

'I was just going to say that . . . you look beautiful in that dress,' he said, ending in a whisper. There was a hint of bashfulness on his face that I'd not seen before.

I was so taken aback by his compliment that I couldn't even muster a polite thankyou, and instead just stood there trying desperately to limit the size of the smile that I could feel bursting through my facial muscles. Ten seconds must have passed by the time my legs remembered how to walk, and by the time I got to the dinner table, I was positively flushed.

'He's just having a quick shower,' I said as I sat down.

'Hey, Alex,' Finley whispered dramatically.

'Yes, Finley?'

'You look *beautiful* in that dress,' he said, before he and Tom broke out in giggles.

'You little shits! Were you eavesdropping?' I spat out.

'Babe, we're in a villa with thin walls, on a dead-quiet desert island with nothing but ocean for miles. We didn't have to strain our ears *that* hard,' Tom quipped, looking positively delighted with himself.

'Please, don't embarrass him . . . or me,' I begged as I poured myself a glass of white wine from the ice bucket.

'Okay, my love,' Finley replied, pretending to zip his mouth and throw away the key, then launching into an incredible story about almost having dinner with Beyoncé. At the story's crescendo, his eyes flicked behind me and lit up. 'Here he is! Welcome back to the land of the living, Mr Billings!'

Leo was walking towards us, barefoot, in grey linen shorts and an off-white linen shirt, sleeves rolled up. He'd washed his hair and tied it up messily, a couple of rogue wavy strands tucked behind his ears. I looked at Tom, who widened his eyes back at me. We both knew what the other was thinking, and it was definitely not PG-rated.

'Sorry to keep you waiting, kids,' Leo said as he pulled out the chair next to me and sat down. I subtly checked his finger and saw the wedding ring was still absent. 'I'm not sure what happened; I think the week of travel caught up with me. I don't know how you do it, Finley.'

'Vitamin B shots in my arse and a very, very talented Japanese masseur who travels with me everywhere on tour,' he replied matter-of-factly.

I didn't realise it at the time, but that night a core memory was created. In years to come, I would often remember the taste of the lobster, the cool buzz of the wine and the sound of my friends' laughter. I never wanted that dinner to end; I never wanted these friendships to end. I looked at Tom and Finley, so totally free and at peace with how they felt about one another now, and desperately hoped to God that it would end well for them. And, of course, I wished the same for Leo, who more than anyone I knew deserved happiness and peace.

Once the lobster and wine had been consumed and the plates cleared, Finley held up his hands, his green eyes twinkling. 'I've got a surprise for you all.'

I gasped. 'Oh my goodness, is it a private island in the Maldives?'

'Smartypants,' he sang back. 'I can't tell you. But you'll know when it happens.'

Tom scrunched up his face. 'How will we know?'

'You'll just know.'

'And when is it happening?'

'Soon. Now, no more questions. Why don't you two take a little walky-walky?' Finley looked at Leo and me, making walking movements with his index and middle fingers, like some sort of half-pissed *Play School* presenter.

I looked at Leo. 'I suppose we'd better do what he says.'

Finley gave a satisfied wink as the two of us walked across the front of the house towards the sand.

'So . . . is Henry your boyfriend?' Leo asked as we stepped off the deck and onto the warm sand.

I let out a loud laugh. 'Henry? No! Why would you think that?'

Leo brushed his hair off his face and shrugged. 'Well, he's come up a lot today . . . and you said you'd been seeing him.'

I suppose I could understand how he'd made the assumption, but I was mortified that he thought I'd been seeing someone when in reality all I'd been doing was pining for him.

'I meant I was seeing him for financial advice!' I said. 'We're just friends. He and his sister are handling all the Mark stuff for me. She's some badass lawyer.'

Leo's face relaxed. 'Right. That makes sense. Sorry.' He rubbed the back of his neck, clearly embarrassed.

We walked side-by-side in comfortable silence for a minute or two, my mind still mulling over his assumption.

'Tessa rang this afternoon.' He cleared his throat. 'She had some news.'

'Is everything okay?'

'Everything is fine. Everything is actually great. Their visas were approved today.'

'Leo!' I squealed. 'That's fantastic!' I reached out and grabbed his elbow. 'They're going to love it here! Well, not here. Back home, I mean.'

'I'm pretty sure they'd love it here too,' he replied.

'Who wouldn't?' I said, looking out over the moonlit ocean and then back at him. He looked nervous. 'What's wrong? I thought you'd be happy!'

His pace slowed. He took a deep breath, and as I stared back at him I could see his hand was trembling. A sense of foreboding immediately hit me.

'I know, I'm sorry. I am happy. It's . . . Jack,' he replied, looking at his hands and then at me. 'I promised him that when the visas came through, and we knew that we'd all be in Australia together, that I would do something.'

'Right,' I said. 'Can you tell me what it is? Or is it, like, an uncle–nephew secret?'

'Well, that's the thing.' We both stopped walking as he faced me. 'The promise relies *entirely* on me telling you something.'

An overwhelming fear hit me as the words came out of his mouth. Was he about to tell me that he'd met somebody in London? Was that why he'd taken his ring off? My insides started to tremble, and a wave of nausea hit me. I wrapped my arms tightly around myself.

'Oh,' I whispered, trying desperately to sound relaxed as I braced myself for what was coming. 'Whatever you have to say, I can take it.' I swallowed. 'I promise.'

He nodded his head, his face illuminated by the tiki lights along the shore, and closed his eyes for a moment. I focused on the sounds of the waves lapping nearby on the sand, counting them as I waited for some sort of reprieve from his excruciating silence.

And then finally, his eyes were open and staring directly into mine. 'I'm in love with you, Alex,' he finally whispered.

A quiet gasp escaped my mouth. I brought a hand up to cover it.

'I wanted to tell you that night when we were dancing at the Ivy, but when the moment came I couldn't find the words. Then I had to go back to London, and I didn't want to tell you until I knew I wouldn't have to leave you. So I spent every second of my time there trying to figure out a way home. To you.

'When I lost Laney, I felt like my life had hit a dead end. And I'd accepted that—it was the price of loving so deeply, and I was at peace with it. Honestly . . .' He paused. 'And then you walked into the bar that day, with your bright dress

and your shopping bags and your gin martini and your inces-
sant chattering . . . and I eventually realised that it was you all
along. You were the bright light that had always been waiting
for me on the other side of that miserable darkness.

'I understand if you want to go and live your amazing,
colourful, happy life with someone carefree and easy because
I *know* you don't need me.' He paused again. 'All I can hope
for is that you *want* me. And that you believe me when I say
that I love you. And I'm here. And I'll never leave you wondering again.'

A loud bang cracked through the sky above us, shocking us
both. Fireworks. Finley's surprise.

I took a step forwards towards Leo, reached up and gently
traced my fingertips along his lips. I remembered my new
year's wish on the shores of Malapascua. How I had begged
the universe for another chance. How I'd promised myself not
to let love get in the way of my future, never for a moment
thinking that maybe good, proper, real love was a part of it.

'You . . . love me?'

'I do, Alex, I do. Very much,' he replied quietly.

I slowly leaned forwards and rested my forehead on his chin,
breathing him in for a moment before looking back up at him
through grateful tears. 'I think I hoped you did all along.'

And then finally, my lips were on his. Slow and deep at
first, then quickening as I finally let myself disappear into
him. Nobody had ever kissed me the way Leo was kissing me,
as if his entire life depended on it, as if he'd wanted to do this
since the moment we met.

He wrapped his arms around me, pulling me towards him until it felt like every part of us was touching, until I could feel his heart beating strong in his chest against mine. His hands in my hair, his scent enveloping me, my heart echoing the explosions in the sky.

I felt weightless, like all the fear I'd been carrying around had suddenly disappeared from my shoulders. I had been so scared of loving Leo. So scared I might not be enough for him. And I'd been scared that he might never be able to love me back after everything he'd been through.

The sky continued to erupt in loud explosions above us as I looked up at him, my cheeks wet. 'I'm tired of being scared,' I told him softly.

His eyes were ablaze with understanding, his whole face soft and open. 'So am I.'

And so I cast it all into the ocean. I sent my fear and my disappointment and my grief into the sky, shooting it off inside makeshift fireworks as I felt my pain explode above me. Big, beautiful colours burning bright and hot and then disappearing into complete nothingness.

I willed it all out. I kissed him some more. And finally, I let the door of my heart swing wide open.

'I love you too,' I told him, between kisses. 'Very much.'

As the fireworks ended in one final thunderous explosion, I looked into Leo's honey-coloured eyes, the last bits of falling light illuminating his perfect face. There in his arms, I knew that I was forever safe.

There was no fear left. All that was left was him. And deep in my heart, deep in my bones and skin, right down to my fingernails, I knew.

I knew that I wanted to love Leo Billings for the rest of my life.

‖‖‖‖‖‖

'Do you think Goldie secretly always hoped we'd fall in love?' I asked the next morning, my fingers tracing patterns on his bare chest as the warm morning breeze came off the water and swept gently through Leo's room.

Leo looked up at the ceiling contentedly. 'I know for a fact that she did.'

I sat up on my elbow, resting my chin on his shoulder. 'What? How?'

'She called me from Switzerland,' he replied, weaving one of his fingers through my curls. 'We spoke the night before she passed. I think that, with everything that happened with Laney, she wanted me to hear it from her. She wanted to make sure I understood. Before she hung up, she asked if we'd fallen in love yet.'

I gasped. 'That cheeky minx! What did you tell her?'

'I told her that I was working on it. And then I packed my bags and came home. That bit was her idea too.'

I buried my face in the pillow, too happy and overwhelmed to speak. Then I looked at him again. 'So this was her plan all along?'

The corners of Leo's eyes crinkled, and he leaned down and kissed the top of my head. 'I think so, yeah. She said she always knew we'd hit it off. That if anyone was gonna get me out of my funk, it would be you.'

'Goldie fucking Miller.' I sighed blissfully. 'What a woman.'

Leo and I stared at each other in happy silence for another moment or so, then I sat up. 'I suppose I'd better turn on my phone and face the onslaught. Are there robes or something in one of these cupboards?' I asked, pulling the sheet across myself.

'Well, Finley did say nudity was encouraged,' Leo replied, smirking as he slipped out of bed and checked the wardrobes. I was too distracted by the sight of his naked body in the sunlight to notice him throwing a robe towards me. I hopped out of bed and slipped it on, standing on my tippy toes to kiss him. 'I'll be right back.'

I slid the glass door open and checked that the coast was clear before scampering over the pool deck to my bedroom, which I suspected would go unused for the next four days. Once inside, I quickly brushed my teeth, washed my face and grabbed my mobile phone, then headed back out. I was halfway across the deck when I heard someone clearing their throat, and looked up to the balcony where Finley and Tom were holding their yoga mats.

'Care to join us, or have you already had your fill of downward dog for the morning?' Tom called out, followed by raucous laughter from Finley.

'Namaste, boys,' I sang out.

The smiles on their faces said it all. I waved happily before popping back into Leo's room and sliding into bed next to him again.

'So, I just got an email from Victoria Milligan.'

'What?' I nuzzled in closer, trying to get a good view of his screen.

'Yep. We've been summoned by Mark. Nine am Friday. The day after we get back.' He looked at me, totally unaffected. As if it were a routine dentist appointment, as opposed to a meeting that would determine the future of our careers.

'How do you seem so chill about this?'

He let out a contented sigh. 'Well, I just spent the night making love to Alex York on a private island in the Maldives. So I've hit the jackpot. Nothing that weasel says to me could make me believe otherwise.'

'Making love? Oh God, that's like the sexual equivalent of the old thumbs-up emoji. Please never refer to us having sex that way ever again.'

Leo threw his head back and laughed. 'Okay, I promise.'

I leaned in and kissed him on the lips in quiet disbelief that I got to do that now. Kiss Leo any time I felt like it.

'Well, on the phone yesterday, Henry said he and Miriam had gone over the contract with a fine-toothed comb and seem pretty confident that, legally, they can't fire me.'

'They still might fire *me*.'

'I say we just spend the rest of the trip squeezing every ounce of hedonistic pleasure out of this holiday before we need to fly back. Let's just go all-in and enjoy ourselves in blissful ignorance.'

Leo crawled on top of me, kissing my forehead, my lips and then my neck as he whispered, 'If blissful ignorance includes a repeat of last night, as soon as possible, then yeah, I'm in.' He lowered himself under the covers, untying my robe and moving his lips from my neck to my breasts, my stomach and belly button as I melted back into the bed, then gently opened my legs. For a moment I wondered if anybody else in the history of the universe had ever been this happy.

᠃ᑊᗷᑊᑊᗷᑊᑊ᠃

Alex York, 7:00 am: We're in love and we had sex and it was the best.

Missed call, Vanessa Blake, 7:05 am

Missed call, Vanessa Blake, 7:05 am

Vanessa Blake, 7:06 am: CALL ME!

᠃ᑊᗷᑊᑊᗷᑊᑊ᠃

It wasn't until the taxi pulled up outside May and Billy's at 8 pm on Thursday night that either of us remembered that I lived with my mum's sister and her husband and we would therefore now have to deal with either the fanfare that would come with announcing we were a couple or pretending we weren't and sleeping in separate rooms. Both seemed exhausting. I hadn't even stepped out of the taxi when I spotted May on the front porch, chatting on her phone, grinning like she'd just won the fifty-million-dollar Powerball. She quickly hung up and started to wave.

'She knows,' I said to Leo as I stared through the passenger-side window at the house.

'What do you mean?'

'Look at her! She's sick with anticipation! Bloody Tom's given her the heads-up, I bet you. She was just on the phone, no doubt giving Mum a play-by-play. I wouldn't be surprised if she's put rose petals on my bed.' I looked at him seriously. 'I am so sorry if she's put rose petals on the bed. I promise I will get my own place soon.'

Leo laughed as he opened the car door and made his way towards the boot where the taxi driver passed him our bags. I skipped ahead towards May. 'Please, I beg you, don't make a thing out of this,' I pleaded as I hugged her tight.

She brought her mouth to my ear as she whispered, 'I knew from the second I laid eyes on him.'

'You did not!' I whispered back, rolling my eyes.

'I did so, ask Billy! Anyway, I won't embarrass you. I'm not a *regular* aunty, I'm a *cool* aunty!'

'The *Mean Girls* line gets you officially off the hook. Touché, May,' I replied, as I kissed her cheek.

Seconds later, without saying a word, May had wrapped Leo in the tightest hug known to man, letting go only after I suggested he may be running out of air.

There were no rose petals on the bed; she had, however, changed my sheets and placed a chocolate on each pillow. When Leo spotted them and held his up towards me, I laughed so hard I cried. Maybe that Bondi penthouse wasn't *such* a bad idea after all . . .

֍֍֎֍֍

Ordinarily I would have spent hours choosing the perfect 'fuck you Mark Holdsworth' outfit for our meeting, but that morning I was too happy and content to care. In what I could only describe as an act of defiance, I wore a black Prada tracksuit, which to be fair cost over two grand, but was still a tracksuit. I teamed it up with chunky fuchsia Balenciaga sneakers and my hair in two perfect space buns on top of my head and no make-up. If Mark Holdsworth was going to treat me like a child, then I may as well dress like the coolest fucking child on the planet. I didn't bother bringing a handbag. His boring-arse office didn't deserve one.

Leo and I made out in the elevator up to Mark's floor, which would have served as the perfect antidote to any pre-meeting nerves—if I'd had any. Minutes later, we were sitting outside his office. Victoria was tapping busily away at her keyboard, but she shifted her head slightly towards us and flashed me a brief wink from one glinting eye.

'You know, Victoria, you should be running this place. I reckon you know more than all of those old guys combined,' I mused out loud in her direction.

'Tell me something I don't know,' she replied, without taking her eyes off her computer screen.

Leo was called in first, leaving me to wait alone. I pulled out my phone and checked the rant video one last time. It had reached forty million views. Beyoncé had even 'liked' it, which had rendered Tom mute for four and a half minutes due to the fact that he was in the background of the video for three seconds and she now 'knew he existed'. I'd had journalists from all over the world reach out, begging for comment; I'd been invited to be a guest on dozens of podcasts and gained one hundred thousand Instagram followers.

It only strengthened my resolve.

Less than five minutes after he walked in, Leo opened the door and raised his eyebrows at me, holding it open for me to enter. 'You got this,' he whispered as I passed, closing the door behind him as he left. I'd expected him to stay, so I stared at the door for a moment or two after he'd shut it before directing my attention towards Mark, who was in his usual spot. I plonked myself down in the chair opposite him, crossed my legs and grinned sarcastically.

'Well, let's make like P!nk and "Get The Party Started", Mark,' I said confidently.

Visibly confused at the reference, Mark removed his glasses, folded them up and placed them next to his keyboard. He clasped his hands together, closed his eyes and sighed. It all seemed a little dramatic, to be honest. The last time I'd sat on this side of his desk he'd been dismissive, high on his own power. This time, he looked resigned. Defeated.

'Alex, I've got two documents to show you.' He opened his eyes and passed two manila folders over the desk towards me. 'The first is a letter from me. An apology for my behaviour, which I hope you'll accept. The second is an amended version of your contract, which stipulates that no changes or additions will be made to the talent line-up of the show for the duration of the current two-year contract. Should you be happy to sign it, you can do so at your leisure. The board would like to make it clear that you have their full support, and they're proud to have such a strong, talented woman at the helm of the breakfast show. Do you have any questions?'

Henry was right. The company really wanted to avoid any bad PR, which suited me just fine. At this point, I could have been humble in the face of Mark's defeat, but false humility had never exactly been my thing and I couldn't let the moment pass without a little friendly advice.

'For you? No. But I would like to say one thing.'

Mark looked back at me apprehensively. 'Go on.'

'I hope to God your daughters have someone looking out for them in this world the way Goldie looked out for me, and the way I try to look out for my team, because I'll tell ya what, Mark, with bosses like you, they're sure as hell gonna need it.'

And with that, I grabbed the documents and stood up. 'Looking forward to working together *well* into the future,' I said. He twisted his face into something that almost resembled a polite smile and watched me leave. 'Oh, and I'll have Goldie's old office, thanks. Not much privacy at my desk,' I called out over my shoulder.

I didn't look back, but I could almost hear the steam escaping his nostrils. Checkmate, Mark Holdsworth.

17

It was strange seeing Leo so nervous. I mean, he'd been nervous nine months ago on the beach in the Maldives when he told me he was in love with me, but nerves go hand in hand with admissions of undying love and affection that may or may not be reciprocated. This was different. This time he was going out on a limb and doing something he'd never even come close to doing before. After years of making responsible decisions, he finally chose to listen to the small voice inside that was telling him what he truly wanted to do. Even if it was a little crazy. Tonight, the fruition of that dream had arrived.

Tessa, Mum, May and I had shared a cab into the city, leaving Jack with his new best friend, Uncle Billy, who had promised to teach him how to make sous-vide duck. Theirs was a friendship none of us had seen coming but that we all gladly welcomed. Jack spent most weekends at May and Billy's house, happily taking over my old bedroom once I'd finally moved out (I bought a penthouse, but not in Bondi. Henry claimed that Bronte Beach was so close that it still counted—a fact I continue to dispute).

When we arrived, I looked around in awe. The long, blue, marble bar had gold edging and chandeliers hanging above it, reflecting specks of golden light on the bartenders below. Behind them, rows and rows of whisky and gin, too many to possibly count. A photographer approached us for a photo, Leo nervously placing his hand on the small of my back as I tucked myself in next to him, beaming proudly towards the camera. As it flashed, I spotted Malik, completely in his element, keeping a close eye on the bartenders and an even closer eye on the drinks they were sending out.

'The place looks amazing, darling,' I told Leo. 'You've done it. You've actually gone and done it! And it's bloody packed!'

'Well, I'm pretty sure Finley's attendance has something to do with that. I can't believe he's here.'

'He loves you. And he also takes full responsibility for us getting together, so I think in a weird way he feels like he's as much in this relationship as I am.' I giggled, grabbing a martini off a tray as it went past and taking a sip. 'My God, that's good.' I sighed happily. 'So, no regrets?'

Leo looked at me, eyebrows raised. 'What, do I regret punching a man who continually disrespected and undermined the woman I love? Do I regret resigning so she could shine in all her glory, continuing radio domination without having to explain to people that her boyfriend is *technically* her boss? No, my love. I regret nothing.'

I didn't know it at the time, but Leo had had his resignation letter printed and ready to submit the day we both met with Mark. On a personal level, I knew it made sense. He did the job because he was good at it, not because he loved it. Not like I loved it. And Leo Billings was so smart that he could do anything he wanted.

And it turned out, what he really wanted was to open a martini bar.

As for Darren Chase, public sentiment about him had soured after his true colours had been exposed. He chose not to press charges against Leo, perhaps fearing more attention, perhaps satisfied that Leo's resignation was revenge enough. His contract had been paid out, and he had disappeared soon after. Rumour was that he changed his name and went to attempt some sort of a career revival in regional Queensland.

'Speak of the devil,' Leo called out, his eyes darting over my shoulder to Tom and Finley who had just arrived and were walking towards us. I gasped when I saw them.

After a brief, speechless moment, the words finally came. 'Are you . . . both . . . wearing . . . custom Gucci?'

'Nothing but the best for the social event of my calendar year, my darlings!' Finley yelled, exuberant. They looked like they'd both stepped off a 1970s yacht full of millionaires who'd spent twenty-four hours existing on nothing but magic mushrooms and/or French champagne. It was utter perfection. 'Now, obviously, as the unofficial celebrity ambassador of the launch I've prepared a little ditty. You don't mind if I steal the stage for a couple of minutes do you, Leo, my love?'

Leo shook his head, shocked and obviously delighted at the prospect. 'Of course, Finley! Just say the word!'

Tom rolled his eyes at me. 'And I thought *I* loved being the centre of attention,' he whispered, obviously as delighted as Leo.

'Right well, this is me saying the word,' Finley said with a grin. 'Let's do it now so I can get pissed on martinis like everyone else, hey?'

Two minutes later, Finley grabbed the microphone without waiting for an introduction. The last time I saw him stand up on stage in front of a crowd like this was the night I discovered the truth about him and Tom. Leo and I were still the only ones who knew about them, apart from their parents who were all as delighted as we were that their boys had found love.

'Hello, everybody!' Finley announced as he walked onto the stage, the beading on his lapel shining under the glittery lights. 'If I could get your attention, please, I'd love to welcome you tonight. I'm Finley Stark, but I suppose you all know that already, don't you?'

The crowd cheered ferociously, a sea of iPhones appearing just above eye level.

'I'm glad you've all got your phones out, because I'm gonna need someone to put this on the internet. In fact, I'm gonna need you all to put this on the internet. Because I've got a new song that I wanna play for you tonight. It's a song that nobody on the planet has ever heard.'

The crowd cheered again. I looked at Tom, who looked back at me and shrugged. It seemed he was as surprised as everybody else.

'I wrote this song about the first time I fell in love. And I mean, like, proper, deep in your bones love. Not the fake shit most of us pop stars sing about.' He paused, finding Tom's eyes in the crowd. 'I want to dedicate it to the love of my life, who's here tonight . . .'

I heard Tom gasp as he reached out his hand towards me to steady him.

'We could have chosen fear, baby. But I'm so glad we chose love. I chose it then, and I choose it now. I choose it forever. Thomas Winter, this is for you, my darling.' He strummed his guitar, cleared his throat and looked back to the crowd. 'It's called "Love or Fear".'

The cheers were loud before, but now they were deafening. The crowd scrambled to catch a glimpse of Tom, who, with tears streaming down his cheeks, had a smile on his face big enough to light up the universe.

Finley's tearful and joyful serenade began and, before long, half of the room was either searching through their handbag for a tissue or wiping their eyes with their sleeve. The song was raw, vulnerable and altogether stunning (it unsurprisingly went on to spend a month on top of the UK charts and become his most successful release).

Once he had sung the last line and strummed the last chord, an almost holy silence fell upon the room. Finley gently placed the microphone on the ground, hopped off stage and walked towards Tom, the crowd parting before him. I let Tom's hand go and stood back, finding Leo's arm. Slowly, carefully and lovingly, Finley took Tom's face in his hands, leaned in and kissed him.

And then he pulled back, kissed him again quickly and looked to the crowd.

'I suppose Goldie Lane is officially open. Now let's all enjoy the best goddamn martinis on the planet!'

Cheers reverberated through every corner of the room as glasses were thrust into the air. Through a gap in the crowd I spotted Joanie, who beamed when she caught Leo's eye, the two of them finding each other in the crowd and embracing. Above them hung a giant, ornate gold chandelier.

A couple of metres away, May and Tessa giggled like schoolgirls as Malik cleared their drinks and placed another two down in front of them. It was hard to believe they'd only known each other for a couple of months, but I suppose that's what a chosen family is. The ones you meet along the way who very quickly feel like home. Henry and Georgia chatted away animatedly on a chaise lounge, and nearby Vanessa had her mobile phone out and was showing Mum pictures of her latest adventures on the Galápagos Islands.

I stood there alone, surrounded by more love than I ever thought possible, overcome by the life I had somehow found myself living and the people I was sharing it with.

I'm not sure what happens after we die, but I'd like to believe that the very best of us lives on in the people we love. And as I looked around that night, I couldn't help but hope that in another universe somewhere Goldie and Laney had found each other. I imagined them, happy and free, sipping on cucumber martinis and toasting to the loves they left behind and the futures their love made possible.

'Cheers, girls,' I whispered as I subtly raised my glass to the ceiling, took a sip and walked towards Leo, whose hand was outstretched, ready to hold mine. Just like he promised it always would be.

ACKNOWLEDGEMENTS

To my friends and family. Emma, I would not have had the time, capacity or headspace to write this book without your love and care for Buddy. We do not deserve you! Thank you Adrian for the late night plot chats as we lay in the dark, exhausted, and for always putting my creative dreams first and never telling me to go get a job. Ha! Buddy—being your Mama is the best job I've ever had. Mum, Janny and Wazza for your love, support and spare rooms. No girl is complete without her group chats: Clarashnia and Sunday Ladies Lunch—thanks for giving me life.

To the formidable women at Allen & Unwin. Tessa Feggans, you were the perfect person to hold my hand from day one. Big love to editor-extraordinaire Courtney Lick and to publisher Cate Paterson for getting this thing out into the world with such care. Big love also to Bella Breden, Shannon Edwards and my Kiwi team, Abba Renshaw and Grace Wang.

Abigail Nathan and Dannielle Viera, without you both this book would be full of plot holes and spelling mistakes. Hazel Lam—thank you for the glorious cover art!

Thank you Craig Bruce for always telling me I was a writer, even when all I did was talk. Thanks to my amazing management team at Profile, especially Bec and of course Mel Harvey, who read my early words and encouraged me to write the book.

The first readers—Violet, Georgia, Marlei, Tash and Jordon—for your encouragement. And Vanessa who finished it, crying, while getting a Brazilian wax. Tom—the funniest human being I'm ever likely to know. Writing you into these pages was one of the most enjoyable parts of this whole process. May you continue to look twenty forever, babe. To Fifi and Kate. Not many people become friends with their idols, so I must be extra lucky. Your kind words mean the world.

Big love to whoever makes the instrumental Taylor Swift covers that I listened to for two years while I wrote this book.

If you've gotten to the end of these acknowledgements, you may have had the same realisation that I did while writing them. That I am surrounded by unbelievably talented women. I cannot think of a better way to exist in this world. #YTG